NIC TATANO

I've always been a writer of some sort, having spent my career working as a reporter, anchor or producer in television news. Fiction is a lot more fun, since you don't have to deal with those pesky things known as facts. I grew up in the New York City metropolitan area and now live on the Gulf Coast where I will never shovel snow again. I'm happily married to a math teacher and we share our wonderful home with our tortoise-shell tabby cat, Gypsy.

You can follow me on Twitter @NicTatano.

It Girl

NIC TATANO

Harper*Impulse* an imprint of
HarperCollins*Publishers* Ltd
77–85 Fulham Palace Road
Hammersmith, London W6 8JB

www.harpercollins.co.uk

A Paperback Original 2014

First published in Great Britain in ebook format by Harper*Impulse* 2014

Copyright © Nic Tatano 2014

Cover images © Shutterstock.com

Nic Tatano asserts the moral right
to be identified as the author of this work

A catalogue record for this book is
available from the British Library

ISBN: 978-0-00-759175-6

This novel is entirely a work of fiction.
The names, characters and incidents portrayed in it are
the work of the author's imagination. Any resemblance to
actual persons, living or dead, events or localities is
entirely coincidental.

Automatically produced by Atomik ePublisher from Easypress

For Myra, my real life It Girl

CHAPTER ONE

"My network's twenty–million-dollar-a-year morning anchor just got arrested for soliciting a prostitute."

While I've made a habit of getting major exclusives as a television reporter, this latest juicy scoop brought the conversation at our dinner table to a screeching halt.

And the next words you hear should tell you that you need to get out of your conventional mode of thinking.

"She hired a prostitute?"

That's right. *She.*

See what I mean? You naturally assumed said morning anchor was a man looking for a hookup with some silicone babe on a Manhattan street corner. But nooooo, in this case we're talking about television's reigning "It Girl" who heretofore was assumed to be pure as the driven snow by the network executives who hired her.

At least they got the *driven* part right.

Snow White in handcuffs.

Film at eleven.

This simple text message from my contact at the cop shop meant the bigwigs who ran my network would be looking for a replacement. Immediately. You can't exactly get the kids ready for school while watching an anchor who thinks *half 'n' half* is something other than what you put in your coffee. Anyway, it wouldn't take long for the vultures who wanted the job to start circling.

I would not be one of them. But even the chance that the network might pluck me from the local affiliate for this job from hell sent a chill up my spine.

Yeah, you heard me. Twenty million dollar job from hell. It was a gig this intrepid television reporter didn't want.

And in the back of my mind I knew, thanks to Murphy's Law, they'd want me for it.

Sonofabitch. I hate it when people offer me huge contracts.

My best friend Layla raised one perfectly plucked dark eyebrow like a question mark. "Veronica, you gonna throw your hat in the ring?"

"Hell, no!" I said, as I grabbed my wine glass and took a bigger sip than normal. A pre-emptive strike in case said hat ended up in said ring.

Since you're probably wondering why a local TV reporter wouldn't want a network anchor slot that pays a fortune, I should probably tell you a little about my method of deductive reasoning. I'm Veronica Summer, the top hard news reporter for the network's New York City flagship affiliate. The local version of an "It Girl." And at the age of thirty-two, this tall, green-eyed redhead has her career just where she wants it. I get the lead story almost every night, take no prisoners, and am generally considered to be the best old-school journalist in town. So the last thing I need is a job that forces me to talk about purses, hair color and breast feeding at the crack of dawn. There's a network job I want, a dream job, and that aint it.

Even if it pays about a hundred times more than my current salary.

"Why the hell don't y'all apply?" asked Savannah, the sultry Southern brunette who is the most logical in our group.

"Because the morning show is a bunch of soft bullshit," I said. "That's not me."

"I watch that show while I'm on the treadmill," said Layla,

who probably saw the dollar signs that came with the job before anything else. "They do *some* serious interviews. You could still do your Brenda Starr thing."

"Yeah, and that's about ten percent of the show," I said. "The operative word being *show,* not *newscast.* The other two hours are a flying Mongolian cluster of fluff consisting of musical guests, dieting tips and how to avoid picking up killer germs from shopping cart handles." I threw up my hands and shook them. "Run for your lives!"

Layla sat up straight and smiled as a cute guy walked by our table, then twirled a few strands of her jet black hair as she made eye contact. "You're gonna get a call."

"Pffft," I said, waving my hand like I was shooing a fly even though I knew she was right. "They've got a deep bench at the network. I'm not even a blip on their radar."

The discussion was thankfully interrupted as dinner arrived. Our regular waiter, a cute thirtysomething guy named Frank, slid a huge plate of fettuccine Alfredo with shrimp in from of me. I licked my lips. "Lotta cheese, as usual?" he asked.

"You know what I like," I said. His cheese grater hovered over my plate as he carpet-bombed my dinner with parmesan. I was thinking that even with twenty mil per year I'd still eat at this place. Loud and brassy, always busy with hardly any space between the tables, it had great food and portions large enough to end up with a to-go box for a midnight snack. The waiter finished serving and moved on to another table, while I turned my attention to one of the many flat screens that hung around the perimeter in the hopes of changing the topic. "Hey, the Mets are actually winning." I twirled some pasta with a shrimp into a neat ball and popped it in my mouth. Nothing like butter, cream, cheese, pasta and crustaceans to take your mind off things.

"Don't change the subject," said Layla. "You need to apply."

"They don't have someone like y'all," said Savannah. "You're pretty, smart, have the quickest wit of anyone I know. I'm sure men wouldn't mind waking up to you."

"The jury's out on that," said Layla, "because she throws them out the night before."

"I meant *on television*," said Savannah.

"And it pays twenty... million... dollars," said Layla. "Cha-ching."

I shook my head as I dabbed my mouth with a napkin. "The outgoing anchor has been there ten years. They're not going to pay that much for someone new."

"So you wouldn't do it for ten million?" asked Layla. She lowered her voice and said, "Cha-ching," again.

"It's a moot point," I said. "I'd take the evening anchor job in a heartbeat, but I'm not the kind of person they want for mornings. The 'P' word is a necessary skill set for that show."

"'P' word?" asked Savannah.

"Perky!" I said. I playfully batted my lashes as I widened my eyes and turned my voice into that of a high-pitched brainless bimbo. "It's what all morning shows want! Someone upbeat and cheerful before the sun comes up! Good morning! It's a beautiful day! Let's all be happy while you get your precious little snowflakes ready for school!" I went back to my normal sarcastic tone. "Can you picture me on a morning show? Hey guys, I'm Veronica Summer. What the hell are you guys doing up? Fuhgeddaboudit! Go back to bed and let the little bastards make their own damn school lunches!"

"Yeah, you're not exactly little miss sunshine in the morning. But you could fake it," said Layla. "You're good at faking things."

"Funny," I said, sneering at her. "Trust me, they're not going to call."

I really wanted to believe that as the discussion finally ended.

But dammit, they called the next day.

***

The network morning show is called, quite simply, The Morning Show. How much they paid someone to come up with that

4

incredibly clever title is a closely guarded secret. Rumor has it that ten years ago network executives went off on a three day retreat to revamp the morning offering and come up with a new name for the thing. After a long weekend running up a huge bill at some exotic getaway in the Bahamas and countless hours of brainstorming someone came up with the ground-breaking idea to add capital letters to the concept.

The people in Congress have nothing on network executives, who have raised lack of productivity to an art form.

Anyway, The Morning Show's executive producer Gavin Karlson was already seated at the last table in the restaurant when I arrived a few minutes after twelve on Saturday afternoon. The huge teddy bear of a man in the camel's hair sport coat and starched white shirt stood up to greet me, towering over me by nearly a foot. "Veronica, nice to finally meet you."

"Same here," I said. A waiter came by and pulled out my chair. "Thank you," I said as I sat down and he handed me a brown leather-bound menu with a gold tassel in the middle. Natural light spilled through the windows, giving rich tones to the dark paneled walls of the old place.

The fortyish egg-faced bald producer (a dead ringer for Doctor Evil) studied me with his piercing gray eyes, probably looking to see if I had that starry-eyed look most prospective network anchors have on interviews. I smiled casually, as if this were just a run of the mill two hundred dollar lunch with a co-worker. Besides, I didn't want the job anyway. But when a network exec invites you to lunch at the city's oldest and most expensive restaurant, or even a hot dog stand, you jump, because you never know what's down the road. Don't burn a bridge before you even cross it. "So," I said, "getting any sleep lately?"

He shook his head and smiled. "You kidding? This has been the worst week of my life. Between bailing Katrina Favor out of jail in the middle of the night and dealing with the tabloids, it's been hell."

I tried to hold back a smile as I recalled the local front pages the day after she'd been arrested. "When you've got stripper name like Favor, it's a hanging curveball over the middle of the plate for the headline writers. Some of those were pretty brutal."

"Yeah, but you have to admit they were clever. We all got a kick out of *Party Favor*."

"She put you in a tough position."

"She put herself in a tough position. Pun intended."

"Hey, you could moonlight writing headlines. But seriously, I guess it must have been tough to let her go."

"Actually, it was an easy call to fire her. Thank God for the morals clause in her contract." He looked around to see if anyone in the half-empty restaurant was paying attention, then leaned forward a bit and dropped his voice. "Between you and me, we were going to replace her anyway when her contract expired next year."

"Really? After ten years?"

"Her favorability ratings were slipping, she was a bear to work with and her salary was way out of line. Then again, I'm not the one who signed her to that ridiculous deal."

"Oh, so this gig no longer pays twenty million." I playfully tossed my napkin on the table. "I'm outta here."

"It still pays a helluva lot. More than you're making now."

I replaced my napkin, took a sip of water, then glanced at the menu, which, of course, did not include prices. "Hell, I'm sure these entrees cost more than I'm making now. So what's good here?"

He looked quizzically at me, as if wondering why I was more interested in food than begging for the job. (Because I actually *was* more interested in the food.) "Uh, everything. I always get the broiled salmon with dill sauce. Save room for tiramisu."

"Sounds good. Make it two," I said, snapping my menu shut as I leaned back in my chair. "So, I'm sure people have been beating a path to your door since the news broke."

"Women will eat their young for this job. No offense."

"None taken. Hell, I agree with you. Last time we had an anchor opening we could have made a fortune with a pay-per-view catfight between a few of our reporters."

"Anyway, with sweeps coming up we need to have the replacement in the chair soon. I don't need weeks of speculation in the papers or the newsroom."

"I'm sure you have many qualified candidates."

"We do. You're one of them."

I couldn't help but smile. "I'm flattered. But I must admit I'm curious as to why you're talking to me. I mean, I'm not exactly someone with a morning show or anchoring background. And I'm not known outside of the tri-state area."

His smart phone lit up and vibrated. He looked at it, didn't answer, and turned back to me. "Well, the day after Katrina got arrested, we all sat down and threw out names of possible replacements. Yours was one that came up a few times. You're an excellent journalist, and our co-anchor said you've got a sharp wit. I had no idea you two went to college together and are close friends."

"Yeah, Scott and I go way back. We just don't see each other much because of the hours. I'm getting off work when he's coming in. Ships passing in the night."

"Well, anyway, he thought you'd be a good choice, and I think it's important that co-anchors actually like each other. Scott and Katrina were oil and water."

"So I've heard. He was about to shoe polish the toilet seat in her private bathroom and Saran Wrap the bowl. Splish-splash."

He laughed a bit. "I would have paid good money to see that. Anyway, we've been thinking of adding a harder edge to the show. So we need a real journalist as opposed to a traditional morning show host."

I sat up straight and widened my eyes, feigning interest. "Harder edge as in..."

"More political interviews, investigative pieces. We would get you out in the field to do stories, so you wouldn't be chained to the desk."

"Hmmm. By the way, you said my name came up a few times. May I ask who else thought I might make a good replacement?"

"You may ask," he said, with a wicked smile.

I shook my head as I rolled my eyes. "Typical management. You should know Jedi Mind Tricks don't work on me. Besides, I can just ask Scott."

"I figured you would. Anyway, we're doing a few tryouts tomorrow morning starting at nine when no one's around. Attempting to make the search as quiet as possible while keeping the knife throwing in the newsroom to a minimum. Scott's coming in and we're going to do a mock show with Friday's script. I'd really like you to come in if you're interested."

I wasn't, but turning down this man was career suicide. I'd never be considered for anything at the network again. I knew the "harder edge" was bogus, just a carrot to try to gain my interest. I'd just bomb the tryout and be on my way back to my real job. I forced a little excitement into my eyes and smiled. "Sure, I'll be happy to," I said, as I picked up my water glass.

"Great, I'll email you the script so you can look it over. Oh, one more thing that might pique your interest. One reason we want Katrina's replacement to do hard news is that this is the stepping stone to the evening anchor position. We see the person we hire as the heir apparent."

My glass froze in midair. Whatever attempt I was making at being casual went right out the window as my jaw dropped. That dream job I mentioned earlier? Yeah, this was it. Known as *The Chair*, the job was referred to with reverence by reporters, as if it could be spoken in italics. Gavin had dangled the ultimate carrot. "The morning show anchor will eventually replace Bill Recker?"

He nodded and smiled as he licked his lips, now having my attention and soul firmly tucked away in his pocket. Ruthless bastard. "He's retiring in three and a half years. That's not common knowledge by the way, but he's sixty-one and tired of the grind. Wants to sail around the world on his yacht before he's too old to do it. But he wants one more presidential election, and then he's gone. So the plan is to keep Katrina's replacement on mornings till he walks out with a gold watch, then slide that person into *The Chair*. Well, actually, it would be three years on the morning show, and then..."

And then he dropped another enticing piece of produce.

"Six months covering Senator Dixon's presidential campaign."

And just like that, the job in which I had no interest was now a job I *had* to have.

***

"I forbid you to take this job."

My latest boyfriend's words out of the blue stopped me just as I was about to apply the whipped cream to his washboard abs. I sat up and put the can of Reddi-Wip on the nightstand. Obviously my plan for round two on this Saturday afternoon human dessert bar had been doused with a bucket of cold water. "*Excuse* me?"

"You heard me," said Alexander Dumont, my significant other for the past four months. He put his hands behind his head and locked his fingers. "I forbid it."

The night's dinner reservations at the city's trendiest restaurant went right out the window. I got off the bed, stood up, folded my arms in front of me and stuck out one foot like an angry teacher even though I was wearing nothing but a bright red thong. "Who the hell are you to *forbid* me to do anything that pertains to my career?"

"I'm your boyfriend, the man who is going to take care of you. And if you take this job and start getting up at two o'clock in the morning, we won't be able to continue our relationship. I already put up with you working nights."

I raised one eyebrow. "Oh, you *put up* with that, do you?"

"Every other guy I know has a girlfriend who works normal hours. Or a wife who stays home."

"Well, these are the normal hours for my job. And I'll never be a Stepford wife. I don't need someone to take care of me. I can take care of myself. Always have."

"You could get them to put you on the day shift."

"The eleven o'clock newscast is the station's signature broadcast, and I'm the lead reporter—"

"Yeah, yeah, I've heard about how important it is for viewers to go to bed watching your channel so that's what they're watching when they turn the TV on in the morning. Real rocket science."

"What I do for a living is important, Alexander. And I love what I do. You should know that by now."

"I just figured at some point your biological clock would kick in and this little fling with broadcasting would be over."

Now he'd crossed the line. My pulse spiked as my eyes widened. "Little fling?"

"You tell stories for a living. C'mon, it's not a real job."

Annndddd… cue the anger. "And you sell stocks to people. You're nothing more than a legalized bookie taking bets that companies will make money. Wall Street is a glorified casino."

"Don't change the subject. You're not taking this morning show job. You're not a morning person anyway."

"You don't get it. This will lead to the main network anchor job in three and a half years. You know how many people have sat in that chair in the last half century? Three. I'll be the face of the network at thirty-five. And I'll get to cover Sydney Dixon's campaign, and she's a lock to be the next President. I'll get to travel the world, have the President of the United States on speed dial, take trips on Air Force One—"

"Great, I'll see even less of you."

"It's my dream job."

"It doesn't work for me. Or my plan for us. You're not taking the job. End of story. C'mon, get back in bed."

He reached out for me and I shoved his hand away. My blood reached its boiling point, but I'm one of those people who can still think rationally even when I'm seriously pissed off. Reporters often see things in black and white, with very few gray areas. And at that moment, I knew I had to step back and look at the situation as a reporter, not as a girlfriend. I took a long look at the thirty-five year old man my friends considered to be an incredible catch. Tall, classically handsome with (ironically) an anchorman's square jaw, deep set dark brown eyes that matched the color of his short hair, a rugged face. A seriously buffed body to die for and sex that was off the charts. But the realization hit me that the man I had planned to turn into a hundred and eighty pound chocolate sundae didn't even know me.

Or didn't want to.

And just like that, I reached a decision. I knew it was time to cut my losses. "Get out."

"Excuse me?"

"You heard me. Get your underwear off the trapeze and your toothbrush out of my bathroom and whatever other stuff you've got around here and get out. You've got thirty minutes and after that anything I find that belongs to you is going down the garbage chute. We're done."

He reached out for me again. "C'mon, babe, calm down."

I glared at him. "Oh, I'm very calm. You just showed your true colors. You have absolutely no respect for my career, or for what I want to do with my life. Which, since you obviously didn't get the memo, is not yours to mold. And in case you haven't been to a wedding in a while, they took the *obey* part out of the vows, so you can't *forbid* me to do anything. You *put up* with me for the past few months? Well now you won't have to *put up* with anything. Go get yourself a nine-to-five girlfriend."

"You're serious."

I nodded. "We're done, Alexander. As you would say, end of story."

CHAPTER TWO

Scott Winter is known as "America's boy next door." One look at him tells you why.

Not classically handsome but beyond cute, he's got a mop of always-tousled black hair that leaves the impression it's been styled by some babe who ran her fingers through it after having her way with him. Combine that with devilish olive green eyes that make him look like he's up to something, a permanent five o'clock shadow, and a lean face accented by dimples that run the length of his cheeks, and you've got a guy with the highest "Q" rating in television.

That means viewers like him more than anyone else. On any network.

Women *really* like him. And they all want to sleep with him, even though he's happily married to his high school sweetheart and would never, ever cheat.

At five-foot-ten he's the biggest thing on television.

And he's been my friend for fourteen years since the day we met freshman year.

He stepped off the set to greet me as I entered the studio. "Hey, it's The Spitfire!" he said, using my nickname.

"Hi, Scott," I said, as he gave me a strong hug and almost lifted my hundred and thirty-five pounds off the floor.

"There's something I haven't seen between our co-anchors in awhile," said Gavin Karlson.

"Do we have to do a tryout?" asked Scott, as he wrapped one arm around my shoulders. "Can't we just hire her right now?"

"Sorry," said the producer. "This one's not my call. But you've got as much input as I do."

"Yeah, I know," said Scott.

Gavin looked at me. "So, you go by *Spitfire*?"

"My dad gave me that nickname when I was a little girl since he said I was an out of control ball of fire."

"Nothing's changed," said Scott. I playfully slapped his shoulder. "So, you ready to become the next morning show It Girl?"

"I don't know if I'd get that title, but I'd love to work with you."

"It would be nice to see you more. And my wife would be thrilled if you were my partner. She got a little tired of my bitching about Katrina."

"Well, thank goodness for the NYPD Vice Squad."

Gavin interrupted our little reunion. "You guys ready?"

Scott nodded, then took me by the hand and led me up the riser to the set, a grouping featuring a red leather couch and matching chair, a mahogany coffee table and a couple of giant flat screens hanging off the back wall which was painted royal blue. "We haven't anchored together since college. Remember how we always planned to work together?"

I nodded as we both sat down in the anchor chairs. "I'd forgotten about that, but maybe this is it. Just took ten years to get there."

"Why don't you read through the script a few times before we roll tape," said Gavin, who headed out of the studio. "I'll get someone to run the prompter and leave you two to practice."

"Sure," said Scott, who turned to me. "When was the last time you anchored?"

"I filled in a few times this year, but never more than two days in a row."

"Well, just think back to our college days. Like riding a bike.

And remember, this is different than a regular newscast. It's more about personality than anything else."

I couldn't help but smile as the memory of our college newscast flashed through my mind. We had incredible chemistry that only works in television if the anchors like each other. I wondered if it would still show up after a decade apart.

A young brunette entered the studio and sat down at the tele-prompter control station.

"That's Mandy," said Scott. "Mandy, this is Veronica."

She waved and gave me a cheerful smile. "Hi!"

"Hi, Mandy," I said, smiling back.

"Her pace is probably a little faster than Katrina's," said Scott. Mandy nodded.

"Okay, you ready to do this?" he asked.

"Let's rock," I said.

I faced the camera and the words filled the prompter.

"Welcome to the Morning Show, America. I'm Scott Winter..."

"And I'm Veronica Summer. Thank you so much for joining us this Friday morning."

And just like that, I was twenty-two again, anchoring next to my closest friend in the business, looking at a future that was suddenly very bright.

Until I began to stumble through the script like I was twenty-two.

****

The job I didn't want that became the job I had to have had quickly become the "what if" moment I'd look back on for the rest of my life.

Remember my original plan to tank the tryout? This was worse.

The prompter may as well have been filled with Chinese. Even after three practice runs, I had become the victim of the classic rookie anchor mistake: stumbling out of the gate and becoming a snowball rolling downhill as I focused so much on the first screw-up I continued to make more.

Thankfully the mock interview segments we taped didn't require me to actually read, or it would have been even worse.

I knew it was gone. *The Chair*, the presidential campaign, rides on Air Force One, all history.

I shook my head as I looked at Scott. "I sure screwed the pooch on this opportunity."

"Pffft. Don't worry about it. They know you're not used to anchoring."

"Yeah, but they could find a small market anchor who could read the prompter better than I did."

He shrugged. "Not the biggest factor on this show."

Mandy the prompter girl walked toward the set and extended her hand. "It was nice meeting you," she said, her sad look telling me she knew she'd never see me again.

"You too," I said.

The door to the studio opened. Gavin Karlson walked through it and headed toward the set. For some odd reason he was smiling.

I dipped my head and looked up at him through sad eyes, like I'd been a bad student caught by the teacher. "I promise to buy *Hooked on Phonics* this afternoon."

He chuckled a bit. "Don't beat yourself up. You were fine."

"Amazing. You're channeling my mother."

He turned to Scott. "She obviously doesn't understand what we're looking for."

"Nope. Sure doesn't," he said.

"Let me guess," I said. "You're looking for an actress to play the *before* role in a stuttering commercial."

Gavin laughed as he sat down on the couch in the seat previously occupied by our mock interview subject. "Veronica, morning shows are all about personality. I could put any number of people in the chair to read a prompter flawlessly, but I need someone who has both incredible chemistry with Scott and who can connect with the viewers. Especially the female ones."

I cocked my head toward Scott. "I think *every woman's dream* over here has that covered." Scott tried to hold back a smile and blushed a bit.

"You still don't understand," said Gavin. "We need a woman that every man wants and who every woman wants to be. Someone who's going to attract men but not turn off the women. Someone who's approachable in the eyes of both sexes. If we paired some ice queen with him we'd lose the women even though they love Scott."

"But you said you wanted a harder edge to the show," I said.

"I do," said Gavin, "but it's still crucial that the new co-anchor bring great chemistry to the equation. The fact that you two have been friends for years really came through the screen. It's obvious you like each other. When we brought Scott on two years ago the women responded, but Katrina had no chemistry with him. She started resenting all the attention he got and it showed. She came off like a bitch with some of her snide comments and that turned off a lot of women. I've got a few thousand emails if you wanna read 'em."

"So, I'm still in the running?"

"Very much so."

My spirits lifted a bit and I actually smiled.

Until I saw the competition strut into the studio.

***

Every Sunday for the past five years I've had a standing appointment with my two closest friends. We meet at the same restaurant for brunch at eleven.

And even though I'm about twenty minutes late, I already know the topic of conversation.

Me.

Thankfully, they'll be supportive, which is what I need right now. I guess I should tell you about them.

Layla Starr has been my best friend since high school. The first time I saw her and heard her name, I did the judge-a-book-by-its-cover thing. At fourteen she had reached her current height, five-ten, and current figure, classic supermodel. With huge ice blue eyes that are a striking contrast to her black shoulder length hair, she could have been a model right then. With a name like Layla she was an obvious target for off-color comments from the boys at school.

When she was assigned to be my chemistry lab partner and I caught a glimpse of her killer body and perfect cheekbones, I rolled my eyes knowing I'd be wearing invisibility spray as the males in the classroom would totally ignore me. One of the boys nearly blew up the lab when she came to class one day in her cheerleader uniform that showed off legs up to her neck. Anyway, turned out she was this conservative girl from a strict family much like mine, so we became fast friends. I consider her the sister I never had.

The girl routinely stops Manhattan traffic and gets carded at bars, as the woman has apparently discovered the fountain of youth. She's solid muscle, working as an aerobics instructor, as her body still doesn't have an ounce of fat. You could bounce quarters off the girl's ass.

Savannah is my fish-out-of-water friend, a Southern belle from Mississippi whose main objective in life is to divorce herself from her evil family traditions that exist south of the Mason-Dixon line. This goal came about when, at the age of twenty-two, she graduated from college and was promptly anointed an "old maid" by her mother. After a few months of being compared to her high school cohorts who were already well established in the trailer park and regularly showed off their cereal covered spawn every Friday night at Wal-Mart, Savannah left town with nothing but her devastating looks and incredibly sultry drawl. She headed straight for the Big Apple. Luckily she brought a serious amount of common sense and surprising level of street smarts with her. I happened to meet her the day she arrived while working on a story at the airport, took pity on her and offered her my couch until she got situated. Which she promptly did the next day, as she relocated from my sofa to the apartment of the cute guy who lived next door. He also took pity on her, but in the end she left nothing but an empty husk.

A curvy, five-six brunette whose mahogany tangles end in the middle of her back, she's used her pale green eyes and pouty lips to advance her career as a political consultant who is often the spokesperson for campaigns. Clients seek her out since she's whip smart and can make any man feel like he's the only person in the room. (And by nightfall it often ends up that way.) She can also charm a crowd in a political debate by inserting charming Southernisms into the discussion. Savannah calls herself a "serial dater" but when she says it with that accent it actually sounds charming. She'll pretty much date any decent guy once, as there is apparently a little known congressional bill called "no man left behind." At twenty-eight she's the baby sister in our group.

The girls were already seated at our usual corner table, sipping mimosas as patrons crowded the long buffet line, so deep in conversation they didn't notice my arrival until I pulled out my chair.

Layla looked up and smiled, studied my face, then bit her lower lip. "Uh-oh."

I shook my head and said nothing.

"What?" asked Savannah.

"Well," I said, taking my seat as I flagged down the waiter with the tray of mimosas, "so much for my dream of anchoring the nightly news."

"What happened?" asked Savannah. "Y'all look like someone ran over your dog."

"I couldn't read the prompter. I stumbled through every script. Worse than in college."

"You haven't anchored in forever," said Layla. "I'm sure they know that. How did you do with Scott?"

"That part was okay," I said, as my mimosa arrived. "And the producer said we had great chemistry."

Savannah smiled. "There you go! Chemistry's important. I hate it when anchors don't like each other. Did the producer give you any other feedback?"

"He said I was still in the running, and I believed him," I said. "Until..."

"Until what?" asked Savannah.

"The competition walked in." I took a long sip of my drink. I needed liquid courage before discussing she-who-must-not-be-named.

"And said competition would be?" asked Layla.

I swallowed hard. "Noelle Larson."

Both raised eyebrows and said nothing for a minute. They knew what the implications were. The clanging of silverware and glasses replaced the conversation. The smell of a roast wafted by as a chef wheeled out a huge steamship round.

"Oooh, that looks good," I said.

"I thought Noelle got out of the business when she left the other morning show," said Layla, who obviously wasn't going to drop the subject.

I nodded as I leaned back in my chair. "She did, last year. But rumor had it that she was waiting out her non-compete clause for something else. Rumor was apparently true." I shook my head and stared at my drink. "There's no way they'll pick me instead of her. I mean, she's a morning show icon. And you should have seen her. Six foot blonde, short skirt with perfect legs, four-inch heels. Plus she's had a boob job since America last saw her and looks like she could nurse a small village. She was spilling out of her blouse."

Savannah reached across the table and patted my hand. "Well, y'all don't fret your pretty lil' head. They probably don't want someone who's plastic."

"You should have seen the producer," I said. "Practically tripped over his tongue. Then she heads up to the set, says hello to Scott, pretends she doesn't know me and asks if I'm a production assistant. Bitch."

"They won't pick her," said Layla. "She's older than Scott. It'll look like a cougar newscast."

"She's only forty and she's got a history of delivering ratings in the morning," I said, slugging down the rest of my drink.

"And she's too tall," said Layla. "She'll tower over him."

"Right," said Savannah. "That poor little thing will look like a munchkin next to her."

"Look, I appreciate you guys trying to find excuses to keep me in the running," I said. "But it's game over. What the hell, I've still got a great job. Let's eat."

"It's not over, sweetie," said Layla. "Remember, Scott's gotta have some input as to who they hire."

"He does," I said. "But I can't compete with a real life silicone Barbie doll."

***

As I headed down to the newsstand for the Monday morning papers, I decided it was in my best interest to totally forget about the job, relax and smell the roses. (Or, in the case of this part of Manhattan, the lovely residue of a garbage strike.) It was pointless to worry about something that was out of my control, and with Noelle Larson in the picture the job was a million-to-one longshot anyway. It dawned on me I was probably a courtesy interview to appease Scott.

Yeah, let's go with that.

The air was cool and crisp. At ten o'clock commuters were out of the way and the five block hike to the newsstand was an easy one. I liked buying hard copies from a human being, bypassing the electronic version or the delivery to the door of my apartment. And midtown was still populated by those classic green newsstands, with the dailies in a stack weighted down by half a brick while every magazine available hung from the sides. Besides, it forced me to walk every day and get some exercise, which I loathed. (And canceled out the candy bar I always bought with the papers.) I reached the newsstand, grabbed the city's three dailies and a Fast Break (a wonderful concoction of chocolate and peanut butter) and handed a five to Hal, the grizzled, fiftyish guy running the stand who always had a three day growth of silver whiskers.

"I think you're both, Freckles," he said, using his personal nickname for me.

"Excuse me?"

He pointed at my newspapers as he looked over the top of his silver reading glasses. "Page Six," he said, as he handed me my change.

Uh-oh.

Page Six was the city's clearinghouse for gossip, and obviously it had something to do with me. I opened *The Post* and saw the headline above side-by-side pictures of myself and Noelle Larson. The huge bold typeface screamed at me.

RED / HOT
Chase is on for Katrina Favor's job

So much for keeping it quiet.

The paparazzi had apparently snapped a photo of me entering the network headquarters yesterday, and done the same with Noelle Larson. Her photo was under the "hot" part of the headline (it was no contest, considering the length of her skirt) while I filled the side of the page under "red."

"Damn," I said out loud.

"Like I said, Freckles, you're both," said Hal. "Red hot Veronica, that's what I'm gonna call you now."

"Gee thanks, Hal," I said, as I leaned against his stand to read the article.

By Gemma Farrington

It's a network catfight in a game of musical chairs.

Producers of The Morning Show didn't waste any time holding tryouts Sunday morning for Katrina Favor's now empty co-anchor spot. Sources tell us that network execs are scrambling to find a replacement after Ms. Favor's arrest last week following her embarrassing dalliance with a male prostitute. Co-anchor Scott Winter was dragged in on his day off Sunday as the network shuttled a parade of info-babes onto the anchor desk. And with ratings sweeps just around the corner, the decision will come quickly.

Despite the long hours of tryouts, we're told the short list has but two names on it. Former morning show queen Noelle Larson, who left her post at the competition a year ago due to a contract dispute, and NYC reporter Veronica Summer, the fiery redhead who makes corrupt politicians run for cover.

While Larson's assets (both journalistically and physically) are well known to viewers, Ms. Summer is a wild card in the deck, having no anchoring or morning show experience. She's also a local reporter, so is unknown to a national audience. While this might seem to leave her at a disadvantage her off-camera relationship with Mr. Winter makes her a formidable challenger. The two attended college together and are said to be close friends; Ms. Summer was even a bridesmaid at Mr. Winter's wedding.

Chemistry could be the deciding factor in the choice, even though Ms. Summer does not seem to possess the typical morning show perkiness that has become the industry standard for women. It's no secret that Katrina Favor did not approve of Winter's hire two years ago, and their relationship off camera was said to be ice cold.

Who would you rather see sitting next to America's Boy Next Door? His attractive best friend from college with whom he has a warm (yet platonic) relationship? Or the towering blonde with the mile-long legs and the cheerful attitude that will give you a cavity? Vote in our Internet poll. Results on Wednesday.

"*Sources tell us*, my ass," I said aloud.

"Story not true?" asked Hal.

"It was supposed to be a secret."

"Well, I voted for you," he said, holding up an iPad.

"Thank you, Hal." I grabbed another candy bar and tossed him a buck. "Think I need a double today."

I turned and headed back to my apartment, feeling naked as it seemed every person on the street was staring at me. I'm used to being recognized, but not like this. I forced a smile at everyone, but it was through clenched teeth.

Gavin Karlson was pissing me off. I knew damn well he was the "source" and was using the newspaper to float a trial balloon. Yeah, he wanted to keep it quiet. Bullshit. The damn story would be in the paper until Thursday, the day after the results of the "poll" were released. And the whole thing would no doubt be picked up by every entertainment publication in the country.

And speaking of the poll, did it mean I really was on the short list of two? Or was this simply a ploy to find out if people wanted to wake up with Noelle again?

Inquiring minds wanna know.

It was time for this reporter to start digging.

CHAPTER THREE

As an Emmy Award winning reporter, you'd think I'd be able to investigate my own life. But despite the tabloids seemingly permanent pipeline to that network "source" I've not been able to find out a damn thing about the decision to replace Katrina. Even Scott has been no help, apparently being left out of the loop after pleading my case to the network. (He also told the bigwigs his apprehension about working with a glamazon who made him look like a hobbit when she stood next to him in heels that took her up to six-foot-four.)

Oh, and that resolution I made to forget it and smell the roses? Fuhgeddaboudit. That barn door has sailed, as we say in the news business.

By Friday I had turned into a teenage girl hoping for a date to the prom. Every time the phone rang I jumped, waiting for news that would at least resolve the situation. Luckily Savannah has asked me to lunch, obviously noting I had become a walking frayed nerve ending.

While Layla is my best friend, Savannah is a world class expert at putting things in perspective with that Southern way of looking at things. (The laid-back and relaxed view of life, not that of her relatives whose family trees are of the pine variety with reunions that might have been accompanied by banjo music.) And since she works in politics, she always knows how to spin things. The girl could make a colonoscopy sound like fun.

Since I would be off to work in an hour I sadly bypassed the glass of wine I really needed in favor of club soda with lime. Savannah had chosen a quiet, elegant restaurant featuring soft violin music instead of my usual preference, a loud place with flat screens filled with ballgames that served kick-ass fried cheese.

"Y'all look so pretty today," she said, as always starting things off with a compliment.

"Considering I've hardly slept all week, I'm sure you're being polite."

"Well, you can't handle this all by yourself, sweetie. If you don't let go of the worry, you're fixin' to have a nervous breakdown."

"I think that happened when I saw my picture in *The Post*."

"Hey, you did well in the poll. Against Noelle, that's saying something."

I nodded slightly, realizing she had a point. I had expected a landslide in favor of the competition, but I actually came in a close second with forty-eight percent of the vote. "I was surprised at that, considering the photo of her that they ran."

"Did y'all forget that morning shows are predominantly watched by women? They don't want to tune in and watch a girl who looks like a wanton harlot."

"Wanton harlot?"

"Genteel Southern way of calling her a cheap bimbo." Savannah sipped her glass of wine as she looked over the menu. "That dress she almost wore was not exactly appropriate."

"Yeah, but a few years ago her producer was quoted as saying her legs were worth five share points. Why do you think they never put her behind a desk?"

"Let's not talk about that trollop anymore."

"I guess we could talk about the boyfriend I no longer have."

"You havin' second thoughts about throwin' your dog off the porch?"

I chuckled at the Southernism I'd never heard before. "Hell, no. He needs to move to Connecticut and find himself some Junior Leaguer who will bring him his slippers when he gets home, put on her kneepads and service him when the lights go out. Then send him a thank you note for not taking more than ten minutes."

She snapped her menu closed and waved for the waiter. "Ah'm sorry that didn't work out, but it's for the best. You don't need a man like that. You've got too much goin' for you."

"But not quite enough for the network."

"Will y'all stop it? You're young, you've got that beautiful red hair and those darling little freckles and gorgeous eyes and a great body. Plus you're smart and you've got a great job that you love." She leaned forward and gave me a soulful look. "And friends who love you."

"I know, I shouldn't complain. I really do have a lot to be thankful for. And I do appreciate you guys more than you know. But the shot at the evening anchor job comes along once in a lifetime."

"I guess we're not going to get off that subject. By the way, did you find out who is leaking all that information to the newspaper?"

"I don't have concrete proof, but it's gotta be the producer. However, he may have been under orders from the network president. That's the one thing that worries me about the job."

"What's that?"

"That if I get it, there's someone there I already can't trust."

***

My cell rang just as I left the station for my dinner break. I pulled it from my purse and felt my pulse quicken as I saw the name of the caller.

Scott.

"Hey there," I said. "Up past your bedtime?"

"It's Friday. I can be a night owl and stay up till eight. Might sleep in till four."

"Wow, aren't you the wild child. So, what's up?"

"I have good news and bad news."

I stopped walking and leaned against a store display window. A cute guy recognized me and smiled, so I smiled back. "Give me the bad news first."

"Let me preface this by telling you something I've never told anyone. The air duct in my private bathroom connects to Gavin's office. So I've pretty much heard everything he's said for the past two years."

"Just give me the bad news!"

I heard him exhale deeply. "They offered the job to Noelle."

My heart sank, the color drained from my face as my knees weakened. My body slid down against the glass as I went into a crouch. "Well, I can't say I'm surprised. I'm sure you'll do well with her."

"Don't you want the good news?"

"What, that I came in second and should be happy I got that far?"

"You should."

"That's your definition of good news?"

"It's a very important part of it. Because, and listen to my words very closely. She didn't take the job."

My head snapped to attention. "Wow. You're kidding!"

"Hey, I spent an hour in the can this afternoon listening to their negotiations. She wanted Katrina's salary, a five year contract, and a signing bonus. Basically a package worth a hundred and ten million."

"Holy shit!"

"They offered eight million a year for three years, no bonus. Bottom line, she got very insulted, showed her true colors and ripped Gavin a new one. Told him to go screw himself and walked out. She didn't just burn the bridge, she napalmed the damn thing. I thought Katrina was a bitch but this woman has raised it to an art form. Anyway, turns out she had another offer in her pocket from a syndicator that offered more money for her to do daytime talk without getting up in the middle of the night. I just found out she signed this afternoon."

"Scott, I'm blown away."

Long pause. "So, you want the good news?"

"There's more?"

"Do the math, kiddo. You came in second and should be happy you got that far."

My eyes widened and my adrenaline pushed me up to a standing position. "Are you saying..."

"You'll be getting a call Monday. They were busy hammering out an offer sheet late this afternoon."

I tried my best not to scream in the middle of the street, holding it in until I got home. "You know, Scott, you really buried the lead on this one. You could have just told me I got the job right up front."

"Hey, you were the one who asked for the bad news first." Slight pause. "You're going to get even with me for this, aren't you?"

"You know me too well. But I'll let you slide on this one. Listen, thanks for everything you did to make this happen. I know you had a lot of input."

CHAPTER FOUR

My grandfather owned an old fashioned hardware store, and it ticked him off to no end that I enjoyed playing there as a little girl. I mean, he loved me to death and I couldn't get enough of the guy. But to Pops, hardware was a man's game, and no place for a six year old girl who should otherwise be occupied with Barbie dolls or skipping rope. To me the place was a giant metal toy store, where I could do cool stuff with magnets and leave countless colorful chalk marks on the walls using that plumb line thing. (In case you hadn't guessed by now, I'm one of those kids who colored outside the lines in grade school.)

Pops had a display in the front window in a futile attempt to scare the women away by offending them. When women's lib hit the country and skirts first appeared in his store, he took action by placing a small, bright red toolbox in the front window with a sign reading, "Woman's toolbox. Fully stocked. $19.95." Inside were two things: a can of WD-40 and a roll of duct tape. When women asked about it, he replied in this manner: "If it moves and shouldn't, duct tape. If it should move but doesn't, WD-40. If a woman has to deal with anything else, she needs to call a man."

Reporters all have virtual toolboxes. Writing ability, poise, the ability to wing it, a built-in bullshit detector and, most important in New York City, street smarts. The one tool they should give you in journalism class but don't is this thing called negotiating skills.

Because when you're dealing with broadcasting management, you've just entered the world's sleaziest car dealership and you're about to sit down with a man in a polyester suit. "So, what's it gonna take to put you behind the wheel of this morning show, little lady?"

We even have a newsroom acronym that describes the process. BOHICA.

Bend over, here it comes again.

As I headed to Gavin's office on Monday morning, I was armed with very little in the way of bargaining power. Because he has those world class carrots of *The Chair* and The Campaign to dangle. (I've decided the latter now deserves capital letters, like The Morning Show.) And there are a dozen other qualified women who would offer to have his children for the chance. (By the way, upper news management is predominantly filled by poster children for male-pattern ugliness who would otherwise have no shot at even being in the same zip code as a woman who looks like Noelle Larson. Power is the great equalizer in this business.)

Scott has filled me in on the specifics of Noelle's offer, complete with all the little perks they were willing to throw in. Some are standard for morning show anchors, like a limo to take you to the studio. They don't want their bleary-eyed stars scraping wind-shields, shoveling the driveway or getting behind the wheel half-asleep at two in the morning. Others are not, like their offer to insure Noelle's legs for one million dollars. (Should have thrown in a fifty dollar policy rider for her brain.)

Gavin's hot blonde secretary smiled and waved me into his massive corner office featuring floor-to-ceiling windows that offered a great view of Central Park. I had arrived at five minutes till nine. He got up from behind his antique oak desk which was cluttered with papers and extended his hand. "You're early. I like that."

I shook his hand. "I figured if I was late you'd give the job to someone else."

He smiled and gestured to one of the two chairs opposite his desk. "Your agent on the way?"

"Don't have one." Big smile from Gavin. Management hates dealing with agents.

"I'm surprised, but I'm not gonna complain. However, I am rather curious as to why you don't employ one for something like this."

I was glad I hadn't as I looked around the office. Half a dozen Emmy Awards sat on the wooden credenza behind his desk, while the bookshelf cubicles were filled with more award statues I didn't recognize. The walls were covered with photos featuring Gavin with various celebrities. There was a class system in television, and I wasn't in the top one yet. He was.

"Look, I could bring some shark in here to play hardball and maybe get another ten percent out of you, and then I'd have to turn around and give him ten percent of the gross instead of the net. Do the math. And I don't want to get off on the wrong foot. Besides, I'm old fashioned and think we're adult enough to make a deal in a civilized fashion without any lawyers in the room."

"Well, that's refreshing."

"I said no lawyers *in the room*. That doesn't mean I won't have mine look over the contract. Which I'm sure is fine."

"Fair enough. And since we're putting our cards on the table, I'll be honest. We offered the job to Noelle and she turned it down. But you were a close second anyway."

"I'm sure I'm a helluva lot cheaper."

He tried to hold back a smile and was unsuccessful. "This is still a helluva lot of money we're talking about." He opened a red folder, took out a single sheet of paper and slid it toward me. "This is the basic offer. I'll give you a more detailed contract to take home and review with your attorney, but the broad strokes are covered here so you don't have to wade through the legalese."

I grabbed the sheet of paper and tried my best not to let my eyes bug out, but when the word "million" ends up next to "salary" it's hard to keep a poker face.

It wasn't Katrina's money, or Noelle's. But for a girl who grew up in a hardware store, it was enough to buy enough duct tape to circle the planet a few times and hose down the entire globe with WD-40. The salary was more money that I could possibly spend, even after taxes. Three year contract, five million per. A list of wonderful perks. "That's extremely generous," I said. *For someone who's never anchored or done a morning show,* I thought, but didn't say.

"We want you to be comfortable."

"Hell, Gavin, I could eat lobster every day on this. Even after my income tax funds jobs for ten government slugs."

"So, thoughts?"

"Well, this looks fine, but I do have two small requests."

He rolled his eyes. "Oh geez..."

"No, no, these aren't going to cost you anything. One has to do with a staff writer at my affiliate. George Winson."

"Don't think I've ever met him."

"We'll, you're heard his words for years if you've watched our newscast. Anyway, he's sixty-two with a kid in grad school and the current News Director is trying to force him to quit so he can hire someone younger and cheaper. He's got three years till retirement and I'd love to bring him along."

"I thought this wasn't going to cost me anything."

"It's not. I'd like you to subtract his salary from mine. Basically, I wanna pay for him. He's a good friend and I'll need a fabulous writer for this gig anyway. Personally I love to write but I can't do it at three in the morning."

"Sounds very doable. Katrina's writer just quit anyway. She didn't like Scott."

"Great. Pay him a hundred grand, and make my salary four-point-nine million."

"That's incredibly generous of you, Veronica. I'd heard you were great to work with but I've never heard of something like this."

"When people are good to me, I have their backs."

"Very nice. What's the second thing?"

"My salary is *never* to be made public. Never, ever. I don't want newspapers referring to me as a five million dollar a year anchor, and I don't want people in the newsroom resenting me because of my salary. When I sign this contract I want it buried in that warehouse at the end of *Raiders of the Lost Ark*."

"Fine with me. If you don't tell anyone, it will never get out."

"No leaks to the tabloids."

He shrugged and said, "Yeah, sure. Not a problem." I studied his face, looking for anything that might confirm my suspicion that he was the leak to Page Six, but I saw nothing. If the guy had a tell, I'd have to figure out what it was.

We chatted for about an hour, going over the parameters of the job, what was expected, my stories in the field and after-hours appearances. Of course, I was pretty much giving him the husband-tuning-out-wife-bobblehead, nodding at everything while my daydream had already time-warped a few years into the future. It showed me covering the presidential campaign and anchoring the evening newscast.

I left at ten, heading directly for my lawyer's office with contract in hand, but I knew I'd sign it.

And then I learned something. I'd often heard anchors who make millions bitch about all the pressure they were under, and I'd always scoffed at it, thinking, yeah, must be real tough taking home that much dough.

I wasn't scoffing anymore, as I broke out in a cold sweat.

***

When you're a single woman living in a one-bedroom Manhattan apartment that costs two grand a month, you dream of a walk-in closet.

This job comes with one. Sadly, it's located at network headquarters.

It also comes with a clothing allowance. Actually, if you imagine your sugar daddy is a billionaire. All of my new clothes cost me nothing.

The wardrobe consultant took me shopping on the company dime and now I have about fifteen new outfits that will supposedly make me look my best, blend with the set, set off my hair and eyes, etc. While I usually slip into a size seven quite easily, a few things needed slight alterations. So I've been on a pedestal in one of the network's wardrobe rooms while a middle-aged pudgy woman named Nancy sizes up the turquoise skirt I'm currently wearing. I kept looking at the rack holding my new wardrobe thinking everything hanging on it probably cost more than I made last year.

Nancy was about to go to work on altering the skirt when she was interrupted by a polite knock on the door. "You decent?" I recognized the voice as Gavin's.

"Yeah, come on in," I said.

He opened the door and walked into the fitting room, sleeves rolled up and red tie loosened. I noticed he had a sizable bay window that was previously covered by his suit jacket. "Just checking on the wardrobe progress. Nancy, how are you?"

"Fine, Gavin." Nancy stepped back and pointed toward my skirt. "Okay?"

Gavin walked completely around me, checking out my outfit, which, I must admit, felt a little creepy. Okay, my skin crawled. He ended up facing me and smiled, then turned to Nancy. He held up four fingers and she nodded. "Okay, you two have fun." He turned and left the room, closing the door behind him.

"What the hell was that all about?" I asked.

"Gavin likes to have input on the clothes before they hit the air."

"Well, we already bought 'em." I furrowed my brow. "What was the deal with him holding up four fingers?"

"That means I need to hem this skirt four inches shorter than it already is."

It was already about three inches above the knee. "Good God, I'm not Noelle with the world's longest inseam. This skirt will be up to my ass."

"Gavin's a leg man," she said. "And you've got a pair of good ones. They'll never see a day behind the desk anyway, since the female host always sits in the leg chair."

"The *leg chair*?"

"Yeah, it's the one at the end of the couch. Scott's behind the coffee table, but his co-host gets the leg chair which offers camera two an unobstructed view. You'll also be required to wear stilettos or platforms."

"And all my hemlines will be halfway up my thigh?"

"When you stand, anyway. When you sit, well…"

CHAPTER FIVE

Here's the thing about my new shift. Getting up at two in the morning isn't a big deal.

Knowing you have to fall asleep eight hours earlier, is.

I'd gone to bed at six, a ridiculous hour for someone who's been a night owl her entire life.

And all I could think of was, "I have to fall asleep. I have to fall asleep." And of course, I couldn't.

At seven, I got up and drank a glass of wine.

At eight, I took an herbal sleep aid.

At nine, I turned on the light and picked up a novel.

Somewhere around ten, I fell asleep, and was in the middle of a wonderful Christian Bale dream when the alarm jolted me out of bed.

"Alexander, hit the snooze button," I muttered. Before the fog cleared and I realized that I had *thrown my dog off the porch* and the snooze button would not exist for the next three years.

I wasn't remotely rested for the biggest day of my career.

I staggered to the shower with all the energy of an extra in a zombie movie, thankful that I'd been told not to bother with my hair and makeup with the phrase *we have people to do that for you.* Just as well. I would have looked like I'd combed my hair with an eggbeater.

The hot water from the shower woke me up a little. When I emerged my Siamese cat Pandora was waiting at the bathroom door with a happy face, as if to say, *Cool! You're up! You're nocturnal too! Let's play!*

I threw on jeans and a sweatshirt, having been told not to put my outfit on till I got to the studio. No wrinkles on the morning show. (Clothes or face.) I grabbed the hanging bag that contained my outfit, headed out the door and one minute later found a lean, middle-aged man in a dark suit standing next to a limo with the engine running.

He tipped his hat at me and smiled. "Morning, Miss Summer. I'm Charlie."

"Morning," I said, though it came out "mohreen."

He laughed as he pointed at my mouth. "Forget something?"

"Huh?" I brought my hand up to my face and felt the toothbrush sticking out of my mouth. I yanked it out, and shook my head. "Dear God."

"It's a tough shift to get used to," he said, laughing as he opened the door for me.

I considered spitting out the toothpaste but the thought of paparazzi lurking in the shadows stopped me, so I just swallowed it and got into the car, which was toasty warm. I leaned back, closed my eyes, and immediately fell asleep.

***

One nanosecond later, or so it seemed, the sound of the car door opening awakened me.

"Good luck today," said Charlie.

"Thanks," I said, stifling a yawn as I got out of the car and staggered toward the door. I actually heard my heel clicks on the pavement, the streets being quiet without any traffic.

The door swung open as I approached and I was greeted by Scott's cheerful smile and obviously over-the-top perky face.

"Morning, sunshine!"

"Bite me," I said.

"Yeah, I've been there," he said, ushering me in the door and wrapping one arm around my shoulder. "You'll get used to it."

"I feel like shit. I probably look like shit, but I can't focus my eyes enough to look in the mirror."

"You look fine. Get any sleep at all?"

"Four hours, but it seemed like four minutes."

"You just have to adjust your body clock." He led me down a hallway toward the network's newsroom.

"I'm not even *in* my body yet," I said, as we headed into the newsroom which was already a beehive of activity.

Gavin looked up from a desk and headed in my direction. "Well, you made it," he said, extending his hand.

"My body's here. My brain will arrive at five."

"As long as it's in the chair by seven, you'll be fine." He turned to Scott. "Get her down to makeup."

Oooh. A chair. I can sleep.

***

I discovered you can't catch a few zzzzzzs when your hair is being styled and your face painted. I was still in my roll-out-of-bed spring collection as this was being done, so as not to mess up the turquoise suit that's been chosen for my first day. Personally, I think it's a jacket with a matching belt. The skirt is *that* short.

The clock struck three-thirty, the makeup and hair were done and all of a sudden I heard a rumble from the pit of my stomach. The hollow feeling reminiscent of a hangover washed over me, and I knew I had to eat something or I'd pass out.

I walked briskly to the newsroom and grabbed Scott's forearm. "Where are the vending machines?"

He looked up at me, studied my face and nodded. "Ah, you're right on schedule. Time for your first breakfast."

"First breakfast?"

"If you think your body clock is screwed up, wait till you deal with your stomach. It's living in a parallel universe. I need to explain morning show weight gain syndrome later."

"I'm gonna get fat?"

"If you're not careful. Here's how it works. You usually eat breakfast, right?"

"Sometimes. Why?"

"Well, your body thinks it's time for breakfast because you've been up awhile. Of course, you'll burn so much energy during the show you'll need to eat breakfast again at nine. And we're not counting any snacks during the show. Then you get home and you eat lunch and dinner, except you're eating dinner at your normal time but it's time to go to bed, which is the worst thing to do. So you can pack on the pounds real easy. I gained ten my first month."

"Again, I'm gonna get fat?"

"Like I said, if you're not careful. Anyway, it's time for our dinner break."

"I thought we were eating breakfast?"

"Figure of speech. Follow me." He turned to the staff. "We'll be back after dinner."

Everyone nodded as he led me out of the newsroom and down a brightly lit hallway that made me shade my eyes as we headed to the front door. "Where are we going?"

"Across the street. The little bakery opens up early for us."

"Great. Just give me a bear claw or something."

"Not what you need. You'll slide right into morning show sugar crash syndrome. The guy who runs the place has a special breakfast that I've eaten every day for the past two years and haven't gained an ounce."

"I thought you gained ten pounds?"

"That was before I started eating here."

We left the building, crossed the street and headed for a place that looked closed. The sign above the door read The Little Bakery.

Sort of appropriate for people who worked on a morning show called The Morning Show.

Scott reached the glass door and tapped on it. I could see a light on in the back and shadows moving around. A man emerged from the back, backlit so I couldn't see his face, and made his way to the door. He turned a key and opened it. "Morning, Scott."

Scott moved through the door. "Hi, Angelo. This is our new co-anchor, Veronica."

He stuck out his hand, though I still couldn't make out his face. All I could tell was that his shadow was tall and well-built. "My pleasure," he said.

I shook his hand, which was dry (no doubt from working with flour) and smiled. "Hi, Angelo."

"C'mon back," he said, then turned and led us past the display cases which were half-filled with cookies, breads and pastries. The smells filled my lungs, a combination of sugary sweetness mixed with the aroma of freshly baked bread.

We emerged in the kitchen, already full of activity as bakers in white aprons shoved dough into stone ovens. I could finally see Angelo, who looked as Italian as his name. Maybe thirty, thick black hair and deep brown eyes, a rugged complexion on a lean face. About six feet without an ounce of fat. How he did that working in a bakery was a secret I wanted.

Scott led me to a small table for two that was set off in the corner. There were already two large glasses of orange juice on the table as we took our seats. "So what are we having?" I asked.

Angelo smiled at me. "The only thing that can get you through your show. A real Italian breakfast." He headed for a stove, put something onto two dishes, returned, and slid the plates in front of us. "Sausage bread and eggs," he said. "Protein, carbs, and my special blend of spices designed to give you energy and keep your metabolism up."

"It looks wonderful," I said. And it did. Next to a couple of sunny side up eggs were two slices of hot bread that had veins of crumbled Italian sausage running through it. It was a lot more than I usually ate for breakfast, but I was starving.

"Get a piece of bread and dip it in the yolk," said Scott, who demonstrated.

I followed his lead and tasted something wonderful. The sausage, hot bread, egg and spices blended beautifully and seemed to instantly satisfy my hunger and wake me up at the same time. A sip of what was obviously freshly squeezed orange juice washed it down perfectly. "This is fantastic," I said.

"Glad you like it," said Angelo. He turned to Scott. "She seems nicer than the dragon lady."

I couldn't help but raise one eyebrow. "Dragon lady?"

"Let's just say Katrina is not on Angelo's Christmas card list," said Scott. "I only brought her here once."

"She's a *gavonne*," said Angelo.

"A what?" I asked.

"Italian slang for a person with no class."

"I'll have to remember that," I said. "So Scott, you do this every day?"

He nodded. "When I first started Angelo noticed I was buying nothing but pastries after the show. He told me I was approaching the vampire shift the wrong way."

"I've been getting up at two in the morning for years," said Angelo. "Sugar is not your friend on this shift."

"Anyway," said Scott, "he invited me to stop by for breakfast. And I've been coming here every day at three-thirty sharp ever since."

"Well, save a chair for me, Angelo," I said.

***

At one minute till seven my heart slammed against my chest for the first time in my television career. I'd never, ever been nervous, but this was more pressure than I'd ever felt.

And even though I was putting up a brave perky face, Scott

noticed. He knows me too well.

He reached over and gave my hand a squeeze. "Hey. You're with me. Nothing can go wrong."

He looked into me with those incredible eyes of his, and seemed to suck whatever anxiety I had out of my body. I felt myself melt into the leather chair as the tension evaporated. Then I felt a burst of energy and took care of the most important thing: I yanked down my skirt as far as it would go, which, for some reason, wasn't very far in the *leg chair*. Gavin must have designed the thing. I tried shifting into different positions, but no matter what I did America would get a great shot of my thighs.

"Thirty out!" yelled the floor director.

Half a minute before millions of Americans woke up with me.

Half a minute before every TV critic in the land sat poised holding a red pen filled with venom.

Half a minute before my first guest, the President of the United States, would be ushered from the green room.

The old line hit me. *Americans worship success. But they root for failure.*

"Ten out!"

So, this was it. They say there are forks in the road of life, moments during which your future can take off or do a swan dive into the dumper.

And as the light red light on top of the camera lit up, I knew this was a make or break moment.

***

The next day I knew how Sally Field felt when she won the Academy Award.

They liked me! They really liked me!

The reviews were positive across the board, from television critics to entertainment magazines to the Big Apple tabloids. My life felt like one of those movie posters with one line quotes from critics, like, "You'll stand up and cheer!" or, "The best morning show host since Katrina the bimbo!"

In reality, no one stood up and cheered at that hour of the morning, but apparently the country was comfortable with me. Some highlights from my own personal movie trailer:

"Veronica Summer brings a long overdue dose of journalistic credibility to The Morning Show."

"Summer is smart, informed, upbeat, and obviously has good chemistry with her college buddy Scott Winter. She looks like a solid choice out of the gate."

This one was my favorite, touching on the fact that I had no idea what a Louis Vuitton purse was supposed to look like during a fashion segment. *"Nice to see a morning anchor who knows more about the Middle East than designer handbags. Her interview of the President was tough but fair."*

However, as someone who has made a living being a credible journalist, I was a bit put off by the amount of ink used to describe my appearance. And it was a barrel of ink.

"The spunky copper-top has a mound of red tangles and killer legs bound to get any man's motor running in the morning."

"Scott Winter's wife must be incredibly trusting to let him spend the middle of the night with a woman who should be in the Sports Illustrated swimsuit issue."

"Only a matter of time before Playboy makes Ms. Summer an offer."

But the most telling comment came from Hal the newsstand guy. Actually, it was more of a scary prophecy that he offered as I arrived for my daily haul of print and chocolate.

"So, big star now," he said. "Guess you'll have some handmaiden pick up your papers from now on. Just remember, I knew you before you were famous."

"I can still do my own shopping," I said. "But if I ever do get the big head, please let me know."

"I won't hold back, Freckles." He turned to take some money

from another customer, then looked back at me. "So, how you gonna handle the dating thing now that you're a household name?"

"What do you mean?"

"Well, I guess if I was in your shoes, I'd be wondering if a guy was really interested in me or my salary."

CHAPTER SIX

Hal's prophecy, such as it was, would apparently be put to the test very soon.

Two weeks into my new job and six weeks since I "threw Alexander off the porch" my friends thought it was time for me to put myself back on the market. My love life, or lack thereof, was the subject of our Sunday brunch conversation.

"I met a guy who I think might be a good match," said Layla, attacking a slice of london broil.

"See if he wants to have dinner at four," I said, stifling a yawn as I sipped a virgin mimosa. (Orange juice.) "He'll save money taking me to the early bird special."

"So, who is he?" asked Savannah, even though I knew damn well the two of them had already conspired on this project.

"You two reading off a prompter?" I asked.

"Smart ass," said Layla.

"I know how your devious minds work. Just get on with it."

"His name's Rob. He's a media buyer for an ad agency. Smart guy, funny, extremely cute. Thirty, never married. He already knows who you are."

"See, that's not fair," I said. "He knows what I look like and I don't—"

Layla interrupted me by shoving her iPad under my nose with

a photo of this prospect, who, I had to admit, *was* extremely cute. My eyes widened and I absent-mindedly licked my lips.

"You were saying?" asked Savannah.

"Her prompter went out," said Layla.

Suddenly I was waking up. "He's uh, attractive."

"Yeah, right," said Layla. "Did you think I would fix you up with a guy who rings bell towers? Anyway, I told him you were available and that you two might hit it off."

"So," said Savannah, "I made a call and got you two a reservation for Saturday night at The Firefly."

My eyebrows shot up. "The Firefly? That place is booked six months ahead."

"Not if you know the owner," said Savannah. "And, we got you show tickets." She slid an envelope toward me.

I opened it up and saw two orchestra seats to the hottest Broadway musical. "How did you get…"

Savannah playfully batted her eyelashes and shrugged.

"Never mind," I said. "I don't wanna know."

"So you're good for Saturday," said Layla. "Rob will pick you up at six."

"Guys, I really appreciate this, but I've been spending Saturdays in bed."

"Yes, and y'all need some company in there," said Savannah.

I exhaled and shook my head. "I'm guessing I have no say in the matter."

"No," they said in unison.

***

A few minutes before my date, I knew I was in big, big trouble.

Because I was ready to go to bed. And no, not with Rob the media buyer or anyone else for that matter. Bradley Cooper could have walked in naked and I would have handed him the remote and told him to not to wake me. Though the thought did cross my mind that a wild night of sex might serve as an adequate sleep aid.

The week had been a roller coaster of sleep cycles. A few hours here and there, but not a single night with eight hours straight.

And right now I wanted about twelve hours of uninterrupted snoring.

Trust me, if my friends had not gone through all this trouble to get me "back in the saddle" as Savannah had put it, I would have called the guy and asked for a rain check. That not being an option, I slugged down one of those energy drinks (to which I had become almost immune), drank two cups of coffee and downed a chocolate bar. If that wasn't enough caffeine to get me through the evening, so be it, and my date could carry me home.

Still, despite my lack of energy I had managed to get gussied up enough to make a nice impression. (I should also mention that since I scored this gig, I am sought after by the paparazzi constantly, so I have to get dressed up and put on makeup just to shop for groceries. No more shoving my hair into a baseball hat and going out in sweats, which pisses me off.)

The doorman rang the buzzer, which told me my gentleman caller was here.

I looked at the clock and shook my head, knowing I had to stay awake for at least four more hours.

Great way to approach a first date, huh?

***

Rob the media buyer came as advertised, appropriately enough. His photo didn't do him justice, as he was even cuter in person. About five-ten, slender, with sandy brown hair and hazel eyes, he wore a sincere smile that brought long dimples into play.

Had I been wide awake, I probably would have been as excited as a schoolgirl and ready to jump his bones.

Alas, I was already fighting the sandman as we placed our order in the city's trendiest restaurant, which looked like a throwback to the gaslight era. Antiques everywhere, the only light provided by candles. A bubbling fountain in the center. Rose petals on the tablecloth. If I were in the mood I would have considered it incredibly romantic. Though we had a corner table in the back, I was getting constant stares. I politely smiled at everyone as I wondered if it would break some etiquette rule to dine while wearing sunglasses. I would make it a point to face the back of the restaurant any time I eat out in the future.

Rob was indeed a good match as we did have a lot in common. Thankfully he was carrying the conversation, as I found myself drifting in and out of consciousness. A quick look at the huge old grandfather clock told me I had three and a half hours to go. I was considering falling asleep during the play with the excuse that I was bored.

"The ad rates for your show have gone up since you started," he said. "Madison Avenue likes you."

"Good to know," I said.

The conversation segued nicely to sports, with his favorite teams, the Giants and the Mets, also being mine. His words began to fade and got a hollow sound as the tuxedoed waiter arrived with the soup course. He slid the china bowl in front of me and I tried to focus, but suddenly the world began to spin. I saw little black spots and knew from past experience I was about to pass out.

I grabbed the arms of my chair but I couldn't stop myself and the world went dark.

When I awakened, my vision cleared and I saw Rob and a waiter standing over me, both fanning me with napkins. My face felt very warm.

I had fainted, and gone head first into a bowl of lobster bisque.

"Do you need a doctor, Madame?" asked the waiter with a French accent.

"I'm fine," I said, right before I passed out again.

***

My eyes flickered as bright sunlight spilled onto my face.

Obviously, it was no longer Saturday night. I stretched my eyes open and looked up at industrial white ceiling tiles and a large fluorescent light that definitely wasn't the one in my apartment.

"Morning, sunshine."

I leaned up and saw Layla and Savannah seated at the foot of the bed, which was also clearly not my bed.

I was in a hospital room. "What the hell happened?" I asked.

"You passed out on your date," said Layla, who got up and moved toward the bed. "Twice. He called nine-one-one and they brought you to the emergency room, then checked you in for the night."

Savannah stood up. "I'll go get the doctor and let him know you're awake."

"What time is it?" I asked, as I stretched my arms out and yawned.

"Eleven on Sunday morning," said Layla. She sat on the edge of the bed. "I was beginning to wonder if you were ever gonna wake up. You've been out about seventeen hours."

"How did you know I was here?"

Layla reached for the end table, grabbed a bunch of newspapers and handed them to me. "Well, everyone kinda knows you're here."

I sat up and looked at the front page of New York's most popular tabloid. There I was, passed out on a stretcher, hunks of lobster in my cream-covered hair and mouth hanging open like a trophy bass, under the blaring headline.

MORNING ANCHOR GOES BOBBING FOR LOBSTER

"Dear God!" I said.

"Yeah, not exactly a Kodak moment."

I unfolded the paper and turned to the article.

Veronica Summer apparently doesn't need a spoon when

eating soup.

The new co-anchor of The Morning Show did a header into her twenty dollar bowl of lobster bisque last night while dining at The Firefly, one of Manhattan's hottest restaurants. Her dinner companion, a young man who was not identified, called 911 after she passed out, was revived, and passed out again. A waiter at the restaurant confirmed Ms. Summer had not had any alcohol. She was taken to NYU's emergency room and admitted for overnight observation. Blood tests revealed no alcohol or drugs in her system.

A source close to the show tells us Ms. Summer has been exhausted trying to adjust to the early morning shift and suggested the weird hours and lack of sleep may have finally caught up with her.

No word on if she'll be back on the set Monday morning.

I rolled my eyes, dropped the newspaper and slapped my head back on the pillow as a doctor entered the room.

"Well, good morning, young lady," he said, sticking out his hand. "I'm Doctor Heller." He was perhaps forty, short and pudgy with thinning sandy hair and hazel eyes peering out of a moon face.

I shook his hand. "Veronica Summer. Sorry to tie up one of your beds for nothing."

He picked up the chart hanging on the foot of the bed and looked at it. "From what I can tell, a bed is what you need. When's the last time you had a good night's sleep?"

"Last night?"

"I meant before we checked you in here."

"A few weeks ago, before I took a morning anchor job."

"Yes, I watch your show. You're obviously doing a good job faking being awake. Your friends tell me you're having a lot of trouble adjusting to the overnight shift."

"I can't sleep more than four hours at a time. And it's also depressing the hell out of me. I've got no life. My whole life revolves around trying to get to sleep."

He nodded. "Have you been taking anything to help you sleep?"

"Wine. Over the counter sleeping pills. Melatonin. Nyquil. I've tried everything. Not at the same time, of course. Nothing works for more than four hours."

"Before you started working this shift, what usually helped you get a really good night's sleep?"

"Sex."

He bit his tongue and smiled. "I, uh, don't think your insurance covers that."

"Sure, it'll cover Viagra for guys but when women need some help, nooooo."

He laughed, pulled a pen and prescription pad from his pocket and started writing. "I'm going to prescribe a strong sleep aid. And this one should be more effective than a boyfriend and won't get you pregnant."

"Ooooh, I like a doctor who's a smartass."

"Occupational hazard when you work in the emergency room. Anyway, this medication has been very effective with my patients who work unusual shifts, like you. Now there is a small chance of a side effect. People have been known to drive while asleep—"

"I don't have a car and I don't know how to steal one. Just give me whatever it will take to knock me out."

He smiled and nodded as he ripped the prescription from the pad and handed it to me. "By the way, you had a ridiculous amount of caffeine in your system. Try to cut back. The thing that's helping you wake up for your show is also keeping you awake when you're trying to sleep. It takes quite awhile for caffeine to get out of your system. If you can simply get your sleep cycle adjusted, you won't need it."

"Got it. Thanks, doctor."

"I'll get you discharged. For today, go home and rest." He nodded at my friends and headed out.

"You know," said Savannah, "you may have something with

your idea."

"She's right," said Layla.

I threw back the covers and started to get out of bed. "What idea?"

"Sex to knock you out," said Savannah.

I rolled my eyes. "Yeah, and you see how my attempt to start a relationship last night ended up."

"Maybe you don't need a relationship," said Layla. "Maybe you could go the *friends with benefits* route."

"Now I know how Katrina Favor did this shift for so long!"

***

If I needed a reason to feel more positive about the job, she was sitting on the interview set waiting for me. Yes, one of the key carrots in the bunch, Senator Sydney Dixon, was my guest on Monday morning. Thankfully the extended stay in the hospital had recharged my batteries a bit. I'd also ditched the coffee and switched to fruit that was high in natural sugar, figuring things like dates and raisins might perk me up but not keep me awake at night. I still desperately wanted coffee, but was determined to give the natural high a try.

The Senator stood up to greet me as I approached the set and extended her hand. "Veronica, so nice to meet you."

"My pleasure," I said, as I shook her hand. Her turquoise eyes locked with mine, and I saw what was known in media circles as *the look*. The one that went right into your soul, seemed honestly sincere, as opposed to the usual blank glare you got from politicians who forgot your name ten seconds after you told them. It was part of the reason she was such a media darling and often received positive coverage bordering on bias. Reporters generally liked her personally, and she seemed genuine in return.

Voters loved her for any number of reasons, not the least of which was her appearance. The forty-five year old Senator from

New Jersey is a stunner, a redhead like me but she's strawberry to my copper. Her body would be the envy of any twenty-year-old, as the former Marine drill sergeant has maintained her perfectly toned figure. But her buffed physique is a contrast to her incredibly sexy face, complete with high cheekbones, full lips, a sharp nose and a distinctive sultry whiskey voice that drives men crazy. It's like a cross between Demi Moore and Lorraine Bracco, and the moment you hear it you know who's speaking. She's known as the Tower of Power in Washington: a six foot babe who can turn heads in an evening gown and crack heads when she needs to. She also answers to Big Red from her days in the military.

That military service is an asset, as is her seemingly perfect normal family. Married to her high school sweetheart who is a school teacher, she's managed to raise two squeaky clean college age kids who spend their summers working with various charitable organizations. If there have ever been any skeletons in her closet, they've been exorcized. No one has ever been able to come up with anything remotely resembling a scandal about the woman.

Put it all together and she's a slam dunk for the next Presidential election. I know it, the public knows it, and the network sure as hell knows it. Yes, there's this thing called bias which drives viewers crazy; in this case the networks are jockeying for position to get in the good graces of the woman who will occupy the Oval Office for four, and maybe eight, years.

That's not to say I agree with everything she stands for, because I don't. But since I'm an old school journalist I'll never share my opinions about politics, religion or social issues.

Anyway, she hasn't officially kicked off a campaign with it being three years away, so today's visit is actually about things going on in the Senate. But there was a problem with one of the cameras, so we had a chance to make small talk while it was being fixed.

"I read about your hospital visit, are you feeling better?" she asked.

"Yeah, once I rinsed the bisque out of my hair. But you should know it does make a wonderful conditioner."

She laughed as she leaned back in her chair. "I'm not surprised you passed out. I couldn't imagine getting up at that hour every day. Though if I run for President, I know it'll be a couple of years without a break and crossing so many time zones I won't even know who I am. I wouldn't want to be one of those candidates who gets up to make a speech and forgets where they are."

"Hey, we love those sound bites. Speaking of the campaign—"

"Ah, nice try, Veronica. No announcement today. I haven't decided."

"Hey, you can't fault a girl for taking a shot."

"Look, I live in North Jersey and I've watched you for a long time. I know you're a solid reporter." She leaned forward and lowered her voice. "As opposed to some other morning show hosts."

"Thank you, that's very kind."

"So what do you want to talk about—"

"Ah, nice try, Senator."

"Hey, you can't fault a girl for taking a shot."

We shared a laugh, and I could see how the woman could charm even the most hard-boiled reporter.

Fifteen minutes later her interview was in the can. It was a spirited give and take; she didn't dodge any tough questions, I didn't lob any softballs, and she avoided anything that sounded rehearsed. She talked rather than recited. Again, I didn't agree with everything she said, but I couldn't help but like her personally as I walked her to the door.

"So, I was talking to Gavin," she said, "and he told me that should I decide to run you would be assigned to the campaign."

I nodded and smiled, thankful that Gavin was actually sticking to his word on something. "Yeah. So we could be tired together."

"Well, maybe by then you'll have learned some tricks and can give me advice. We redheads have to stick together. Although I'm not sure the rest of the media could deal with two spunky ones on the same plane."

"True. As far as attitude is concerned, we could have been separated at birth." We laughed as we reached the door. "Here's one piece of advice I can give you right now, Senator: be prepared to have no social life."

"Already there, honey. Sometimes I go weeks without seeing my husband."

"At least you have one."

"Don't worry, Veronica, Mister Right is out there."

I held the door open for her, revealing a waiting limo. "Thanks for coming by, Senator, and it was great to meet you."

She shook my hand and smiled. "Pleasure was mine. I'll see you again soon."

I watched her energetic walk to the limo, waving at a few pedestrians as she moved.

Funny, the carrot Gavin had dangled was a carrot top. Ironic, huh?

And suddenly the thought of a campaign and Air Force One gave me a shot of energy that topped anything in a coffee mug. Maybe I could do this after all.

CHAPTER SEVEN

Upon further review, maybe I *can't* do this after all.

Three months into the new job, and I've realized my old boyfriend was right. I still don't want him back, but he was right. I'm not a morning person and never will be. You can't force an owl to be a chicken. (That one's from Savannah.)

This truly has become the job from hell. Forbidden fruit, as Alexander would put it. I can almost hear him saying, "I told you so. You should have run off to Connecticut with me and you could be baking cookies, servicing me every night, and thanking me for the opportunity."

I've become a physical wreck. Oh, those great breakfasts at The Little Bakery get me through the show all right. But it's the other twenty-two hours of the day that are killing me.

Here's my typical day:

Get up at two in the morning after being jolted out of bed like I've been hit with a cattle prod by an alarm which, at that hour, sounds like a Chinese gong.

Start the coffee pot, which I've loaded the night before since during my first week on the job I attempted to make some java while bleary-eyed and filled the coffee machine with flour, thus creating the first paste cappuccino.

Take a ten minute hot shower, drink two cups of coffee, stagger down to the limo in jeans or sweats, chasing raccoons away from the door in the process. I look up at what I thought were birds, but which Charlie informed me were actually bats since birds don't fly at night. Appropriate for the vampire shift, so I wave at them. Professional courtesy.

Drink two more cups of coffee after arriving at the station.

Breakfast across the street, which perks me up just long enough to get through the show.

Home by ten. Close the black curtains I've purchased to block out every ray of sunlight and make my apartment look like a hangout for a coven. Eat bowl of cereal, careful to add blueberries instead of the olives I used my first week. (New! Lucky Charms! Now with a full day's serving of olives!)

Resolve to stay up without taking nap so that I will fall asleep at six and get eight hours.

Despite the caffeine content of four cups of coffee, I pass out on couch at noon after watching *The Price is Right*. (I always overbid.)

Wake up at four, covered with drool and somewhat rested. Eat lunch or dinner, depending on what I decide to call it.

Crawl back into bed at six in an attempt to sleep.

Give up at eight and watch television or read.

Fall asleep at ten.

Rinse. Repeat.

Social life? Seriously? Weekdays are totally out of the question. Weekends are spent in bed trying to catch up on sleep. I haven't been out with anyone since I did my swan dive into the lobster bisque and got a nine-point-four from the tabloid judge. I seem to remember what sex was like, but the memory is fading. I'm lonely as hell. My friends still are my friends, but they're on a different schedule, along with the rest of the world.

Sunday nights are the worst. After two days of my body almost getting back to normal, I have to crawl back into my coffin.

I know, I know, there's a big brass ring waiting for me in two years, eight months and twenty-eight days (who's counting) but

I'm not sure it's worth it. I might be dead before then.

So, after two weeks of deep thought I'd decided on a course of action. To hell with the evening anchor job. I want my life back. And there's only one way to do it.

Try my best to get fired.

Oh, I wasn't going to make it obvious, like not showing up or dropping F-bombs on live television. It's going to be something natural. No one's going to be surprised. And no one's going to blame me.

Because everyone on the staff knows how exhausted I've been and what a physical wreck I am.

Now I had to let the whole country know.

***

I was filled with more energy than I'd ever had on this show, then realized I was simply excited about launching my plan. But I couldn't show it. Instead of sitting up straight as the intro music faded I slumped into my chair. Scott started with his usual upbeat welcome to the viewers. "Good Monday, everyone, and welcome to The Morning Show. I'm Scott Winter."

I started to talk and then stifled a fake yawn. "Oh, excuse me. And I'm Veronica Summer. At least I will be at some point."

"She was up past her bedtime," said Scott, always quick with the ad-lib. "Went to bed at eight."

"Just wake me when the prompter says it's my turn to talk."

Scott turned and made eye contact, shooting me a somewhat worried look that our two-shot camera could not pick up. I rubbed my eyes like people do when they first roll out of bed. His eyes widened a bit. Now I could tell he was seriously worried.

"So let's get started," said Scott, turning back to the camera, "because we've got a packed show for you this morning. A very special guest from Hollywood will be dropping by later on. He's just been named the most beautiful person on earth."

"Pffft, whatever," I said, waving my hand like I was shooing a fly. "Eye candy aint gonna cure cancer, so what's the big deal?" I caught a glimpse of Scott taken aback in my peripheral vision. "As for the really *important* stuff that isn't superficial, we'll get you up to date on the budget situation in Congress and take a look at how the new tax laws could effect your paycheck. And later on we'll have a visit from a nutrition expert to show you how to make a very healthy school lunch for your children that won't impact your budget."

"Right," said Scott. "And in the second hour—"

I cut him off. "You know what, Scott?"

Scott turned and gave me a wide-eyed look that I knew meant *What the hell are you doing?* "No, what?"

"I'm thinkin' there are a whole bunch of parents out there who just dragged themselves out of bed a half hour early to make those lunches for their precious little snowflakes. Well... here's a news flash for you moms and dads out there." I leaned forward and raised my voice. "KIDS CAN ACTUALLY PUT A SANDWICH TOGETHER BY THEMSELVES! HELLO, MCFLY!" I leaned back and returned to my normal tone. "Kids, stop playing with Facebook and listen up. You get your peanut butter, you get your jelly, you slap it on two pieces of bread and toss it in your Harry Potter lunchbox with a banana and a juice box. It's not rocket science! Let mom and dad sleep an extra thirty minutes and make your own lunch because they work their tails off so you can have a two hundred dollar cell phone in the third grade and then chauffeur you to every conceivable activity they can think of lest they be thought of as bad parents. Mom and Dad, go back to bed. We're here for two hours anyway and you can catch up later." I waved my hand at the camera. "Go on. Get under the covers. The kids won't starve. Toss 'em a pop-tart and catch some more shut-eye."

Scott's jaw dropped. I took a quick glance around the studio and saw the same reaction from members of the crew.

I flashed a devilish grin at the camera. "And tomorrow, we might

even teach your children how to make an exotic breakfast called...
wait for it... scrambled eggs! If we have time we'll show them how
to do something really tricky... pour milk into a bowl of cereal!
An incredible life skill! Meanwhile, let's check on the latest news."

***

Nothing happened as we went to commercial because I had one
trump card up my sleeve. I knew Gavin Karlson had one hard
and fast rule he'd never broken. He would not, under any circum-
stances, enter the studio until the show was over. He would not
chastise me through my earpiece. He believed, as I do, that yelling
at an anchor in the middle of a show only made things worse.

Didn't matter, I was doing it on my own.

The level of snark had reached an all time high for a network
morning show. I went off on tangents, ranted about stuff that
bugged me like helicopter parents who bubblewrap their kids;
wondered aloud while interviewing our fashion expert why anyone
would pay four hundred bucks for a purse when you could buy
a perfectly good illegal knockoff on the streets of Manhattan for
thirty, because, what the hell, they were all made with shoddy
workmanship in China anyway; slammed the Mets for not having
a decent centerfielder and charging too much to watch a lousy
team; argued that all Central Park mimes were so damn annoying
they should be deported to France; and vented about people who
brought babies to the movies. Get a damn sitter! Scott had tried
to talk me down off the ledge during each commercial break, and
I gave him the bobblehead, then took off again the minute the
red light went on. I figured someone was no doubt compiling my
greatest hits for YouTube (probably labeled "Morning Anchor
Goes Batshit") and whole thing would get ten million hits before
the day was out.

At one minute till nine Scott ended the show with, "We'll see
you tomorrow morning. I think." The credits rolled over a two-shot

as I waved cheerfully to the camera. I'm sure that even my faux perkiness looked sarcastic.

At one nanosecond after nine the wooden door to the studio flew open so hard it banged against the wall and shattered the little glass window in the middle.

No surprise, Gavin Karlson stormed into the studio, eyes narrowed directly at me. "In my office. Now."

CHAPTER EIGHT

I followed Gavin, head down, pretending to be the student headed to the principal's office. He was shaking his head as he passed his secretary, who held up a fistful of pink message slips while avoiding eye contact with me. She was on the phone and every line on the thing was lit up. He grabbed the message slips as he walked into his office, pointed to the chair opposite his desk without saying a word, then closed the door after I took a seat. It was all I could do to keep from smiling. He moved behind his desk, sat down, leaned back and folded his hands in his lap.

"Explain," he said.

"Explain what?"

His eyes became saucers. "Explain *what*? Oh, I don't know... why you were so incredibly obnoxious for the past two hours on national television."

"I don't even remember half of what I said. I'm fried, Gavin. Totally exhausted. If I said things that offended people I'm sorry, but I was basically asleep out there."

"Well, I'm sure you'll be able to read about it in every newspaper in America. Or watch yourself on the Internet."

I thrust out my lower lip in a pout, dipped my head and looked up at him through my eyelashes like a naughty little girl. "It was that bad?"

That question launched him out of his chair. "It was the worst performance in the history of morning television! I think you probably insulted every possible demographic out there! Not to mention what you said to our special guest!"

I played dumb again. "I, uh, don't remember—"

"The most beautiful man on earth! You asked him if his childhood idol was a Ken doll! You may as well have called him a plastic toy!"

I bit my lower lip, more to keep from laughing than anything else. "Oh."

He shook the pink slips at me and the irony hit me. (Maybe I'll get one later today!) "Meanwhile, I'm sure I'll be spending the rest of the day fielding phone calls and answering emails from irate viewers. I'd make you stay and do it yourself, but God only knows what you'd say!"

"Gavin, all I can say is that I'm sorry. I'm so exhausted I'm just not myself."

"Well, then go home and take a pill to knock yourself out." His phone buzzed and he hit a button. "Yes?"

His secretary's voice came over the intercom. "Mr. Fincastle wants you upstairs. Right now."

"On my way," he said. He grabbed his suit jacket from a hanger on the back of the door and put it on. "Great. Now I'm gonna get my ass reamed by the CEO. I'll send you a bill for the Vaseline." He stormed out of his office, leaving me behind.

I got up from my chair and slowly walked out past his secretary. "I guess he's done with me and I can go home?"

"That would be a very good idea," she said, glaring at me.

***

I desperately wanted to get out of the building as fast as possible so I wouldn't have to do what I'd never done.

Lie to Scott.

Alas, 'twas not to be, as he was waiting for me at my desk wearing a worried look. "So," he said, "you still work here?"

"No clue. Gavin got called upstairs."

"What the hell was up with you this morning?"

I shook my head. "I don't know, Scott. I'm just so damn tired I guess the truth came out about everything."

"Listen, you might want to write Gavin an apology before you get out of the building. I've got some clout around here but I might not be able to save you on this one. Meanwhile, make sure you get enough rest so that it doesn't happen tomorrow. "

"The point may be moot. I might not be here tomorrow."

"I'll see what I can do."

Oh, shit. The last thing I needed was for him to go to bat for me. "Really, Scott, don't put yourself in the line of fire for me. My screw-up, my problem. You don't need to take a bullet for me."

"Bullshit. We're a team, remember?"

Damn Boy Scout. Then again, I knew I'd do the same for him if the roles were reversed.

***

Charlie dropped me off at my apartment without saying a word. Didn't even get out of the car to open the door for me like he always did. As soon as he pulled away and turned the corner I had a spring in my step, my fake yawns no longer needed. Just as I was about to head up the stairs a well-dressed fortyish businessman in an expensive gray suit spotted me and smiled.

"Hey, Veronica Summer. Great show this morning," he said.

I rolled my eyes. "Yeah, right."

He stopped walking. "No seriously, it was hilarious. You aren't fake like all those other people on morning shows. That rant you went on about kids making their own lunches was hysterical. My wife actually went back to bed. Our teenagers bitched about it but they made their own lunches. After they left we started talking about taking back the house and our lives."

My face tightened. "You actually *liked* what I did this morning?"

"Are you kidding? I'm telling you, I was doubled over laughing. What a great way to start the day. I know it's April Fool's Day and all, and it was probably a put-on, but you really ought to consider doing that every morning."

Oh, shit.

I'd completely forgotten it was April first. Would viewers think the whole thing was a joke? Would such a small oversight ruin my master plan? Would Gavin let me off the hook because he'd think it was me trying to be funny?

Dammit! I needed to get fired here and the universe was conspiring against me!

"I'd never miss a show if you keep it up," the man said, then looked at his watch. "Anyway, thanks for the fun wake up call and for making our kids more self-sufficient."

"You're welcome," I said, as he moved on.

The spring in my step disappeared. The man actually *liked* my snarky persona. Surely he was one out of millions. Seriously, how many people liked being insulted?

I shuffled up the stairs, heart racing as I dreaded reading the comments on the Internet.

What if the businessman had a typical reaction?

***

Thirty minutes later I was having another Sally Field moment, but with a small difference.

They like me. Sonofabitch, they really, *really* like me. The sarcastic, snarky, insulting me.

The complaints about my performance were few and far between. The laurels on the Internet were everywhere, some touching on the April Fool's angle but most gushing about my brutal honesty and total lack of political correctness. My network email account spilled over with compliments, most of them from moms who had actually gone back to bed and made their bratty kids feed themselves. The tabloids had a few very short stories, all of which were waiting for an official comment from the network.

A single tear rolled down my cheek.

I'd made it worse.

It would be ever harder to get fired.

CHAPTER NINE

My first surprise of the morning came when Charlie opened the door to the limo.

Which wasn't empty.

Scott offered a soft smile as I got in and waited for the door to close.

"So, they send you to soften the blow of the pink slip?" I asked, noting the soundproof window behind the driver was up.

"Nope. You still work here."

Dammit.

"You didn't ride over here just to tell me that."

"Very perceptive. I spent a lot of time eavesdropping after you left."

"And...?"

"It got real interesting as the day went on. Gavin came back from Fincastle's office looking like he'd had a prostate exam with an umbrella."

"I would've liked to have seen that. His walk, not the exam."

"The expression on his face was better. Anyway, by that time the phone had started ringing off the hook. All the calls fried the switchboard and the network's website crashed. When the smoke cleared it was apparent that the overwhelming majority of viewers loved what you did. Right before lunch Fincastle comes down to Gavin's office, and he's very calm. They have this long conversation about how you may have stumbled onto some little bit of broadcasting gold. Anyway, they're waiting for the overnight ratings to see if we got a bump in the second hour. And they've got the April Fool's Day excuse if they decide to rein you in."

"Bottom line?"

He shrugged. "Hard to tell. You may have changed morning show strategy forever. They may want you to keep doing what you did yesterday."

So much for my brilliant strategy. People actually like sarcasm in the morning. Who knew?

"What time do the overnight ratings come in?"

"Usually a half hour before we hit the air."

"So I'm not gonna know if I'm supposed to be perky girl or snarky girl till then? Or unemployed girl?"

"Basically. They're not ready to decide if they love you or hate you. Only the overnight ratings know for sure."

I shook my head and leaned back. "Talk about guys who don't have a backbone."

"I was actually thinking of other male body parts that usually come in pairs."

I couldn't help but laugh despite my fatigue. "So what do I do?"

∗∗∗

I now know what a defendant feels like waiting for a verdict. The great ratings jury is still out.

For three and a half hours I've been sitting on the fence, as Gavin has been holed up in his office the whole time with the blinds drawn. The coward has been communicating with the staff on the phone and via text messages.

I'm not one of those people.

With the exception of Scott and my writer, the staff has been avoiding me as if I were a leper. The hairstylist barely acknowledged

I was in the chair and practically yanked the hairs out of my head with her brush. The makeup artist did everything she could to avoid eye contact while she worked at warp speed in order to be done with me as quickly as possible. They don't want to take the chance of guilt by association, which is the typical *rats deserting a sinking ship* strategy in this business. Of course if the overnight ratings got a huge bump in the second hour, they'll all act like life-long friends tomorrow. Nice to know I'm working with a bunch of spineless wimps who need to check with management before deciding which way the wind is blowing.

Anyway, with the jury still deliberating, I have three possible verdicts:

Guilty, death by hanging. (I get fired! Yay!)

Not guilty by reason of insanity (now known as the April Fool's Day defense), two and a half years probation, no sleep or social life.

Not guilty, free to be as snarky as possible for the remainder of my contract. No sleep or social life, but I don't have to attempt to be perky.

And if the final option turns out to be the one, I'm going to turn into a sarcastic diva and demand everyone who ignored me this morning get reassigned to another show.

Scott and I were going over our scripts on the large rectangular table that sits at the head of the newsroom. He looked up at the clock every few seconds. "Will you please stop doing that?" I asked.

"I just want this to be over."

"It would've been over if our dickless managers could make a decision using their own brains."

And then Gavin's door opened.

Everyone stopped. The room went silent as he headed straight for me.

A smile slowly grew across his face as he looked at me.

Sonofabitch.

***

69

It was now time for Plan B.

Gavin sat down at the head of the table as Scott closed the door of the conference room. I grabbed a chair at the opposite end, while Scott, looking confused, took a seat in the middle. Giant photos of Bill Recker and the other great news anchors of the past covered the walls. Would I be up there with them?

"Why are you sitting way down there?" Gavin asked.

"I assumed you'd want to be as far away as possible from the person who turned in the worst performance in morning show history." I leaned back, folded my arms and glared at him.

He smiled and laughed a bit. "Well, Scott will tell you I do have a tendency for knee-jerk reactions." I continued to glare and said nothing. Scott looked back and forth, like he was in the wild west watching a gunfight about to take place.

Gavin leaned forward. "Anyway, bygones. The viewers loved what you did, as evidenced by the overwhelming support we received in emails and phone calls."

"Bygones, my ass. You had to wait till now to tell me that?" I said. "I've been here three and a half hours wondering if I'm going to be fired."

I wasn't letting him off the hook and he began to squirm. For once I had the upper hand over management because I now knew damn well yesterday was no doubt a ratings bonanza and all of a sudden they needed me and my sarcastic attitude on the air. Desperately.

There were now two possible outcomes, as the game had changed and I was the one who had moved the goalposts.

One, I act as obnoxious as possible with Gavin and hope he fires me for insubordination. Which, unfortunately, is unlikely to happen because management will put up with a difficult anchor for high ratings. (see: *Favor, Katrina*)

Two, I act as obnoxious as possible with Gavin, he doesn't fire me, but I tuck his family jewels away in my pocket for the remainder of my contract while getting to act sarcastic on the air.

I still don't get my life back, but I can at least be myself and have fun during my days as a zombie.

Gavin finally breaks the silence. "I, uh—"

"You, uh, had to wait for the overnights before making a decision. I'm not stupid, Gavin. Until five minutes ago I could have just as easily been fired if the ratings in the second hour had crashed."

He bit his lower lip and looked down at the table. "But they didn't. They went up sixty percent in the second hour. And the last fifteen minutes set a record for this show."

"So, bottom line, you want snarky girl this morning and for the next two years and change. Meanwhile, you won't need to use your April Fool's Day excuse to explain my actions yesterday."

Gavin's eyes widened as if he suddenly realized he was no longer dealing with Katrina the idiot. Then he slowly nodded. "You're obviously a very perceptive person, Veronica."

Finally I flashed a sinister grin. "You know, snarky girl has had time to think, and she's more than willing to tender her resignation—"

Gavin put up his hands like he was being held up. "No! No! Please don't overreact, Veronica."

Dammit.

Finally Scott chimed in, obviously noting this was about to escalate. "Guys, everything's gonna be fine." He stood up and walked toward me, then extended a hand. "C'mon, let's do a kick-ass show. You can be as sarcastic as you like."

CHAPTER TEN

CRANKY MORNING ANCHOR IS NO APRIL FOOL

By Jonas Fender

Viewers of The Morning Show on Monday came away with a new experience: being greeted by a crack of dawn host who hates getting up as much as the rest of us. For two hours Veronica Summer went on an unsurpassed snarky rant that forever buried any inclination a critic might have had to refer to her as "perky", which has long been the industry requirement for women on the morning shift. The woman left in her wake a handful of insulted guests, shocked parents, and the PC police ready to haul her in for questioning under hot lights. Anyone expecting a cheerful "good morning" came away thinking one of two things: Ms. Summer had completely lost it on live TV and would surely be fired, or it was one of the most elaborate April Fool's jokes in network television history.

April second proved the latter to be false.

Or was it?

If Veronica Summer and the network's intent was an April Fool's joke, it came away as a ratings bonanza. If it wasn't, the ratings spike no doubt saved her job. Ratings skyrocketed to record levels in the second hour of the show as the Twitterverse exploded about her performance, while a network source said viewer comments and phone calls were overwhelmingly in favor of snark in the cornflakes on a regular basis. That same source told us Executive Producer Gavin Karlson held a very heated closed door session with Summer right after the show ended, which makes this reporter wonder if the network was indeed in on the joke. If it was a joke.

But that was before the overnight ratings arrived.

So on April second, the spunky redhead returned in the same mood, leaving co-host Scott Winter to play straight man and mop up the sizable amount of sarcasm she spewed all over the studio.

The ratings went even higher.

Same deal April third. April fourth. And April fifth. The ratings continued to climb like the stock market on a bull run.

Ms. Summer seems to be thoroughly enjoying "being herself" while holding nothing back as far as personal opinions are concerned. Though when she has a serious interview, she wears her journalist hat quite well and obviously has the gravitas to hold her own with heads of state. But when the interview subject falls under the pop culture umbrella, for which she obviously has no use, she really lets loose. Any future reality show guest might do well to wear body armor.

It will be interesting to see if this strategy plays well long term. If it does, will it signal the end to the parade of morning anchors who give you a cavity? Will those cheerful hosts be shown the door while the competition conducts a search for people who can be both sarcastic and appealing?

Time will tell.

I stifled a yawn as Layla and Savannah sipped their Sunday brunch mimosas. "I'm still exhausted, but I did have a hell of a lot of fun this week."

"Have you told Scott that you were actually trying to get fired?"

asked Layla.

"That little detail must never leave this table," I said. "It would break his heart."

"Maybe it's working out for the best," said Savannah, always the optimist.

I shook my head. "Getting fired would have been the best outcome, but this is better than having to fake it."

"Regardless," said Layla, "you were hysterical. A couple of people at my gym nearly fell off the treadmill they were laughing so hard."

"So what's up for this week?" asked Savannah. "Management staying the course?"

"Surely you know our network executives won't tamper with a ratings hit. I'm their new best friend forever even though they were ready to have me drawn and quartered Tuesday morning."

"Sounds like politics," said Savannah. "So are y'all gonna continue actin' like a toad in a dry well?"

Layla and I furrowed our brows while trying to decipher this Southernism.

"Would *youse guys* prefer I simply used *pissed off*?" she asked. "Or I can go with *panties in a wad*."

"Either is fine," I said.

"So," asked Layla, "what guests might be the recipient of your flying cutlery this week? That is, if anyone's stupid enough to sign up for a visit."

"It's actually just the opposite." I smiled as I reached into my purse. "They're lining up for abuse. The bookers' phones are ringing off the hook with Hollywood people saying *whip me, beat me, make me feel cheap*. But I haven't looked at the guest list this week." I handed a single sheet of paper to her. "Here, knock yourself out."

Layla unfolded the sheet as Savannah leaned over to take a look. Suddenly their eyes bugged out.

"Whoa," said Layla.

"What?" I asked.

Savannah licked her lips. "Dexter Bishop is on your show tomorrow."

My face tightened. "Who?"

"*Who?*" They asked in surprised stereo and looked at me like I had two heads.

"Sorry, I don't recognize the name."

"Y'all never heard of *Bish the Dish*?" asked Savannah.

I shook my head. "No. Who is he?"

"He's that gorgeous British judge on *Dance Off*," said Layla. "Basically the reason most people watch that show. He's also sarcastic as hell. The two of you could have been Siamese twins, conjoined at the brain."

"What's *Dance Off*?" I asked.

"Good God," said Savannah. "It's on your own damn network and I think it's the number one show in America. It's that contest where celebrities pair up with professional dancers and once a week someone gets voted off the island, like on *Survivor*. And please don't ask what *Survivor* is."

I rolled my eyes, reached across the table and snatched the paper from Layla. "They really expect me to interview someone from a show I've never seen?"

"I'll do it if you don't want to," said Layla. "Damn, he's beyond hot." She reached into her purse and pulled out an iPad, did a quick search, then handed it to me. "This is who will be sitting next to you tomorrow. You lucky bastard."

I looked at the tablet and my jaw dropped. The guy was so perfect he almost looked computer generated. Maybe thirty-five, medium length dark hair that cascaded over his forehead, deep-set olive green eyes, a jawline that had been carved out of granite and the deepest dimples I'd ever seen. "Damn."

"Or as we say in the south," said Savannah, "day-umm."

"So, you wanna come over and do some binge watching on Netflix?" asked Layla.

"I'm not wasting my day off watching that reality garbage," I said.

"Consider it research," she said.

"You'll be the envy of every woman in America," said Savannah. "That man gives me the vapors."

"Whuh?" I asked.

"Sorry. He makes me hot and bothered. Mostly hot. I'd have biscuits in the oven and my buns in bed for something like that."

"Yeah, but there's probably nothing upstairs. Anyone who works on a reality show has to be shallow," I said.

"So dive into the pool, hit your pretty lil' head and let the man give you mouth-to-mouth," said Savannah.

"Whatever," I said. "You guys can live vicariously through me tomorrow."

"Great," said Layla. "I'll be eating corn flakes while you wake up with an English muffin."

***

For most of the world "homework" ends the day you're done with college or, for those who frequent Wal-Mart, ninth grade. For reporters, there's an assignment every single day.

Nothing can sink a reporter's career like being unprepared. The Internet is filled with television news gaffes featuring people who failed to do their research and ended up looking stupid by asking a dumb question. Of course I've always done my homework, and I read a lot anyway, so that's never been a problem.

But today's homework made me feel like I'd gotten an assignment to do a term paper in Latin.

Because I had to do some research on this Dexter Bishop guy. Of course Layla said, "I'll be happy to research him for you. Make me your assistant for the day."

You should know that nothing irritates me more about network television than reality shows. They manage to tick me off me on several fronts. First and foremost, they have replaced scripted shows, which means a whole lot of writers and actors and technical people have lost a ton of work. Second, they usually feature people who either: might have a future as a crash test dummy; are inbred to the extent that they could be their own grandfathers; have enough body piercings to set off the metal detector at LaGuardia Airport from ten feet away; or a combination of all three. Bottom line, the networks save a ton of cash by simply having a few photographers follow a bunch of idiots around then pay an editor to make said idiots look as stupid as possible.

And then millions of idiots watch them.

While *Dance Off* is not technically a reality show as it is categorized as a "competition," it does fall into that group of shows favored by people whose lips move when they read. In this case, "celebrities" (and that's a real stretch in some cases, since the show is filled with has-beens and never-will-bes) are paired with professional dancers, train for awhile, then perform in front of a live audience. Viewers then vote via phone and the couple with the lowest score is outta here. The winning couple gets a garish trophy that is uglier than the leg lamp in *A Christmas Story* and choose a charity to which the network makes a decent donation.

And, as I'm told is always the case with these competition shows, there are judges who rip these people to shreds.

And, as is always the case, there's a sarcastic British judge.

In this case it is the aforementioned Dexter Bishop, a/k/a "Bish the Dish."

Just what I need for a Sunday afternoon. Research on a "celebrity" who is famous for being famous.

A nice breeze floated through the open window as the clicks from my keyboard mixed with the sounds of traffic and the occasional cooing of pigeons on the window ledge. I typed "Dexter Bishop" into the search engine and was greeted with the first batch of more than ten million possible results. Along with the massive amount of reading material, I noted a handful of images across the top of the page.

What the hell, may as well start with the eye candy. I mean, I am a thorough reporter. I'm a journalist, but I'm not dead.

Click.

What came up on the screen made me think a drool guard like the ones they have at Chinese buffets might be a good accessory for my laptop. The man not only filled out a three piece suit like a model, but some tabloid shots of him on the beach revealed a perfect body underneath the gray flannel. Not an ounce of fat was evident on this chiseled physique, his hairless torso highlighted by toned pecs and a six-pack that would be a wonderful place to rest one's head.

I mean, if I was interested in this sort of man.

I clicked on a clip of video and his soft British accent filled the air. And I'm a sucker for British accents.

Stop it, Veronica. He's plastic. He's an android. (Though I'd love to hear him say, "Resistance is futile" like Captain Picard on Star Trek.)

I shook my head in an attempt to jolt myself back to reality, reminding myself that the Ken dolls of the world are bad for one's health and that spectacular looks and complex human emotions are usually mutually exclusive. I clicked back and opened the magazine article which was the top hit on the search.

Dexter Bishop's story was right out of Hollywood, only it took place in the United Kingdom. A struggling theatrical dancer who doubled as a dance instructor, he'd tried out to be one of the staff dancers on the original British version of the show. Apparently the producers liked both his personality and the fact that he was a teacher, so they installed him as one of the judges. He became the star of the show, his classic looks blended with biting commentary making him a favorite with viewers. When the show came to the United States (Hollywood loves stealing British stuff, not being able to come up with their own ideas) Dexter Bishop came with it, and enjoyed the same success across the pond. *Dance Off* is my network's highest rated prime-time show.

And, oh yeah, he'd been named the world's most eligible bach-elor this year. Though he was apparently either not dating anyone (yeah, right) or extremely private about his personal life.

What followed after that article were a laundry list of glowing pieces about the guy, websites for women who had a crush (*www.IwannahavesexwithDex.com*) and speculative articles about his future (would he star in a movie, stick with *Dance Off*, open a chain of dance studios?)

Finally, I'd had enough of that superficial garbage and slammed my laptop shut.

Besides, it was six o'clock and time to go to bed.

But dammit, when I closed my eyes all I could see was his face.

CHAPTER ELEVEN

"Coming up this hour," said Scott, "we'll visit with an expert on snakes who will tell you how to identify which ones are poisonous and which ones are not." Then he turned to me. "Speaking of venom, I assume you're recharged with a fresh supply after the weekend."

I reached over and playfully slapped his arm. "Stop it. You act like I'm a big meanie."

"Anyway, who's in your crosshairs this morning?"

"Well, coming up after the break, I'll be talking to Dexter Bishop, a judge on our network's number one show *Dance Off*."

"I love that show."

"Never seen it. But anyway, the guy has been named the world's most eligible bachelor so we'll find out if the brain matches the face and body."

"You mean, see if he passes the *Veronica Test*?" He turned to the camera. "That's a thing she came up with in college. If a guy couldn't spell IQ, he was outta here."

"You know me too well, my friend."

***

I adjusted my microphone as he strutted, and I do mean *strutted*, into the studio. Everything came to a screeching halt. The jaw of our female cameraperson hung open while the clipboard belonging to the gal who was our floor director made an audible bang when it hit the ground. I caught some movement in my peripheral vision and saw words flying by at warp speed in the teleprompter, as our young prompter operator had squeezed the control knob too hard. "Earth to prompter girl!" I yelled, jolting her back to reality.

"Sorry, Veronica," she said, turning the wheel the other way to cue up my introduction. "I was, uh, distracted."

I rolled my eyes at her and turned just as our guest approached me with his hand extended.

"Pleasure to meet you, Miss Summer," he said, in a smooth British accent. "Pleasure" came out "plezh-ahh."

I took his hand and shook it as I locked eyes with this Greek god and he sent me into some sort of a trance. I tried to say something but the words got stuck in my throat as I took in the total package. My jaw opened slightly but nothing came out.

I'd never seen a man so perfect. Incredibly, the photos on the Internet didn't do him justice.

Down girl. Stop thinking with the wrong head like a man.

"Uh... yeah." Gulp. "Nice to meet you too."

We both sat down as a production assistant came over to attach a microphone to his lapel. Her hands shook as she tried to do this while staring at his face and it ended up on his shirt pocket.

"I can take care of that, darling," he said, taking the microphone with one hand and patting her hand with the other. She turned red as a beet and smiled at him as he clipped the mike to his lapel. "I'm good," he said.

She just stood there.

"Uh, you need to get out of the shot," I said.

She turned to face me. "What? Oh... sorry." She moved off the riser and behind the camera.

"Ten seconds out," said the floor director, in the softest, most sultry tone I've ever heard come from her. (Instead of her usual, fingernails-on-the-blackboard nasal Brooklyn scream.)

Dexter Bishop stole a glance at my legs and smiled as the clock ticked down. I tried my best to focus as the red light came on.

"And, welcome back. Joining us today is Dexter Bishop, one of the judges on our nighttime hit *Dance Off*. Welcome to The Morning Show, Mister Bishop."

"Thank you, Veronica. It's a pleasure to be here. And you can call me Dex."

Plezh-ahh. Damn, that accent gives me chills.

"So, you'll have to help me out here a little bit. I don't watch your show."

He shrugged. "Not a problem. I don't watch yours either." He shot me a little wink.

Oh, so you wanna play?

Let's rock.

"Luckily, our promotions department has informed me that you're going to release the names of this year's contestants, right here on our show this morning." I turned to the camera. "For those of you in the newspaper business, stop the presses and get out the *Japanese Bomb Pearl Harbor* two-inch type." I turned back to him and noted his eyes had narrowed a bit.

He pulled an index card out of his inside jacket pocket. "Well, Miss Summer, we have quite an interesting lineup of celebrities for this season. Our contestants include Desdemona French—"

"That singer who's always in alcohol rehab? She can barely stand up, much less dance."

"She assures us she's been sober for a year. Besides, I thought you believed in second chances in this country."

Now it was my turn to glare. "This is more like a fifth chance for her. Anyway, who else you got that's not on the police blotter?"

"Daniel Hardestine, who has recently—"

"The former child star?"

"Yes, exactly."

"What's he, like, thirty years old now?"

"Something like that."

"The guy hasn't done anything in years. At least not that I know of."

"He's trying to resurrect his acting career, and viewers do so love to see their old favorites. It's that whatever-became-of factor."

"Whatever became of him is that he let himself go and wasn't cute anymore."

"I assure you, he's slimmed down considerably and the dancing will tone him up even more. He's also gotten a hair transplant and is quite a nice looking chap. You won't recognize him."

I gave a quick eye roll to the camera, then asked him about the rest of the "celebrities" on the list. As suspected, they weren't exactly A-listers, but considerably down the alphabet of fame. "Can't you get any big names on this show, or are they so expensive they might blow the budget?"

"You know, Miss Summer, there's no reason to act like a solicitor."

My eyes bugged out. Did he just call me a hooker? "*Excuse* me?"

"You're questioning me like a solicitor."

"Look, buddy, you don't have to like me but don't compare me to a prostitute!"

"I said no such thing."

"Well, solicitation is what hookers do on street corners!"

He started to laugh. "My dear, an attorney is sometimes called a solicitor in my country. I'm sorry if my comment was lost in translation, but you were treating me like a hostile witness in a trial."

"Well, I'm sorry I'm not up on current British slang."

"Trust me, the term was around long before the United States existed."

"Oh, still ticked off about that little thing called the Revolutionary War?"

He leaned forward, locking eyes with me. "Perhaps if you Yanks learned to brew a decent cup of tea instead of dumping it in Boston Harbor, you might be more relaxed. You have to actually *boil* the water... maybe you've heard of the concept?"

"Well, you people *across the pond* still haven't figured out that beer and soda don't taste good warm. You're supposed to put them in this new fangled invention called a *refrigerator*... maybe you've heard of the concept?"

He leaned back and exhaled audibly. "Can we please get back to my show?"

"Fine."

"Fine."

"So, *Dex*, why do you suppose anyone wants to watch this stuff?"

"Because *this stuff* as you refer to it is elegant. It's a tad old-fashioned, though ballroom dancing has been making a comeback. It is dance partners working as one, as a team, dressed to the nines, to create something beautiful." He paused, then hit me with a question. "Don't you like to dance, Miss Summer? You've certainly got the legs for it."

I'll ignore that second part. (But nice to know he noticed.) "I love to dance. Took six years of ballet."

"So perhaps if you sampled our show you might enjoy it."

"I don't really want to watch a bunch of amateurs—"

"In fact, I have a better idea. Instead of watching our show, you could take the journalism approach and do the *reporter involvement* thing. We do have one slot open... how would you like to be one of our celebrity contestants? Take your morning show viewers along for the experience."

I raised one eyebrow. "You can't be serious."

He shot me a huge grin. "Yes, it would add so much to our show since it is filled with *amateurs* as you call them. So you'd get a chance to put some money where that rather ill-behaved mouth of yours is."

I had another zinger ready to fly but heard "wrap" in my earpiece from the producer. *Dammit, he got the last word.* "Well, we're out of time. Thanks for coming by."

"My plezh-ahh... I think."

"We'll be right back."

The red light atop the camera went out, the floor director yelled, "Clear!" and Dexter Bishop took off his mike and placed it gently on his chair. He didn't say a word to me, didn't look at me, as he got up and headed for the door. It swung open just as he reached it. Gavin walked through, shook his hand and smiled.

My eyes locked on them as they appeared to be having a nice conversation. Dexter then pointed at me, still smiling, and Gavin nodded as a huge grin grew across his face.

Oh, shit.

***

Layla handed the lunch menu to the waitress, waited until she was out of earshot, then turned to me. "You know, I love you Veronica, but sometimes you're a complete idiot."

"What the hell did I do?"

She pretended to search the heavens for an answer. "Oh, I don't know. You had the world's most eligible bachelor on your show and you treated him like dirt."

"Pffft. Not my type."

"Bullshit. He's every woman's type. He's your type but you won't admit it. And you might be his type since he noticed your legs."

"C'mon, Layla, you think I wanna get involved with someone who produces reality show garbage?"

"It's not a reality show, it's a competition." She grabbed her wine glass and took a sip.

"Semantics."

"You need to get the damn 'J' off your forehead."

"The what?"

"That invisible journalism tattoo you wear. Not everything in life has to be serious. Some things are meant to be fun and mindless, like cute guys. You need to learn to relax and take off your reporting hat once in awhile."

"I know how to have fun. I just don't want to watch that sort of show."

"You know, maybe you should watch it just once. It's actually a lot of fun. You like Broadways musicals, the Joffrey Ballet, right?"

"Sure."

"Well, this is a little bit of both. Professional dancers, choreography, great music, and a lot of personality thrown in. And you get to see some of your old favorite stars who had dropped off the radar."

I shrugged. "Whatever."

Long pause. "So, you gonna be a contestant—"

I put up my hand. "Don't even go there."

"Sorry, I thought it was a fun idea. Might get you out of the house. Spend some time with a bunch of cute guys. You should see the professional dancers on that show. Serious eye candy. But hey, you're on your way to being a cat lady so stay home."

"I only have one cat."

"That's how it starts."

"When the hell would I have time for a dance competition? I can barely make it through the day as it is. What am I supposed to do, anchor the morning show and then fly to Hollywood?"

"They shoot the thing in New York."

"Oh. Still, even if I wanted to do it, there's the time factor."

"I suppose. You still could have been nice to Dexter Bishop. I'd give my right arm for a shot at that."

"Too plastic."

"Just because he's on a show you consider superficial doesn't mean he's the same way. Maybe he's playing a part. Did your little bit of research turn up anything bad? Any scandals, drunken brawls, visits to drug rehab?"

"No. What's your point?"

"The guy's either squeaky clean or very good at hiding his bad habits. But you won't get the chance to find out since you were so rude to him."

My cell phone hummed which thankfully interrupted Layla's lecture. Scott was calling. Since I feel it's rude to talk on a phone in a restaurant I excused myself and headed out the door before picking up. "Hey."

"Hey, yourself. You doing okay?"

"Something tells me I'm about to *not* be doing okay."

"Depends on your point of view."

"Ohhhkaaayyyyyy..."

"You know, the Justice Department has nothing on my eaves-dropping skills."

"Dammit, Scott, just spill."

"Gavin and Dexter Bishop were on a long conference call with the entertainment division."

The color began to drain from my face. "Oh, no..."

"Put on your dancin' shoes, girl."

CHAPTER TWELVE

I've never had an argument with a boss at three in the morning, but I guess there's a first time for everything. In this case, I'd had a sleepless night (are there any other kind for me these days?) going over my defense strategy in my head for what I knew was coming.

And it wasn't even just from Scott's little bit of snooping. The blogosphere was buzzing with the possibility of my being a contestant on *Dance Off*. The show's Facebook page was loaded with comments begging the producers to put me on the roster. Twitter went wild as someone started a hashtag #Veronicainheels in which people speculated how I'd look in various revealing outfits that are apparently the norm for this show. Once I did a little research on *that* my blood pressure spiked; there was no way I was gonna parade myself in "costumes" that were one step above a bikini and platforms. They made my current network micro-skirts look positively Victorian.

And of course there was the scheduling issue. I'd be dead from exhaustion.

So when Gavin greeted me at the door with a huge smile as I emerged from my limo, I was loaded for bear.

"Morning, Veronica. We need to talk—"

"No. I'm not doing it."

He held the door for me and I blew threw it, leaving him in

the wake of fast heel clicks provided by my best power walk. "You don't even know what I'm going to say."

"Yeah, I do. You want me to be on *Dance Off*, and that's not happening. I'm a journalist, not Ginger Rogers."

"Can we please talk about this in my office?"

I put up my hand so the back was facing him. "There's no point. End of discussion. You can go back to laying out this morning's show."

And then he dropped another big, friggin' carrot which landed with a thud and stopped me dead in my tracks.

"If you do it, you can come in at ten a-m for three months."

Again with the produce.

I spun around to face him, brow furrowed. "Say that again?"

He smiled and gestured toward the open door of his office. "Please, let me explain."

The prospect of actual sleep was intriguing, but what about The Morning Show? Were they gonna take me off after just a few weeks, screw with the incredible ratings and the new "business model" which revealed that "perky" was no longer attractive for a morning show host? "Fine," I said, as I walked into his office and grabbed a chair opposite his desk.

Gavin closed the door, moved behind his desk and plopped down into his burgundy leather rocker. "Okay, here's the proposal."

I folded my arms tight. "If you wanna marry me you gotta get down on one knee. And give me a big-ass ring."

"It never stops with you, does it?"

"Nah, part of my charm."

"The network wants you on the upcoming season of *Dance Off*."

"Wow, what a news flash. Let's break into programming. Gavin, I'm exhausted as it is—"

This time he put up his hand to cut me off. "Let me finish. During those three months you would not be required to be *live* on The Morning Show. We think we can pre-tape about ninety percent of it. Scott can do the live news segments at the top, and we'll just bring the guests in later for you to interview. When you arrive at *ten o'clock*, tanned, rested and ready after a good night's sleep."

Ruthless bastard.

"We're going to pre-tape a national morning show?"

"As I said, Scott takes care of the breaking news of the day, and then we roll tape. It's not that big of a deal, it's only for three months and the viewers will be aware that you're working nights. Besides, the cross promotion with having you on a prime time show could take the ratings even higher."

"That's an interesting concept, Gavin. But there's one key element you seem to have forgotten."

"What's that?"

"That little deal we have about me getting *The Chair* after three years."

"Nothing's changed on that. What's your point?"

"My point is that after parading my half-naked body in front of millions of Americans in those revealing costumes I won't have a bit of credibility left. You think viewers will trust an evening news anchor who used to strut her stuff in stiletto heels and dresses up to her ass? I won't have a bit of gravitas left."

He smiled, shook his head and leaned back. "Veronica, we're a celebrity nation. Nobody cares about that crap anymore. Every major network anchor does stuff like this. They show up on sitcoms, tell jokes on late night talk shows, dress up on Halloween. We've got celebrities in Congress, for God's sake. What's the difference?"

"The difference is that *I* won't consider myself credible after this."

"Well, I'm sorry you feel that way but the decision has already been made."

"Excuse me?"

"There's a little clause in your contract that reads *other duties as assigned*. It's in the section on promoting the network. And don't blame me, because the network president signed off on this."

I scrunched up my face, pondering this no-win scenario. Sure, there was the attractive prospect of actually getting to sleep for a few months, but the fallout could be journalistic suicide. I played a low card, which wasn't remotely a trump. "I'm a lousy ballroom dancer."

"After six years of ballet? I hardly think so. You'll pick it up."

Memo to self: stop volunteering personal information on live television.

"Maybe I won't be very good compared to the other contestants and get voted off in the first week."

"We already thought of that. The entertainment division assures me it isn't going to happen."

I sat up straight as my eyes widened. "You mean the show's *fixed*?"

"I didn't say that. Why don't we just say that those in power have a lot of faith in your ability as a dancer."

I rolled my eyes. "Good God, Gavin. Reality shows aren't even on the level?"

"Look, Veronica. At least you'll get back to a normal schedule for three months and you'll probably have fun."

"Yeah, right. I guess I have no choice."

Gavin said nothing as he looked at me.

"One more question, Gavin. Was this your idea?"

"Nope. It came from the Executive Producer of *Dance Off*."

"Then I wanna talk to him."

"You already did. The EP is Dexter Bishop."

***

The moment our show was over I ripped off my microphone, threw it onto my chair, grabbed my purse and headed for the door, barging through several staffers like a shopper after a Black Friday sale. I headed out into the street breathing like a snorting bull about to gore a matador in the family jewels.

And Dexter Bishop was dressed head to toe in candy apple red.

As luck would have it his production office was only two blocks away, so I didn't need a cab. I forced smiles at pedestrians who recognized me, waved at the cabbies who honked their horns, blew a kiss at the utility worker who hit me with an old fashioned wolf whistle, and was at the door to Bishop Productions in five minutes.

The impeccably coiffed blonde silicone babe receptionist smiled as I headed into the building, her hair the only color in a lobby with walls of black marble. "Ms. Summer! I just heard the news! Welcome aboard!"

"Where's Dexter's office?"

"Top floor. I'll tell him you're on your way—"

"Don't bother. I want to surprise him." Yeah. With a kick to the groin.

The elevator was already open and I stormed in, glared at the huge photo of Dexter Bishop that filled the back wall of the car, punched the button labeled PH, and ground my teeth as the door closed and I headed up. I wasn't even sure what I was going to say, as my anger had pushed reason to the back burner hours ago. I just knew that as mad as Alexander had made me on the day I threw him out, this was worse.

The elevator slowed, came to a stop, and the door opened. Sunlight spilled into the car from the huge windows which provided light to the large glass top desk that sat in the middle of the room. A massive flat screen television practically filled one wall while a deep red leather couch sat in front. The opposite wall was covered by a built-in bookcase, featuring several Emmy awards lined up in a row.

Dexter Bishop put down a coffee cup, got up from his chair and started to move toward me. "Miss Summer, how nice of you to drop by, and just in time for tea. I can't tell you how excited—"

My palms slammed into his chest and shoved him back a few steps. "How *dare* you!"

"Now calm down—"

My eyes filled with fire as they narrowed into gunslinger mode. "*Calm* down? Oh, you want *calm*?" I kept moving toward him and he backed up as I held a finger inches from his face. "You screw with my career, my reputation, and you expect me to just brush it off?"

He put up his hands but I slapped them away. "Please, Miss Summer, let me explain." I continued moving toward him, he backed up behind his desk, his knees hit his chair and he plopped back into it.

I stopped my charge, grabbed the arms of the chair, and looked down at him. "Fine. Explain yourself."

"It's simple. You're going to be this season's *It Girl* on our show. One of the reasons we had one slot open was that we had not found the right person. But during our little bit of snappy repartee yesterday, I knew you would be perfect for the show. When you dropped that little tidbit about your experience with ballet, it sealed the deal."

"That *deal* wouldn't have been sealed unless you had approval from the news division."

"Gavin gave it to me rather quickly."

Oh really. "Did he also tell you that I have a deal to take over the evening newscast when my contract ends on The Morning Show?"

"No, he left that part out."

"Well, that part won't happen if I lose all my credibility as a journalist on your show."

He furrowed his brow. "How would you lose credibility?"

I let go of the chair, stood back up and folded my arms. "Network anchors don't usually flaunt their wares in skimpy outfits. Who will take me seriously after this?"

"Miss Summer, we've had network journalists on our show before. James Devlin, Alecia Florence—"

"They're has-beens! They were never main anchors!"

"Look, I won't put you in a position in which you're not comfortable. It's important that you enjoy your weeks on the show."

"What about the revealing outfits?"

"I'll button you up like Dame Judi Dench on competition nights if you prefer."

"Yes, I prefer."

"However, we will need to show off those fabulous gams of yours."

"No ridiculous hemlines up to my ass?"

"They'll be longer than the frocks you wear on your current show." I was beginning to run out of steam and he smiled at me. "May I get up now? And won't you please have a cup of tea with me?"

"I don't want any damn tea." I backed up a few steps and he stood. "You know, you guys could have talked with me about this before making a decision."

"Gavin knew you wouldn't want to do it. So the point is moot. Come now, let's have some tea and chat."

He reached out and took me by the shoulders but I twisted away like his hands were on fire. "Hey!"

"My, aren't we touchy."

"*We* aren't touchy. You're the one who grabbed me."

"I did not *grab*, I was merely trying to settle you down."

I spun on one heel and headed for the door. "This girl doesn't want to settle down."

And as I reached the door, I realized that statement was technically a lie.

CHAPTER THIRTEEN

Shit lists.

Everyone has one. Most of us are on one. Members of the media could play the journalism version of Six Degrees of Kevin Bacon with shit lists.

Gavin Karlson is on Veronica Summer's shit list. Since Veronica is on Dexter Bishop's shit list...

Those aren't the only lists causing me stress right now. Nooooo. I've got a whole bunch of lists to deal with. Of course there's the list of "celebrities" for the upcoming season of *Dance Off*, and the network has been so kind as to put my name at the top of every media release.

But there's one more list that will affect me directly; the list of prospective partners for the competition. And that's the one which has my friends all but drooling in their salads this afternoon at the casual outdoor restaurant we've chosen. With six female celebrities in the contest, there are a half dozen male professional dancers who will be paired with them. And work closely with them for the next three months for several hours per day.

While I have no idea which one will be my partner, or if I can even request a particular dancer, I've been getting "reviews" of the potential prospects from what I now refer to as "my entourage" since Layla and Savannah are determined to crash the live audience as often as possible. Meanwhile, they're divided on who I should get as a partner, but agree on the fact that I'll end up with a hot guy regardless. The network gave me a media kit with photos of all the possibles, which I haven't looked at but is in the hands of my friends.

"You want Sergio," said Layla, as she grabbed his eight-by-ten glossy and slid it next to my plate. "He's a hunka hunka burnin' Latin love. God, that accent makes me melt." One look at the photo told me I wouldn't care if he sounded like Melanie Griffith after inhaling helium. Tall, dark and lean, the guy's huge bedroom eyes seemed to leap out of the picture. The rest of his ripped physique jumped a few hurdles as well, as the revealing costume showed nary a flaw.

"I suppose he'd be *okay*," I said, trying but failing to hold back a grin.

Savannah shook her head at me. "Not for you. I caught him on a talk show last week and there's nothing upstairs. He's dumb as a bag of rocks. Pure eye candy, and that's it."

"Your point being?" asked Layla.

"She'd get bored talking with him," said Savannah.

"Again, your point being?" asked Layla. "His conversational skills are not on the table. Anyway, I think he's leagues ahead of the others."

Savannah grabbed her choice from the stack of photos. "Salvatore is the guy for you." She slid it across the table and I scooped it up. "Looks great, good head on his shoulders. And those are perfect."

My eyes bugged out at the guy's massive shoulders. A classic hunk of beefcake, he wasn't the typical slender dancer. Not particularly tall, Salvatore's ice blue eyes peered out of a chiseled face framed by black hair. "I could do worse," I said. I was glad a cool breeze wafted by, since I was starting to feel a bit warm.

"Or, if you don't care for him," said Savannah, who daintily handed me her second choice. "This boy would have me sweatin' like a whore in church."

I took in the total package that was Kyle Westin, who possessed the classic boy next door look. Tousled brown hair, hazel eyes, a perfectly proportioned body stretched out over six feet. I absent-mindedly licked my lips as I read his bio, which included a degree from an Ivy League school.

"You like?" asked Savannah.

I nodded. "Very much. Damn, he's cute."

"And obviously very smart. So you'd have things to talk about."

"Your point being?" cracked Layla.

"Y'all hush," said Savannah. "The others are fine for exercise, but I know what she needs in a soulmate. She needs hot *and* smart. Who has a lot in common with her."

"Having things in common is important," I said, still staring at the photo.

"Hell," said Layla, "if you want hot, smart and snarky, you might as well just leapfrog all these guys and go for the brass ring."

I looked up at her. "Brass ring?"

"Dexter Bishop."

***

"Welcome back on this Friday," said Scott. "And this will be the last day in the next few months that my partner will be getting up before the sun. She's off to start training on Monday for her appearance on *Dance Off*. Hopefully she will not dust off her *robot* from college." He turned to me. "So, Veronica, you ready to prove you don't have two left feet?"

"I'll be honest," I said. "I'm a little nervous about all this. I mean, this isn't exactly what they teach in journalism class."

"Well, politicians tap dance around your questions all the time."

"Very true. But our viewers should know that I'll be doing double duty and will be here every day."

"Right, just not live. You'll get the same attitude, just on tape.

97

Meanwhile, we'd like to invite you to tune in Sunday night at eight when all the contestants on *Dance Off* will be paired off with their partners. Do you have any preference?"

I do, but I'm not saying lest Dexter Bishop stick me with someone else out of spite. "Well, as I mentioned when Dexter Bishop was here, I've never seen the show, so I have no preference and don't even know any of the players. Hopefully they'll pair me up with someone who can make me the best dancer I can be."

"Sounds like you're actually looking forward to it."

"I'm looking forward to getting some sleep, Scott. That's a great incentive to work hard and not get voted off the show."

I caught some movement out of the corner of my eye and saw Scott's expression change to one of surprise. "We, uh, apparently have a special guest," he said.

I turned and saw a smiling Dexter Bishop heading in our direction. I shot a quick look at Scott and his expression told me he had no idea this was coming.

And Gavin moves to the top of my shit list.

Dexter stepped onto the riser and extended his hand to me. "Good morning!"

I forced a smile and shook his hand. "Hello, Mister Bishop. So, what brings you by this morning?"

He leaned over, shook Scott's hand, and grabbed a spot between us. "Well, as you already mentioned, we're going to announce the pairings live on Sunday night. But this season we're adding a little twist."

"You've already got me on the show. Isn't that enough of a twist?"

"Ah, Miss Summer, you must always freshen up a good show to keep the viewers interested. I believe you Yanks like to call things *new and improved*. With that in mind..." he looked over his shoulder. "Gentlemen?"

I turned just as the parade started.

All six of the professional male dancers pranced onto the set while "It's raining men" played in the background. They lined up, like some sort of hot guy buffet.

"You brought Veronica's entourage?" cracked Scott.

Dexter chuckled a bit. "Actually, these are her possible partners for the competition. As for the twist, we're going to let the *viewers* decide who she should be dancing with for the next three months." He gestured toward the guys. "Miss Summer, if you'd be so kind as to stand next to each of our dancers to let people see how you look as a couple and then we'll let the viewers vote—"

"You've got to be kidding," I said. "I'm not some bachelorette on a reality show, so—"

"Viewers may vote with your cell phones," he said, turning to face the camera, "and each text will cost one dollar and will be donated to Miss Summer's favorite charity." He turned back to face me with a look that said *I'm in charge here*. "And your favorite charity would be...?"

You ruthless bastard. You know damn well I can't refuse to do this now.

"The Wounded Warrior Foundation."

"Marvelous! They do wonderful work," said Dexter, who then locked eyes with me. "I know those veterans will greatly appreciate what you're about to do on their behalf."

I forced a smile, having no choice. There was no way I was gonna take money out of the pocket of a recovering vet. "Happy to help out," I said. Then I figured, what the hell, let's give it right back. "And I know you'll be more than happy to match whatever funds are raised." I playfully batted my eyes as it was his turn to force a smile.

"Absolutely," he said, eyes not giving away a thing. "It will be my pleasure. Now, if you'll be so kind as to spend a few seconds with each of our dancers while we flash the number for the appropriate text on the screen. As you like to say on election day, vote early and vote often!"

I stood up and moved toward the line of dancers as Scott picked up the ball. "Okay, *Dance Off* fans, here's your chance to play matchmaker for Veronica."

An old disco instrumental played as I reached the group. Salvatore was first in line. He kissed my hand, then wrapped an arm around my shoulders as I stood next to him. I looked at the monitor and saw them flash a number across the bottom of the screen as Dexter Bishop did what amounted to play-by-play. He directed me to move on to the next guy, Sergio, who actually looked a little sleazy compared to his photo while his strong earthy cologne practically knocked me over. He winked at me, said, "Give yourself to me," in a thick Latin accent, then grabbed one hand and twirled me around so that I landed with his arms wrapped around my waist. I forced a smile but I knew this was one guy I didn't want to end up with for a partner. Next up was Kyle, who came as advertised. He simply nodded and said hello, but kept his hands to himself as he moved close to me. So far, I had to agree with Savannah's choice.

Until number six.

If viewers were watching closely on a high-def flatscreen they no doubt saw me gulp while I blushed like a high school girl.

Oh.

My.

God.

My heart melted as the incredible guy named Bradley smiled at me and gently took both my hands. A lean six feet, with broad shoulders and slim hips filling out a dark gray three piece suit; dark, wavy hair that called out to my fingers while his spectacular gray eyes searched mine. He let go of one hand so we could stand side by side to let the viewers get a good look, but I couldn't stop looking at him.

I realized I needed to take control of the situation.

I turned to the camera, raised both eyebrows and mouthed "Wow" then pointed at him and made that "call me sign" with my thumb and pinky raised to the side of my head. Hopefully the viewers got the massage.

"Thank you, Miss Summer," said Dexter, "and I guess we know where your preference lies."

Now if the show isn't totally fixed, I'm good to go.

But one look at Dexter Bishop told me I wasn't.

CHAPTER FOURTEEN

In television news, the tease is king.

You see them all the time and probably don't even notice them. Teases are those little attention grabbers designed to keep you watching. Newscasts use them all the time. "Congressman caught with transvestite hooker! After the game!" Even if said game is a blowout, that tease will ensure you'll stick around to see which member of the House of Representatives got a *Crying Game* surprise.

In the case of *Dance Off*, the tease started Friday morning with the viewer contest to pair me with the perfect partner. But unlike most news teases which last less than ten seconds, this one has legs. And we're not talkin' about the ones about to be shown off in revealing outfits.

Entertainment websites and newspapers were going wild over this, speculating on who will be voted as my partner and if my blatant plea to vote for Bradley will result in my getting my wish. Of course every website is running its own poll and every dancer has a fan club running a "campaign." Then there are the articles about my reaction to Number Six, one of which said I resembled a "starry-eyed sex deprived woman on her first trip to a Chippendales show with a handful of dollar bills." Apparently I was so entranced by the guy I didn't know I had licked my lips, leading another columnist to write, "Ms. Summer looked like a starving woman just emerged from the desert about to devour the man next to her."

Just reading that sentence made me blush. Though the thought made me smile.

Anyway, as I've managed to "sleep in" on this Sunday morning till ten, I'm encouraged that every poll I've seen has Bradley in the lead by a fair margin. Either viewers think Number Six is the hottest of the bunch, they think we make a good looking couple, or they've taken my subtle-as-a-train-wreck hint and want to avoid making me even more sarcastic on The Morning Show.

For what it's worth, I blew about two hundred bucks yesterday voting with my cell phone until my fingers got tired. Hey, a girl needs to support the veterans, you know? And every time I voted I couldn't help but think I was taking another buck out of Dexter Bishop's pocket.

But before our usual brunch I wanted to swing by the set of *Dance Off* just to get the lay of the land.

The network has several studios in its complex, a few for sitcoms, two for talk shows, and a big one for its long running soap opera *Seduction Place* which offers me the opportunity to occasionally run into some of the most perfect looking men on the planet. (It requires me to walk down a ridiculous amount of hallways, but I need my cardio.) The *Dance Off* studio lies at the opposite end of the building from the newsroom. Our Sunday morning news panel show is done in Washington so on any given weekend the whole place is pretty deserted. Since there are only a few security people and a skeleton crew manning the newsroom, I knew I could probably sneak in without being seen.

Automatic lights kicked on as I headed down the hallway toward the door of studio 5-A, which featured a colorful sign with the *Dance Off* logo. I opened the door and moved into the dimly lit empty studio, which was set up to be half movie theater and half dance hall. One side featured about five hundred seats for the audience, with the front row about one foot off the ground.

The other side featured a Lucite podium and two large round tables with bright red tablecloths. Twelve chairs surrounded each table, while a simple folded white place card sat in front of each chair.

Hmmm. Assigned seating.

Let's see where they put me.

I moved toward the tables and started to walk around the first one, searching for my name and that of the man I now referred to as Number Six. I found his card first. To his left, the card of a has-been child star. To his right, that of the drug rehabbed singer. I quickly checked the rest of the cards.

I wasn't even at this table.

Sorry, Dexter, this just won't do.

I moved to the second table and quickly found my card. Dexter had put me next to one of the dancers who did absolutely nothing for me.

I grabbed my card, carried it to the other table, swapped it out with that of the singer, and brought hers over to my original seat.

***

The audience was buzzing with ten minutes to go before we went live with the selection show. I'd arranged for Layla and Savannah to have seats in the front row, since they insisted on coming to every episode in order to watch me dance. But I know all they want is a shot at *Bish the Dish* so they made me promise to introduce them.

Fine. Have at it. Knock yourselves out.

Dexter was standing next to his podium talking to the director so I walked over to him and gently touched his forearm. "Dexter, can I borrow you for a minute? I have some friends who'd like to meet you."

He offered a smile as the director nodded at me and headed back toward the control room. "Certainly. Lead on."

I walked toward the front row and saw my friends sit up straight like they were in a 1950s Catholic school. Of course they weren't dressed like most of the audience in tee-shirts and fanny packs, since, let's face it, we have become a nation of slobs. Layla wore a revealing red silk top with a short leather skirt that rode up her thigh; Savannah went for an asymmetrical look with her hair pinned up on one side. She'd done her eyes like an Egyptian princess while choosing an emerald green halter dress with a slit that showed off her boobs. If she moved in just the right way. And I knew at some point she would.

I led Dexter to Layla and started with her. "Dexter, this is my best friend Layla. We've known each other since high school."

He smiled at her and nodded his head a bit. "Pleasure."

"Oh, the plezh-ahh is all mine," she said, mimicing his accent while wearing the biggest smile I'd ever seen.

"She's a personal trainer."

She whipped out a business card and handed it to him. "I'd be honored if you'd drop by for a body analysis. No charge, of course."

Yeah, right. Body analysis my ass.

He took the card and put it in his pocket while his eyes took inventory of her body. "I think I can work it into my schedule."

I rolled my eyes at her, then continued. "And this is Savannah. She's a public relations consultant."

And, judging from Dexter's sudden transition to a puppy dog look, she is made of solid Kryptonite.

He locked on her like a heat seeking missile as he took her hand. "Oh my. Aren't you lovely."

Unlike Layla, Savannah kept her cool and gave him a soft smile. "Why, sugah, y'all are so sweet to say that," she said, turning up the Southern accent to the level she refers to as "exponential magnolia." Savannah has always told me no man outside the South can resist her little Scarlett O'Hara thing, as her thick, sultry drawl would make Vivien Leigh sound like a longshoreman from New Jersey by comparison.

"And what a charming accent," said Dexter.

"*My* accent... why, *yours* just puts the peach in my cobbler."

He furrowed his brow. "My dear, why would you endeavor to put fruit in your rubbish?"

I shook my head. "I think you two need an interpreter. How about we head over to the United Nations after the show?"

"Silly boy," said Savannah. "Cobbler is a Southern dessert. Ah just called y'all a main ingredient in somethin' sweet and delectable that you put in your mouth." She smiled, playfully bit her tongue while giving both eyebrows a quick lift.

Dear God, the woman speaks porn.

And now Dexter was the one to blush. "Well, that, uh, clears it up nicely. You work in public relations, do you?"

"Ah do. Veronica will tell you ahm very good at bringin' out the best in people." Then she waved her hand like shooing a fly. "Pffft. But y'all are already successful and don't need help in that department from little ol' me."

"One can always improve oneself," said Dexter. "Perhaps you might have some ideas for me."

Savannah licked her lips as she leaned forward. (What a surprise.) The slit in the dress opened as if on cue, Dexter's eyes dropped and bugged out as he took in the view. "Oh, ah have ideas already about what ah can do for y'all."

The floor director's yell thankfully broke his trance or the scene could have been taped and ended up on late night cable. "Ten minutes!"

"Well," said Dexter, "I must be off. But—"

Savannah's hand shot out toward him with a business card. "Call me," she said simply. "Tomorrow. At two."

"Absolutely," he said, though his look said, *Yes, Ma'am.* "You ladies enjoy the show." He turned and headed back toward the stage.

Layla shook her head as she looked at Savannah. "Well, so much for my complimentary body analysis."

I headed for my newly assigned seat along with all the other contestants, pretending to be looking for my name card. The game of musical chairs continued as I reached the seat to the right of Number Six.

My jaw dropped. The drug rehabbed singer was back in her original seat.

At that moment she politely slid in front of me. "Excuse me, I'm sitting here."

"Sure," I said. I looked at the remaining seats and saw Dexter smiling at me.

Then he shot me a wink.

I glared at him as I moved around the table, then discovered that not only was I not sitting next to Number Six, but I wasn't even at his table.

Seats were quickly being filled as I headed for the other table and found my card.

Next to Sergio.

I looked up at Dexter. He licked one finger, then used it to write an imaginary number one on an invisible scoreboard.

***

And then there were two.

With seven minutes to go in the show, ten couples had been paired up.

You guessed it, like the last kid chosen for a game of wiffle ball, I was still available.

But so was Bradley.

He was still sitting next to the stoned singer while Sergio occupied the seat next to me and continued to shoot me looks more appropriate to a seventies lounge lizard in a polyester leisure suit.

Dexter had been giving me sly winks during every commercial

break.

And with one break to go, he dropped the final tease.

"When we come back, we'll pair up our final couples. We'll find out who you, the viewers, think is the best partner for Veronica Summer. And she might be surprised at your decision. Back in a flash."

"Annnndddd... we're clear!" said the floor director.

I had exactly two minutes to rectify this.

I got up and walked quickly over to Dexter's lucite podium. He smiled as I approached. "Is there a problem, Miss Summer?"

This was now about more than spending a ton of time with a guy who I found incredibly attractive. This was about control, about Dexter not pulling my strings like some puppeteer. About showing the entertainment division I had a set of brass ones and could not be pushed around.

It was time to play my trump card. And play it with a reporter's trick attached.

I moved around the podium, put my thumb over his lapel microphone so no one in the control room could possibly hear me, leaned up and whispered in his ear. "You put me with Bradley or America is going to find out this show is fixed. Got it?"

He looked side to side to make sure no one was in earshot. "You wouldn't do that to your own network," he said in a barely audible voice.

Caught.

"I'll take that as a confirmation the show isn't on the level."

Dexter's eyes widened and filled with fear. His lower lip began to quiver, as if he'd been hooked like a trophy bass. "I..."

"I have good friends at the competition who would love an exclusive." I looked right into his eyes with my best barroom death stare. "So, do we have a deal?"

He gave me a slightly worried look as he gently removed my hand from his microphone. "You'd better return to your seat now, Miss Summer."

I spun around and headed back to my table, then slid into the chair next to Sergio just as the floor director yelled, "Ten seconds!"

And one minute later, I found out who was running this show.

CHAPTER FIFTEEN

"We're clear!"

The floor director's words signaled the end of the show. The audience applause died down as people got up and filed for the exits.

And then my partner for the next few weeks smiled at me. "So, ready to work?"

"You're the boss," I said, hoping Number Six would use that title in places other than the dance floor.

I felt a gentle tug on my arm and turned to find Dexter. "Before you leave, we need to talk."

I playfully batted my eyelashes at him. "Yes, I suppose we do."

"Meet you in the green room in ten."

"Fine."

***

I'm never late for anything. In this business, there's one simple rule: you miss one deadline, you're in trouble. You miss two, you're out of a job.

But in this case I was a little tardy getting to the green room. Okay, more than a little. I wanted to make Dexter sweat a bit.

The green room isn't really green. That's just the industry

name we give to a waiting room for guests. In reality, it's simply a comfortable place with a bunch of couches around the perimeter, a kitchen always stocked with drinks and snacks, and a large flat screen hanging off one wall. I opened the door and found Dexter sipping a soda while pacing back and forth like an expectant father. "Nice of you to drop by," he said, with a little sarcasm as he stopped and turned to face me.

"I was talking to my friend. You know, Savannah? She's like a sister to me. *Always* takes my advice. Where to invest money, how to shop. Who to date, that kind of stuff."

"You already made your point on the set, no need to rub my face in it."

"Just wanted to make sure we're clear on things."

"Yes, it's quite clear you're not some fair damsel in distress. You're more like a damsel who *causes* distress."

"Oooooh, I kinda like that, Dexter. So, what did you want to talk about?"

"Well, since we're going to be working together for the next few months I'd like to bury the hatchet—"

"Where? In my back?"

"Please let me finish."

I nodded and folded my arms. "You have the floor."

"Thank you," he said. "I realize you may be angry that I've had a great deal of influence on your current situation. I want to apologize for not bringing you in on the original discussions."

"That barn door has sailed."

His face tightened. "I'm sorry, I don't understand the colloquialism."

"It's a combination of slang from the newsroom. Stolen horses, ships leaving port. Never mind. Anyway, continue."

"I think it best that we call a truce."

"Okay. And what would the terms of said truce be?"

"No more surprises from me. And you'll do your absolute best to win the competition."

"Sounds fair enough." I walked over to him and extended my hand. He shook it.

"I must say, Miss Summer, you're unlike any woman I've ever encountered in the media."

"That's why they pay me the big bucks."

"One more thing... your dear friend, Savannah..."

"Don't worry, I won't say anything. She's old enough to make her own decisions. But treat her badly and I'll beat the crap out of you."

"I believe you would. But she has nothing to fear. I've never treated any woman badly."

"I'll bet." I turned and headed for the door. "Well, see you tomorrow."

"Oh, by the way..."

I stopped without turning to face him. "Yes?"

"You would have been much better off with Sergio."

Now I had to turn and face him. "That sleazeball? Why, he's a better dancer?"

"He's a better person. That suave Latin lover persona is simply for the cameras. He's actually quite the opposite. As well as being an excellent dancer, better than Bradley. But you're old enough to make your own decisions."

***

Savannah, who was old enough to make decisions not only for herself but the rest of the world, daintily ate her cajun chicken salad as a light breeze blew through the outdoor cafe. We've always loved *dining alfresco* and she likes this little place because she can sit next to the sidewalk to people watch. Well, *men watch* to be more specific. And she doesn't mind the looks she gets in return.

"It's so nice to see you looking so rested," she said, as she watched a tight pair of jeans walk by.

I pointed to my face. "Hey, my eyes are up here."

She smiled as she turned back to me. "Sorry. Just enjoying the atmosphere of the restaurant."

"I would think with Dexter tucked away in your pocket you wouldn't bother looking anymore."

"Doesn't matter if I look at the menu, as long as I eat dinner at home. Anyway, you look good."

"It's nice not to get up at two in the morning. You even sleep better knowing you don't have to get up."

"And all your pre-taped stuff went well?"

"Yeah, no problem."

"Too bad they can't do that on a permanent basis."

"Great idea but they'd never go for it long term. This is a unique situation, so I'll enjoy it while it lasts." I selected a few strands from my dinner-sized portion of linguine with white clam sauce, twirled it into a spoon and popped it in my mouth.

"You eating for two today?"

"Not unless you're expecting a virgin birth. I've got my first practice session this afternoon and I know I'll be burning it off, so I'm splurging."

"I'm so glad you got the guy you wanted. Though I still think Kyle would have been a better choice."

I took a sip of sparkling water and dabbed my mouth with a napkin as a cute guy walked by and checked out both of us. "Speaking of better choices, do you really think Dexter is a good fit for you?"

"Good *fit*? Sweetie, I haven't even slept with him yet."

"Stop taking things literally. You know what I mean."

"One never knows unless one casts her net upon the waters. And I'm not turning down a shot at Bish the Dish."

I shook my head. "He's not right for you, Savannah. I mean, look at the stuff he's pulled with me. He obviously can't be trusted."

Her cell rang, *Tara's Theme* from *Gone With the Wind* interrupting the conversation. She looked at it and smiled. "Right on time."

I glanced at her caller ID and saw Dexter was calling. "You've got him trained already."

"One must maintain the upper hand at the start of any relationship." She speared a piece of chicken and took a bite as the phone continued to ring.

"Only at the start?"

She shrugged and smiled.

I pointed to the phone. "Uh, aren't you gonna answer that?"

She swallowed, then took a sip from her wine glass. "Why?"

"Well... because you told him to call you at two. And it's exactly two o'clock. And he's calling."

"So? Boy can follow directions. I never said I was going to talk with him. I just wanted to see if he'd call. If he was interested."

"The guy practically drooled on the set last night and you're wondering if he's interested?"

"I don't need to be an investigative reporter to know that half the men who say they'll call never do. And y'all should know that the best way to keep a man's interest is to ignore him."

The phone stopped playing music as the call went to voice mail. "You gonna call him back?"

"Don't have to. He'll call again. Probably this afternoon. Veronica, you do know men come with handles so we can lead them around, don't you?"

"You know, you are one devious Southern belle."

"That's the nicest compliment I've had in awhile."

CHAPTER SIXTEEN

The term "orientation" often conjures up images of that first day at a new job during which you have to sit through lectures, out-of-date Powerpoint presentations and often laughable videos about why it's a bad idea to have relationships in the workplace. (In the case of a television network, a studio would be a rather uncomfortable place to hook up. Though it could be argued that some guys could use a teleprompter when it comes to foreplay.)

But this is a different kind of orientation, as the celebrities and dancers were paired up and grabbing a space on the hardwood floor of a practice studio. One wall was covered by a floor-to-ceiling mirror, the opposite had a balance bar. A silver boom box sat on the floor in the corner. Everyone was dressed in workout clothes, ranging from garish yoga pants and a tie-dyed tee shirt (rehab girl) to shorts and leotards. I wore a baggy New York Giants blue sweatshirt and a gray pair of sweatpants.

Dexter Bishop was the only person standing. He was busy arranging a stack of folders on top of a small table which was the only piece of furniture in the room.

And considering I was seated next to Number Six and breathing in his Polo cologne like oxygen, this beat the hell out of a "don't have sex with your co-anchor under the set because a microphone cord makes for an uncomfortable thong" presentation.

"Nice to see you again."

I turned as Sergio took a seat opposite my partner. The voice didn't match the face. "What happened to your accent?"

"Oh, that's just for the show," he said, in a perfect American non-accent. "Sergio is my stage name." He stuck out his hand. "Howie Appleton, nice to meet you."

"*Howie?* Seriously?"

He shrugged. "The middle name is actually worse. It's locked up in a secret, undisclosed location often used by the Vice President."

"So, do you prefer Howie or Sergio when we're off the clock?"

"Trey is fine, since I'm Howie the third. It's one of my family's rather unfortunate traditions."

"Oh." I studied his face, not seeing a hint of the lounge lizard I'd previously encountered. His eyes were warm and friendly, the kind you could get lost in. Suddenly he wasn't the slimy creep I'd previously encountered. "Well, that's a great act you have."

"That's nice of you to say, since I would eventually like to break into acting."

"If nothing else, you could do voiceovers."

"Way ahead of you on that one. Anyway, I really thought we'd be working together. But you'll be fine with Bradley. He's a solid dancer."

"Good to know," I said. Also good to know Sergio isn't really Sergio, he's just a Latin-looking guy named Howie. Is this what Dexter was talking about? "So you can just turn that Latin lover thing on and off whenever you like?"

"I can be a Noo Yawkuh if ya want. So, youse wanna pahty afta woik, or what?"

I laughed a bit and took in his soft smile. "You're pretty good at that."

"Thanks."

"Welcome, celebrities," said Dexter, interrupting us and making everyone face forward. "And thank you for agreeing to participate in our little contest."

Agreeing? That's a stretch.

"You're about to embark on what I'm sure you'll find to be a unique, exhilarating experience. You may be surprised at your own abilities, about what your body is able to do, and how dancing can be an incredible workout. And, if you're doing things right, you'll discover how a dance can turn two people into one in a beautiful manner." He raised one eyebrow and dropped his voice. "Sort of like great sex."

The group laughed. I turned and smiled at my partner, who was in the process of rolling his eyes. "What?" I whispered.

"Heard it a bunch of times before," Bradley deadpanned. "Here comes the part about how dancing is going to change your life."

"These few months you'll spend dancing will change your life," said Dexter, right on cue.

"Not my first rodeo," said Bradley, looking at me with sad eyes.

"What's wrong?"

"Long story."

Dexter interrupted us by clearing his throat. "Uh, Miss Summer, is there something you'd like to share with the rest of the class?"

The group chuckled as my face turned red. "Sorry." I sat up straight and folded my hands in my lap. "Please, continue."

"Thank you for granting me permission," he said with a bow, to more laughs.

Everyone looked at me, probably waiting for a snarky comeback. Dexter shot me a wink, then dared me with a "come on" motion with one hand. I opened my mouth, ready to launch a zinger, then thought better of it.

"Amazing," said Dexter. "I'm apparently the only man on the planet with the ability to render this woman speechless. Though I doubt she has a future as a mime."

I smiled, narrowed my eyes a bit, and said nothing.

He rambled on for the next ten minutes, telling us some video from our rehearsals would be used on air, the rules of the contest, and how much practice the average couple goes through. We were told that there was no time limit as to the amount of practice, that we could put as much effort into it as we desired.

"Very well," said Dexter. "I know you're eager to get started. Your dance partner will escort you to your private studio, where you'll find your outfits for the practice sessions."

"We have practice clothes?" I asked.

"Of course," said Dexter, giving my outfit the once-over. "We cannot have you going around looking as though you're going to clean the loo."

***

"He wants me to wear *this*?"

Bradley shrugged as I held up the electric blue spandex outfit that would no doubt make me look like Catwoman had escaped from a seventies disco. "You've got the body for it."

"Thank you, but that's beside the point." *Though it's awfully nice that you noticed.*

"Look, they do this to all the attractive contestants. It's no big deal. Just sexing up the show. Consider it a compliment."

"It won't leave much to the imagination."

He tried unsuccessfully to hold back a smile. "Your point being?"

"My point being that I was promised I would not be forced to wear sleazy stuff, nothing with hemlines up to my ass."

"That doesn't exactly have a hemline." He moved forward and took my shoulders. "Look, Veronica, you're an attractive woman and this is prime time television. You're worth a lot of ratings to this show. And it's not like you're being forced to pose nude or anything."

"Well, can't I just practice in my sweats until the camera people get here?"

"There are no camera people, Veronica."

"I thought our rehearsals would be recorded."

"They will be." He pointed at a spot on the far wall. "They're *already* being recorded."

I squinted and spotted the hidden camera. "Oh, you gotta be kidding. I thought a camera crew would just come in here from time to time."

He shook his head, then cocked it toward the floor-to-ceiling mirror that covered one wall. "And that's one-way glass."

"Holy shit!"

"Don't worry, they'll bleep that out. But it's just like being arrested. Anything you say can and will be used against you in the court of public opinion."

My mouth dropped open as I stared at the mirror.

You behind there, Dexter?

You want a show? I'll give you a show.

"Anyway," said Bradley, "you need to change clothes. Don't worry, there aren't any cameras or microphones in the locker rooms or bathrooms."

"Well, that's comforting." I grabbed my spandex and headed for the locker room, trying my best to smile for whatever camera was recording me.

Said smile died a grisly death with Bradley's next comment.

"Soon as you're changed we can do your body analysis."

***

You've heard of devil in a blue dress? I'm the demon in blue spandex.

To say this outfit leaves little to the imagination is putting it mildly. At least a hemline up to my ass wouldn't *reveal* my ass. But this thing has done a wonderful job of tightening and separating my cheeks. Oh, and the low cut front and tight waist has the effect of a Victorian bustier as I am now close to spilling out of my outfit, looking as though I've been to a plastic surgeon and asked for an Anna Nicole Smith upgrade.

Somehow I don't think Dame Judi Dench will come to mind

119

when the country sees me in this getup.

Bradley was holding a clipboard as I walked into the dance studio. "Okay, let's rock."

He gave me the once over, stopping, as expected, at my chest. "Wow. Are those yours?"

"Yeah. I've got the receipt around here somewhere." He finally looked up at my face. "Kidding!"

"Oh. I guess I need to get used to your sense of humor."

"Don't worry, it grows on you. So, what's the deal with this body analysis?"

He pulled a pen from behind his ear and moved closer. "I need to get your vitals, find out how flexible you are, how strong you are. So... height?"

"Five-eight."

"Weight?"

"You're asking a woman her weight? Seriously?"

"We're going to be doing a lot of lifts."

"Well, then you'll find out when you pick me up."

"Fine." He put the clipboard down, moved closer, and easily scooped me up. He bounced me up and down as he cradled my body. "One forty."

"Hey! I'm only one thirty-five! Well, maybe before lunch."

He put me down and picked up his clipboard. "That's one way to get a straight answer." He jotted down the numbers on the clipboard.

"You're not playing fair."

"This room is not a democracy. It's a dictatorship. If you want to win, you'll do as I say."

"Yes, Sir."

"Okay, I'm going to check your flexibility." He moved forward and put his hands on my waist. "I'm going to try to rest your ankle on my shoulder. I want you to wrap your arms around my neck for balance. Don't worry, I won't let you fall."

Our eyes locked as I snaked my hands around his neck. My

pulse quickened as he slid one hand lightly down my leg, reached under my knee and lifted it so that it was bent. Then his hand glided down to my ankle and slowly lifted it toward his shoulder, sending a bolt of electricity through my body—

Which was interrupted by a bolt of pain down the back of my leg. "Ow!"

He let go instantly. "Not much flexibility," he said. "You ever do Pilates?"

"No."

"You're going to start. Today. It will improve your flexibility greatly and it's very good for relieving stress. Now, do you do any weight training?"

"No, but I'm pretty strong. Why, am I gonna have to pick *you* up?"

"Dancers of both sexes need to be very strong, as you'll soon find out. Drop and give me twenty."

"You want me to do pushups?"

"Yep."

I shrugged. "Ohhhh-kayyyy." I hit the floor and managed to barely do one before collapsing. He extended a sinewy arm and helped me up.

"Flex your arms. Let me see your biceps."

I assumed the pose of a bodybuilder and his hands slid across my arms, then ended up on my shoulders.

Again with the bolt of electricity.

"No upper body strength. We'll begin with light weights and work up. Do you do any running?"

"I run to the grocery store, run to the dry cleaners."

"I think I'm getting a clear overall picture of your exercise regimen. How many reps can you do with a TV remote?"

"Anything else wrong with me, Doctor?"

He smiled. "You'll be fine. I'll whip you into shape in no time."

"Is there something wrong with my shape now?"

His look down my cleavage and successive smile answered the

question.

***

One Pilates workout, a session with weights, and several waltzes around the dance floor later, I was soaked in sweat as I headed into the dressing room. Whoever said *horses sweat, men perspire and women glow* never danced in a reality show. I was glowing like a stallion after the Kentucky Derby.

"There's nothing wrong with your shape."

I turned and saw Dexter leaning against the wall, smiling at me. "Ah, so you *were* behind the glass."

"There's a control room back there in the center of twelve dance studios, like the center of a clock. I'll give you a tour if you like. It affords me the opportunity to keep an eye on everything." His eyes ran the length of my body.

"And obviously hear everything."

"I can't listen to twelve rooms at once. But as you are this season's *It Girl* I surmised it would be beneficial to keep a close eye on your progress."

"Oh, you *surmised*."

"You *are* important to the show, Veronica."

"By the way, remember that little *no surprises* agreement we had?" I pulled the shoulder strap of my bodysuit and let it snap back. "What's up with the lacquered-on outfit?"

"Again, had you bothered to watch any of our previous seasons, you would know this kind of attire is the norm for those contestants who can pull it off, hence it would not qualify as a surprise. And you pull it off quite nicely, I must say."

I shook my head and rolled my eyes as sweat dripped from my chin. "Whatever. I gotta clean up. You wanna come in and watch?"

"While the prospect would not at all be unpleasant, I do have dinner plans."

"Yeah, I guess even reptiles need to eat."

122

"I'm escorting your friend Savannah this evening."

CHAPTER SEVENTEEN

This couldn't wait till Sunday brunch. I called an emergency meeting of the group for lunch at our favorite Italian restaurant after Dexter dropped the bombshell that he had a date with Savannah. Not that it was unexpected, but I'd forgotten about it after going through the dance version of the Bataan Death March yesterday.

Nonetheless, Layla and I were eagerly waiting Savannah's arrival as we ripped apart a hot loaf of crusty rosemary bread and dipped it in olive oil infused with spices. Seriously, I could simply skip the entree and eat this all day. Crumbs already littered the red-and-white checkered tablecloth, making it look like we'd been there for hours. The air was filled with the smells of garlic, provolone, and the sounds of Dean Martin, while the walls were covered with mostly black-and-white photos of celebrities (and famous members of the Mafia) who'd eaten here over the past seventy years.

Anyway, for the first time since I've known Savannah, I was worried about her. I mean, I know she can take care of herself, but Dexter is obviously a world class playboy and might even be able to fight off exponential magnolia.

"So how was day one?" asked Layla.

"Great sleeping in. But the dancing wore me out. I actually

nodded off at eight. Maybe when I get back to my regular shift I ought to keep doing it."

"I can work your tail off at the gym if you like. We've got a bunch of aerobics classes you'd like."

I spotted Savannah entering the restaurant. "Speaking of working one's tail off, here she comes."

It should be noted that Savannah likes to make an entrance, so I try to get to our meeting places early to watch said entrance and the reaction that accompanies it. Customers and staffers along her path parted like the Red Sea as she sauntered in, swaying those hips while ceiling fans blew wisps of her hair back like she was in a shampoo commercial. Jaws dropped, conversation stopped, eyes bugged out, knuckles were bitten. And the men had an even stronger reaction.

But this time she was not wearing the cat-that-ate-the-canary face she usually exhibits after taking a man for a bedroom excursion that sources say would rival the best roller coaster on Coney Island. The phrase "you must be this big to ride" takes on a whole new meaning with Savannah.

"Hey, y'all," she said, sitting down as a bald, middle-aged man from the next table jumped up and held her chair out. "Thank you, sweetie," she said, shooting him a smile. "Such a gentleman. Ah do appreciate the kindness of strangers." The guy melted and you could tell this made his day. Or decade.

"Okay, we want news," said Layla, not wasting any time.

"Well, I got a new political campaign yesterday," she said.

"Not *that* kind of news," I said. "Kiss and tell. Dish about Bish."

"Very clever," said Savannah, as she reached for a piece of bread. "I'll have to remember that. Y'all ordered yet?"

"Details. Now." I said.

"Ah'm just playin' with y'all. We had a nice time."

"Liar, liar, sheets on fire," said Layla.

"There were no combustible sheets," said Savannah, "as he did not end up in my bedroom."

"So you ended up in his?" I asked.

She grew an indignant look. "I am *not* a carnival ride, despite what you may think. We had a lovely dinner, went to a show, and he took me home."

I needed more than that. "And?"

"Then he asked if I was free sometime this weekend."

I sat up straight. "Let me get this straight... you go out with the supposedly most desirable bachelor on the planet who is obviously smitten with you... and nothing happened?"

Long pause. She looked at the ceiling as if searching for an answer, then back at us. "I think I've reached the point in my life where I need to stop kissing and telling."

Annndddd... cue the chorus of "give me a break."

"No, seriously," said Savannah, who was actually wearing a serious look. "The more I tell you guys, the more you think I'm some sort of wanton damsel of ill repute. And some things should remain private. We had a nice time and that's all you're getting."

"Dammit," said Layla. "Guess I'd better renew my subscription to Cinemax."

Savannah changed the subject but I kept studying her face. Alas, she revealed nothing.

The date either went badly, or...

She's already in love.

With *him*.

***

For the last thirty years or so, the major networks have been running their best shows on Thursday night while pretty much giving up on the weekends. Their theory is that the coveted demographic of people who are between eighteen and forty-nine are out and about on Friday and Saturday night. Of course, they've forgotten that *Dallas* was the number one show back in the eighties and was a staple of Friday night television. As was *Miami Vice*, in

126

the same time slot, no less, and was also a ratings grabber. *X-Files* was a Friday hit in the nineties as well.

The other factor is that movie companies like to advertise their films that are opening on Friday, so they'll pay a premium for Thursday night ads. The higher the ratings, the higher the premium. Hence, you put your best shows on Thursday night.

Or your highest rated, anyway, since *Dance Off* is a Thursday night staple.

On the Friday morning after the first "meet the contestants" show, the media and blogosphere were buzzing. Typical were the comments:

"Ms. Summer's outfit made one wonder if next week she'll sport a headband and break into Olivia Newton-John's *Let Get Physical***."**

"While Veronica Summer has always gotten an A for her journalism skills, her previously kept-under-wraps cleavage looks like a DD."

"This is one hot Summer."

As I walked into The Morning Show newsroom, the staff was electric.

"You did great last night!" said Gavin.

"It was just a rehearsal and a meet the contestants show."

"Yeah, but I can already tell you'll be terrific once the competition starts."

I needed to change the subject. "Okay, is our guest ready?"

"Senator Roper is already in the green room. He wants to talk about that budget bill he introduced. You need to be prepped on that?"

I shook my head. "My *brain* isn't wrapped in spandex. I'm going to get gussied up."

"Great," said Gavin.

Twenty minutes later with my hair and makeup done, I was going over my questions on the set when I saw the Senator headed toward me, escorted by Gavin.

A little background on United States Senator Tad Roper. A sixtyish, old money career politician, Roper is a classic Beltway hack who made his name the old fashioned way in Washington; nepotism. Father was a Senator, grandfather was a Congressman. The family money is legendary, rivaling that of the Vanderbilts and Rockefellers. And along with money and power comes that typical bulletproof attitude. The rules don't apply to him. Actions have no consequences. (Actually that's typical of most politicians.)

One particular batch of rules that doesn't apply pertains to marriage, as his is so transparent you could read a newspaper through it. His wife Bitsie has looked the other way so much you'd think she'd turn to salt. Alas, the woman keeps herself going with credit cards and enough Botox to ensure she could easily get a job in a wax museum. (The media refers to her as "freeze frame" since the expression never changes. If the people with the movie rights to *Batman* ever wanted to give The Joker a wife, she would be perfect.) Anyway, Senator Roper, a/k/a "Roper the Groper" is legendary for his dalliances, but made of Teflon with the voters, sort of like the Kennedys were. People actually seem to get a kick out of his roving eye, as he's often pictured with hot babes he refers to as "constituents." This despite ears that stick out like a taxicab with its doors open, a nose long enough to rob a pay phone and a face so wrinkled it looks like it was made of wool and accidentally washed on "hot." Bish the Dish he's not, but, as they say, power is the ultimate aphrodisiac.

Over the years we've had some spirited encounters regarding his politics, but I've always thought the guy respected me as a journalist. I've enjoyed going toe-to-toe with a man who's a master at spin. When your interview subject is rehearsed you can often talk the person into a corner by throwing a curve ball.

The tall Senator, with his shock of snow-white hair, extended his hand as he stepped onto the riser. "Veronica, nice to see you again." He said this while looking at my legs, making the "see you" part of his greeting literal.

I shook his hand, and then gestured toward the couch, hoping to get a break from the overpowering musky cologne in which he'd no doubt bathed. "You too, Senator. So, you wanna talk budget this morning."

"It's an important bill," he said, as a production assistant clipped a microphone onto his lapel.

"Stand by," said the floor director.

"So, Veronica, do you like the morning shift?"

"The hours are killer, but I'm having fun."

"So I've noticed. As has everyone on The Hill. You've got most of Congress watching."

"You guys get up that early?"

"Hell, no! That's what DVRs are for."

"Ten out! Tape is rolling!" yelled the floor director. I sat up straight, as did the Senator who turned on his toothy smile.

The floor director counted down the seconds and then the red light atop the camera came on. "Welcome back," I said, "and this morning we welcome New York Senator Tad Roper. Senator, thanks for dropping by."

"Thank you for inviting me, Veronica. I know you're pulling double duty."

"Not a problem. So, let's get right to it. Your budget bill is somewhat controversial, and some say it is the first step toward abolishing the Internal Revenue Service and establishing a national flat tax. How do you propose—"

"Before we get to that, I must say I've been very impressed with your versatility. I mean, I don't know a whole lot of journalists who can explain the Middle East in the morning and cut the rug as well as you obviously can."

Great. Just what I need. "Thank you, but we're not here to talk about my dancing. If we can get back to the budget—"

"Yes, of course. As you know, the budget is very tight." He paused and started to smile. "You might say as tight as the outfits on *Dance Off*."

"Very funny, Senator. Can a flat tax actually work—"

Pop!

We both jumped as a studio light blew and one section of the set dimmed.

"Everybody okay?" asked the floor director.

"We're fine," I said. "Senator, this will just take a few minutes to get the light replaced, then we'll start over again."

"Sure." He chuckled a bit. "You know, that last question was amusing, coming from you."

"What's amusing?"

"You. Asking about things that are flat." He stared at my chest. "I mean, considering..."

I pointed at my face. "My eyes are up here, Sir."

He looked up at me, shooting a greasy smile that would rival a car salesman's. "I simply had no idea you were so... you know." Both eyebrows went up. "Well equipped."

Okay, this was getting out of hand. "Senator, are you hitting on me? Number one, you're married. Number two, you're my father's age."

"Hey, I've got the body of a twenty-year-old."

"Well, you'd better give it back. You're wrinkling it."

He glared at me as an electrician headed into the studio with a ladder and a replacement bulb. "Now Veronica, there's no need to get ugly."

"Buddy, if you want ugly, look in the mirror."

"Young lady, I'm a United States Senator—"

"Then grow up and start acting like one." I got up, ripped off my microphone, and stormed off the set.

***

I arrived at the dance studio ten minutes early and found several of the professional dancers on the floor gathered around an iPad, laughing hysterically.

"Play it again," said one of the women.

"Sure," said Bradley, as he tapped the tablet.

"You guys are sure having a good time," I said.

"Thanks to you," said Bradley.

"What's so funny?"

He turned the tablet toward me so that I could see. "As if you don't know."

My eyes bugged out in horror as I watched the off-air altercation between myself and Senator Roper.

The tape was still rolling after the light blew out.

And someone had put the whole thing on YouTube.

CHAPTER EIGHTEEN

"We're investigating."

I didn't need Skype to see the smile on Gavin's face. I could hear it. His seriously lame answer to my question, "How in holy hell did an off-air tape from master control end up on the Internet?" only jacked up my blood pressure.

Then he added the cherry on top of this ice cream sundae from hell.

"It's already got half a million hits."

"That's a good thing? Get it taken down, Gavin."

"It's gone viral. You can't un-ring a bell on the Internet."

"You don't sound terribly concerned."

"Look, Veronica, I'm upset that it happened but there's nothing I can do. I assure you that when I find out who uploaded the thing appropriate action will be taken."

"What, you'll give the person a bonus?"

"Veronica—"

"You're so full of it, Gavin, I'm surprised your eyes aren't brown. You're happy about this. It's one more little surprise from your bag of tricks."

"I had nothing to do with this. And you're not the one who looks bad, it's the Senator."

"Wow, what a consolation. Having a member of Congress hit

on me while commenting about my boobs."

"Veronica—"

"Go to hell, Gavin."

I ended the call while wishing I was on a land line so I could slam the phone. Let's face it, hanging up while angry on a cell phone simply doesn't get the message across. You can only push the button so hard.

Meanwhile, Bradley was tapping his watch. I needed to hurry up and cram said boobs into an outfit that would give me a good idea as to how a sausage felt.

Ten minutes later I blew open the door to the dressing room and marched onto the dance floor. "So, we doing a waltz, disco, or what?"

"Right now we're doing Pilates, since you're stressed."

"I'm not stressed, I'm pissed off!"

He cocked his head toward the camera, reminding me Dexter was watching and listening. "Best to relax before we dance, don't you think?"

I took his reminder to shut up. "Right. Pilates."

***

"Okay, we're done." Bradley grabbed a spot on the floor and leaned against the back wall opposite the mirror.

"We're done? We haven't danced together at all."

Bradley nodded. "Right. You needed to learn some basic steps on your own." He patted the floor next to him as he jotted down notes on his clipboard. "Relax and let's go over the plan for the next session."

I shrugged. "Okay, you're the boss." I walked over to him, sat down, and leaned my sore back against the cool concrete.

"These are some of our goals for next week." He handed me the clipboard.

I took it and mopped some sweat from my face with a towel.

I was expecting to find a rundown of dance routines, but instead I found myself looking at a note.

The cameras can't see my writing from this spot.

I thought after what happened today you might enjoy a night out. Would you like to have dinner with me? No strings.

The anger which I'd maintained all day suddenly downshifted, my clenched jaw relaxed.

He turned to face me, giving me a look that told me I might be on the dessert menu. "So, Veronica, do you think this is... doable?"

Do I think *this* is doable or do I think *you're* doable? Yes to both. I held back a smile, not wanting the cameras to pick up any hint of sexual interest. "Sure, Bradley, I think it's a plan."

"Terrific." He got up and extended a hand. I took it and he helped me up. "Okay, then, see you Monday."

***

Years ago celebrities could dine in remote places and not worry about the paparazzi flash bulbs going off. But in the era of cell phone cameras, Big Brother is always watching. And the odds of a network anchor and someone from the most popular reality show in America flying under the radar were pretty slim. The last thing I needed was a shot of us out on a date or him sticking his tongue down my throat when he dropped me off at my apartment.

So we decided to take a pre-emptive strike. We chose a seriously out-of-the-way place to meet and formulated a strategy to go incognito.

I shoved my hair into a baseball cap, threw on jeans, an old sweatshirt, a pair of oversized sunglasses and headed for a mom-and-pop pizza joint I knew in Brooklyn. At four in the afternoon I assumed it wouldn't be busy and I was right as I couldn't see a single customer through the window. The smell of fresh bread and spices hit me in the face as I opened the door, which rang a little bell attached to the top. I grabbed a table in the back and faced the wall opposite the window. A very Italian-looking cute waiter came by for an order. I told him I was meeting someone and asked for a diet soda.

Five minutes later the little bell above the door rang, announcing Bradley's arrival. His disguise was simple but just as good. He'd slicked back his hair and wore a pair of round gold wire-rimmed glasses along with a Giants football jersey.

We looked like two average people in Brooklyn who wanted a Coke and a slice.

"I like the casual Friday look," he said, as he pulled out a chair and sat down.

"Trust me, it feels a lot better than the spandex sausage casing."

He put up his hands in surrender. "Hey, remember I had nothing to do with that." His smile vanished. "It's... *him*."

"Is this a good time for that *long story*?"

He shrugged. "Good a time as any. You don't know much about the show, right?"

"Never seen an episode."

"Well, what the public doesn't know is that the winning professional dancer gets a sizable bonus. You get a decent payout for second and third as well. So it's to our benefit to do our best."

"Well, that makes sense. I assume you've finished in the money?"

He shook his head. "Not once in five years."

"Seriously?"

"Because of Dexter. For some reason he always pairs me with a celebrity who has no shot at winning, or even doing well. Last season I got Darlene Zimmer."

"That woman was on this show?"

"Yeah. Hard to believe she was once a bikini model. When I got her she was well over two-fifty. And before her he stuck me with Blanche Herrick."

"She's still alive?"

"My point exactly. How the hell can I win with a partner who's eighty? If it weren't for you, I would have gotten stuck with rehab girl."

"Have you ever talked to Dexter about it?"

"Yeah. He always tells me, 'Do your job.' I don't know what it is about me, but he hates me for some reason. He only keeps me on the show because the public likes me."

"Well, that doesn't surprise me. Considering—" I caught myself before revealing my inside information about the show.

He leaned forward. "Considering what?"

"Uh... you know. His ego."

"No, that's not it. What aren't you telling me?"

I exhaled deeply. What the hell, Gavin and Dexter have been lying to me the whole time. Maybe it's time for a little payback. "Okay, but you never heard this from me."

"Fine. I'm a vault."

"You're probably going to get a bonus this time. Because the show is fixed."

***

A large double supreme, a pitcher of beer, and a very funny movie later, we were strolling out of the theater like a happy couple. Once we'd spent thirty minutes plotting after my big reveal, the evening turned into a great first date. Bradley's personality was as attractive as his body: a great sense of humor, a dislike of Dexter that matched mine, and a flair for double entendres that made me think he was very interested in coming up to my apartment for more than a cup of coffee.

As we hit the sidewalk he stuck out his elbow and I slipped my arm through it, resting my hand on his sinewy forearm. No one recognized me for the first time in months, which was a wonderful feeling.

"So, was that what the doctor ordered?" he asked.

I nodded. "Yeah, thank you. I really needed to blow off steam after today."

"Well, you're entitled. And what you told me cleared up a lot of unanswered questions for me."

We only had a four block walk to my apartment from the subway stop, and I didn't want to stop in front of the building where we could possibly be spotted by a photographer. I wanted to take him directly upstairs. "I have an unanswered question of my own."

"Shoot."

"I was wondering if you'd like—"

His cell phone rang, interrupting my question. "Hang on a second," he said, as he pulled the phone from his pocket. I stole a glance at the screen and saw the face of a spectacular blonde. "I gotta take this."

"Sure," I said, quickly reassuring myself that a guy who looks like this surely has some beautiful women in his life. She's probably one of the other dancers.

Yeah, let's go with that.

"Hey sweets, what's up?"

Sweets?

"Don't worry, I said I'll be there by ten." Short pause. "Of course I'll spend the night. You know I love your breakfasts."

Annndddd... cue the cold shower.

"Okay," he said, before twisting the knife. "Love you too." He hung up and turned to me. "Sorry. What were you gonna ask me?"

Oh, I dunno. I was thinking a guy who'd just taken me out for dinner and a movie might enjoy being ravaged in my apartment, but that was before I found out you were gonna ditch me for a roll in the hay with some other babe. "I... uh... lost my train of thought." We reached the front door of my building. "This is my place."

"Okay then. Well, see you Monday." He patted me on the shoulder and took a step into the street to hail a cab.

"Yeah. See ya."

CHAPTER NINETEEN

I thought I'd had an easy day of interviews when Gavin met me as I headed off the set. "I've got a story for you to do," he said, as he handed me an assignment sheet.

"Wow, I get to play reporter today. I could use some hard news."

"This... isn't exactly hard news, Veronica."

I looked at the assignment sheet and the first two words hit me like a dart. "You want me to cover a *Dance Off* event?"

"It will help promote the show."

I quickly scanned the sheet for information. "What's the event? All I see is a location." Which happened to be Layla's health club.

"You'll find out when you get there. Dexter wouldn't tell me when I found out there was something going on. Said it was no big deal and not worth covering. He obviously didn't want cameras. He doesn't know we're covering... whatever this is."

"So if he doesn't want cameras, why are we doing a story on this mystery event?"

He pointed at the ceiling. "Orders come from upstairs."

"Yeah, right."

"Really, Veronica, I'm being honest."

"Wow, that's a switch." Great to be able to talk to your boss like that when you know he would never fire you. "Let me get going before you burst into flames."

***

Layla met me at the door of the health club. "I had a feeling you'd be here."

I moved through the door, followed by the photographer. "So what the hell is going on?"

Her face beamed. "It's really cool. C'mon, follow me."

"Where are we going?"

"The olympic pool."

"The pool?"

"You'll see in a minute."

Layla was dressed in a one piece bathing suit with a towel wrapped around her waist. She led us down a long hallway toward the huge swimming pool I knew was at the end. I had no idea what to expect. Was this the *Dance Off* bathing suit competition? It wouldn't surprise me. Would Dexter and the others be synchronized swimming?

My question was answered as we moved through the glass door and the humid air mixed with the scent of chlorine filled my lungs, while a waltz played from a boom box.

A dozen or so wheelchairs were parked around the perimeter of the pool. Along with a few sets of crutches and metal leg braces.

Dexter Bishop and several of the professional dancers were in the pool, paired off with what appeared to be a bunch of teenagers, moving to the music.

Layla tossed the towel on a chair and beamed. "Isn't this cool? They're dancing in the water with a bunch of kids who can't walk."

My jaw slowly dropped as I took in the scene. Couples moved around the pool to the music. It was clear the professional dancers were supporting the kids, who had become almost weightless in the water. Their smiles were off the charts as they were temporarily free of their physical challenges. "When did you find out about this?"

"When I got here this morning. Apparently it had all been arranged last week by Dexter. They really didn't want any publicity, but I guess the secret's out."

"This kind of secret *needs* to be out. Have they done this here before?"

"Nope." She reached out with one finger and turned my head so I was facing her. "I think you really pegged this guy wrong. You should have seen him with the kids. Damn, Savannah hit the jackpot."

My photographer began moving around the pool, shooting video of the couples as they did the water dance. The waltz came to an end, and applause filled the air.

"Think you guys can do the tango?" asked Dexter. He got a unanimous approval from the kids, then turned to Layla. "Would you play cut number four, please?"

"Sure," she said, as she moved toward the boom box.

Dexter finally noticed me. "Oh, Veronica, I didn't see you there. I also didn't know you were coming." He turned and spotted the photographer. "There wasn't supposed to be any publicity about this."

"Gavin sent me. You can blame him. He supposedly got orders from upstairs."

"Ah."

A teenage boy who looked to be about seventeen looked up at me. "Hey, you're Veronica Summer!"

"That's me. What's your name?"

"Jim Larsen."

"You having a good time in there?"

"Yeah. Hey, you're my role model. I want to be a reporter when I get out of college. Your stories are the best."

I couldn't help but smile. "Thank you, Jim, you're very kind."

"I don't suppose you can get in the water and dance with me?"

"I didn't bring a suit."

The kid's face dropped.

And then it hit me. Yes, it hit me in my fifteen hundred dollar dress and six hundred dollar shoes with the red soles whose brand

I couldn't remember that the network had provided. It hit me that Gavin likes reporters to get involved with a story. Besides, we could use a consumer piece on the effects of chlorine on silk and leather.

"Then again, who needs a suit?" I said.

Layla grew a worried look and lowered her voice. "Geez, Veronica, you can't skinny dip in here."

"I said no such thing." And with that I tossed aside my purse, took off my watch, handed it to her, and jumped into the pool fully clothed.

"Oh. My. God." said Layla.

"You are full of surprises," said Dexter.

I moved toward the teenager, my green silk dress clinging to my body while thinking my drowned rat hairstyle would no doubt make the rounds of the Internet. The kid currently had his arms around the neck of one of the female dancers. "May I have this dance?" I asked her.

"Absolutely," she said, as she helped the young man slide over to me. He snaked his arms around my neck and I could feel myself supporting his weight, which wasn't much in the water. I couldn't tell how tall he was, but he was slender.

"I cannot believe you just did that," he said, his ice blue eyes beaming. "You rock, Miss Summer. You're even more incredible than I thought."

"I'm just an average girl," I said.

"Yeah, right." His eyes were misty, and not from the water. "I'll never forget what you just did."

The music started. "Hold on, kid." I wrapped one arm around his waist, entwined my fingers with his and stuck our arms out to one side. While I'd never taken a tango lesson I'd seen enough movies, and if Arnold Schwarzenegger could do it in *True Lies*, how hard could it be? "Here we go." We began to circle around the pool, following the couple in front of us, which happened to be Dexter and a young blonde girl.

"So, you wanna be a reporter, Jim?"

He nodded. "I do. I've got a ton of your stories on my DVR. I already write for the school newspaper and I've applied to several journalism schools. I want to be an ethical reporter, like you. You're one of the few people on TV who isn't biased, and I want to be the same way."

"Well, good for you. If you ever need help, or a recommendation, feel free to give me a call. I could set up a summer internship for you at the network."

"Seriously?"

"I don't kid around about journalism."

"That's very kind of you."

We continued around the pool to the music, making small talk along the way until the song ended.

"I can't thank you enough," he said. "Maybe someday we can tango on a real dance floor."

"Oh. So you're not—"

"Doctor says I'll walk again, but it might take several years. I can get around a little on those braces, but not much. I was in a car that got hit by a drunk driver. I'm still a lot better off than some of these guys, who are permanently paralyzed."

"Well, you seem to be a very determined young man and you have a great attitude. I'm sure you'll be on your feet in no time."

"You two make a nice couple," said Dexter, wading over to us, still supporting the young girl.

"He's a good partner. And he wants to be an *ethical* journalist."

Suddenly the girl leaned over and whispered something in Jim's ear. He shook his head. "No way, Heather, I can't."

"Go ahead," she said. "She'll probably do it."

"Do what?" I asked.

"Nothing," said Jim. "It's too much. You already ruined your outfit for me."

I shrugged. "It's not mine. It belongs to the network. They have deep pockets and they'll agree it was worth it."

The girl leaned toward Dexter and whispered in his ear. "I think it's a marvelous idea," he said, turning to smile at me.

She looked back at Jim. "Ask her. Any woman who would jump in the pool fully clothed for you would do it."

"Is anyone gonna let me in on this?" I asked.

"Fine," said Jim, who then looked up at the ceiling for a moment. Then he looked back at me. "We have a big dance coming up at our school. Would you be my date?"

In the space of three days I'd gone from what I thought was a great evening with a hunky dancer to getting dumped for another babe to being asked to the prom by a teenager. The kid looked into my soul and I knew I couldn't say no. "Sure, Jim. I'd be honored to escort you to the dance."

"See, I told you!" said the girl.

"Bravo!" said Dexter.

I turned to the girl. "So are *you* going to the dance?"

"I haven't been asked yet," she said, her eyes tinged with a bit of sadness.

I looked right at Dexter and flashed a smile. "You know, I'll bet if you asked Mister Bishop to take you, he'd do it." I playfully batted my eyelashes at him.

His lips quivered a bit.

Gotcha.

He turned toward the girl. "I would, uh, be happy to escort you."

She pulled her body close to his and gave him a huge hug.

Then Dexter looked over her shoulder at me, eyes slightly narrowed. "We can make it a double date."

***

My hair was still a bit damp as I headed toward Bradley with narrowed eyes and a clenched jaw. He looked up and smiled but I refused to return it.

"Hey. I heard you got a nine-point-five from the Russian judge at the pool."

"Yeah," I said, practically spitting the word at him.

He noticed. "You okay?"

"Let's just dance, Bradley."

He studied my face, then picked up his clipboard. "Let's, uh, go over our stuff for this week."

"Fine."

We walked over to our spot out of the network's prying eyes and grabbed a spot on the floor. Bradley clicked his pen and began to write, then turned the clipboard toward me. "So, here's what I'm thinking."

I looked at his scribble. *Are you mad at me for some reason?*

I took his pen and began to write. "How about this?" I asked, as I wrote *How was your second date Friday night?*

He grabbed the pen. *What are you talking about?*

I yanked the pen back, squeezing the life out of it and practically tearing the paper as I wrote *The girl you ditched me for when you said goodnight. The name Sweets ring a bell?*

He rolled his eyes, said, "You gotta be kidding me," then started to write. And write. And write.

He handed it back to me.

Sweets is my sister Janice. Her babysitter could only stay till ten on Friday and I told her I'd stay overnight and watch her daughter. The girl I ditched you for is five years old!!!!!

Beads of sweat blossomed on my forehead. "Oh my God," I whispered, just before burying my face in my hands.

He stood up and extended a hand. "C'mon, we've got a lot of work to do."

I bit my lower lip and looked up at him like a little girl who'd been caught with her hand in the cookie jar. I mouthed one word. "Sorry."

He wasn't buying, giving me back my own death stare. "Let's go, network. I'm gonna work you so hard today you'll want to quit."

***

"All is not lost," said Savannah, swinging her leg provocatively and showing off the red soles of her shoes as she sat perched atop a barstool. A guy across the room was following every move, his head going back and forth like a metronome.

"Oh, please," I said, taking a swig from my bottle of beer. The place was crowded and too many people had already recognized me so I lowered my voice a bit. "He obviously thinks I'm the most insecure girl in the world. He barely spoke to me during our session and worked my ass off like a drill sergeant."

"But your reaction was normal. Any other girl would have reacted the same way."

I shook my head. "Doesn't matter in this case. The guy can have any girl he wants. He wants perfect, he doesn't have to settle for someone who turns into a clingy teenager and gets jealous after pizza and a movie."

"Y'all don't know how to play the game up here."

"Up where?"

"Here. Yankeeland. You're so career oriented and so obsessed with being equals to men that you've forgotten how to be women."

"I haven't forgotten—"

She waved her hand. "Pffft. Y'all are amateurs. We're *more* than equals, sweetie. We play men like fiddles in the South and you don't even have a music store up here."

"What, am I supposed to act like Scarlett O'Hara?"

"You could learn a thing or two from that movie."

"Savannah, it was made in 1939."

"The basic rules of courtship never change."

"Oh, so you're trying to tell me I can apply civil war Georgia cotillions to New York City a hundred and fifty years later?"

"Let me ask you something. Complete this sentence. The way to a man's heart is..."

"Through his stomach."

"Wrong."

"Wrong?"

"Wrong. The way to a man's heart is through the bedroom."

"So, what, I'm supposed to seduce him and then I'll have control?"

"Sweetie, when you got 'em by the Johnson, their hearts and minds will follow. And at that point you can serve a man ramen noodles and he won't leave."

CHAPTER TWENTY

So, after four years of broadcasting school, countless award-winning stories, and a reputation that would be the envy of most reporters, my career has come to this moment of truth.

Would the journalism *It Girl* glide around the dance floor like Ginger Rogers, or simply fall off her four inch heels and land on her ass with her skirt over her head?

Inquiring minds wanna know.

Millions of inquiring minds.

But I've been in glass-half-full mode (said glass being filled with wine) and am counting my blessings. I could have ended up on some of the network's previous lame attempts at reality television before they hit ratings gold with *Dance Off*.

Imagine this intrepid reporter being cast in one of these:

-School of Ink: In an attempt to attract the body-pierced tattooed demographic, the show's hidden cameras served as flies on the wall of a not exactly accredited institution of lower learning. "Students" learned the basics of applying tattoos to women, some of whom posed challenges due to significant amounts of fat. The show infuriated the network's "standards and practices" department (one old biddy who had last been kissed during the Nixon administration) when one customer with back boobs decided she would share with the world the fact that she had not made it through high school by having "flunked out" tattooed above the bra strap. Unfortunately when she stood up some rolls of flab obliterated several letters, leaving only the "f" "u" "k" and "u", thus offering a permanent phonetic version of a four letter word insult.

-**Hands on:** A hunting and fishing show designed to level the playing field for the poor creatures being stalked by having the celebrity host of the week catch something with his bare hands. The series crashed in the third episode when D-list celebrity Hank Jolsen waded into an Oregon river and caught a salmon in his arms. Unfortunately he didn't notice the grizzly bear behind him, who enjoyed the network version of surf and turf.

-**Real Soccer Moms of Arkansas:** Chain smoking women tote their evil spawn around in the backs of pickup trucks and drop them at local activities, the best of which included a watermelon seed spitting contest in which contestants kept their remaining teeth clenched.

-**Family Pines:** A traveling show visits family reunions around the country that are comprised of people whose family tree doesn't branch out. (Savannah loved this show and begged me to get the network to send a camera down to her clan.) Terms like "Uncle Cousin" are commonplace, while the only virgins in the family are those who possess the necessary speed to outrun their brothers. (Mercifully cancelled after one season.)

There were no ratings problems with *Dance Off*, as it had plenty of viewers. Three of whom were my closest friends sitting in the front row as we approached our first live episode.

Layla and Savannah were joined by Scott as a few couples got in some last minute rehearsals on the stage that doubles as a dance floor.

But I was done rehearsing, as I had no desire to endure another minute of Bradley's glare while he pummeled what was left of my ass into submission. So I decided to deal with my stress by spending the last few minutes before the contest with those who love me.

"You're up past your bedtime," I said to Scott, who was getting comfortable in his seat.

"Hey, I wouldn't miss this for the world."

"Maybe you'll be a contestant next year."

He shook his head. "Nah. I don't have the legs for it." He glanced down at my outfit. "Speaking of which, I thought you'd be dressed like an NFL cheerleader."

"It's waltz night," I said. "Somehow hot pants, go-go boots and a halter top don't go with the music. But I'm sure they'll make an appearance in a future wardrobe malfunction."

"Y'all look elegant," said Savannah, taking in my old school pale blue chiffon dress that ended at my ankles.

I lifted one leg a bit and pointed at my shoes. "As long as I don't fall off these things. And after this week I don't have any padding left to fall on."

"You'll be fine," said Layla. "And you know damn well you won't be voted off even if you fall, not with rehab girl in the contest."

She was right. Rehab girl had that look which told you she was still in direct contact with the mother ship.

"Ten minutes! Contestants to the green room!" yelled the floor director.

"I gotta go," I said.

Scott took my hand. "I'd say break a leg, but, you know."

"Thanks, partner."

I turned and headed toward the green room and saw Dexter Bishop heading directly for me, dressed in a tuxedo. I had to admit, he looked dashing. But I would be damned if I'd admit it to him. He smiled as he grew closer. "Best of luck this evening," he said.

I lowered my voice to a whisper. "I thought I didn't need it."

He cringed a bit. "You look lovely in that dress. I presume it meets with your approval. It's from the Judi Dench fall collection."

"It's beautiful, Dexter. I appreciate it." Considering his kind efforts in the swimming pool and the dress, I was beginning to think there was some semblance of a human being inside Bish the Dish. I needed to start cutting the guy some slack.

"Well, best be on your way. The show's about to start."

He headed for the judge's stand and took the middle seat as the two other judges, both thirtysomething female choreographers from Broadway, grabbed the chairs on either side. I headed back toward the green room.

As I entered the room I saw Bradley, decked out in a white tie and tails.

The sight knocked the breath from me. If Dexter looked dashing, Bradley was off the charts.

I paused a moment, flashed my biggest smile, and headed toward him. "Don't you look like the top of a wedding cake," I said.

He turned and looked at me, the glare I'd endured for the past few days nowhere in sight. "You're not exactly chopped liver," he said, like nothing had ever happened. "You're absolutely beautiful in that dress."

I exhaled. "Thank you." I leaned forward and whispered in his ear. "So, am I forgiven?"

I leaned back and looked into his eyes, expecting and hoping for a soulful gaze. Instead, his eyes went quickly to the right. "Cameras," he said, in a barely audible voice.

I took a quick glance and saw that the green room was under surveillance, just like the rehearsal studio.

And I had no idea if Bradley was giving me a second chance or simply playing nice for the audience.

***

Luckily we were going last, so I got to watch all the other couples to size up the competition. A couple of the morning line favorites tripped, and one leggy Olympic ice skater surprisingly did a header, dragged her partner down on the way, and ended up sprawled on the dance floor with his face smack in the middle of her boobs. I would have paid good money to have the network Olympic announcer do the play-by-play of that move. "A double loop... a triple lutz... and a death spiral into a full cleavage."

We were in the on-deck circle, watching on the green room monitor while rehab girl looked positively bug-eyed like she was on horse tranquilizers as her partner led her around the floor. She made it through the routine without tripping even though she moved like Gumby, then quickly walked toward the judges with her partner.

"Not bad," said Corinne Walker, the first judge. "Though I did see you looking at your feet a few times. You were a bit robotic, but that should go away with practice. Just relax next time. I'm giving you a six."

Rehab girl politely applauded, though it was clear she was disappointed.

"I saw some real potential," said Wendy Armbruster, the second judge. "I think as you get to know your partner's moves you'll improve. I give them a seven."

More polite applause and a slight smile.

"Well," said Dexter, "I see you've come a long way since you were staggering away from your car after your last drunk driving incident."

Ouch. Rehab girl's face dropped.

"That was pretty harsh," I said, under my breath.

"That's what he's known for," whispered Bradley. "Viewers love the nasty comments. If only they knew."

Rehab girl's lips began to quiver as Dexter ripped her a new one, said she looked like an android on Ambien and gave her a five. Still, a quick bit of math told me she was ahead of the ice skater, who had a total score of seventeen. Shouldn't be too hard to beat. Especially since the show is fixed.

A production assistant stuck his head in the green room and said, "You're up after the commercial." A quick glance at the monitor told me we had two minutes.

"You ready?" asked Bradley.

"Sure."

"Nervous?"

"Hey, I anchor every day. This is nothing."

I forced a smile after the lie and my heart zoomed into overdrive.

***

"Now let's welcome our final couple," said the off-camera announcer, "Veronica and Bradley!"

The crowd applauded as we briskly moved hand-in-hand onto the stage. We both smiled and nodded at the audience, then turned and faced each other. He took my right hand and raised it while putting his other hand on my waist. The applause quickly stopped and everything went silent for a moment as we waited for the music to start.

We had chosen a golden oldie, Patti Page's *Tennessee Waltz*. Two reasons: one, it was nice and slow, thereby cutting down the risk of my falling on my ass; and two, ratings for the show were highest in the deep South, and the viewers there would no doubt appreciate the nod. Of course I had no intention of ending up with one of the two lowest scores and leaving my fate in the hands of the voting public.

Bradley locked eyes with me.

There was no emotion, nothing. Like he was looking at an android.

He hasn't forgiven me! He still thinks—

And then the song began.

I stumbled on my very first step, turning my ankle slightly.

Luckily I didn't copy the ice skater's move as Bradley's strong hand steadied me and we got back on track. But I was a rookie

152

anchor on the dance floor, blowing the first story and becoming a snowball rolling downhill. Suddenly the dance wasn't a case of muscle memory, but of my rehearsing every step in my head.

I felt like a girl at my first high school dance.

I knew it had to look awful, stiff, without any semblance of grace.

"Relax," he said softly, barely moving his lips so the cameras wouldn't catch it.

I tried my best to exhale but I kept looking at my feet instead of my partner. Now I couldn't wait for the song to end.

Thankfully we made it through without my looking like rehab girl staggering out of a disco. But I knew the damage had been done.

"Smile," said Bradley, under his breath again.

I forced a grin as he led me over to the judges to what could only be described as polite applause.

Dexter, knowing he was off camera, rolled his eyes at me.

"Well, not a great start," said the first judge, Corinne. "But you recovered and made it through without any missteps. I think once you two work together a little more you'll be a fine couple. I'm giving you a six."

And I was expecting a negative two.

I mouthed a thank you and smiled.

"The first steps are always the hardest," said Wendy, the second judge. "But you hit your marks the rest of the way, and I agree you two have potential. A six as well."

I needed a nineteen to avoid the voting process. I had twelve. Do the math.

Dexter needed to give me a seven. One quick look at him told me he wasn't happy about it.

"Well, I guess we'll need to attach a teleprompter to Bradley so you'll know what to do," he said. The crowd chuckled and I forced a smile. "Or perhaps we can get some of those old fashioned footprints people used to put on the floor to teach their children to dance." More laughter.

I looked at Bradley and could tell his jaw was clenched.

"Honestly, I don't think we've ever had a contestant stumble on the very first step, and to one of the slowest songs we've ever played on this show. And that first step could spell your last. I'm giving you two a four."

So much for my "semblance of a human being" concept.

Several boos cascaded down from the crowd.

"So, it's time to vote!" said the announcer. "Who needs to dance off into the sunset?"

CHAPTER TWENTY-ONE

Dexter wimped out last night, bolting out the studio back door right after the show. I'd ripped off my dress, changed into street clothes and stormed off in search of him, but he was long gone.

Coward. And just when I thought the guy had a soul.

Meanwhile I could take heart in that a great charity was making a dollar every time someone texted a vote to keep me on the island.

And I wasn't sure if I was more pissed off about getting a four or the possibility of having to go back to the vampire shift sooner than expected. I knew the show was rigged, but between Dexter and Gavin I'd sooner trust Roper the Groper.

I blew through the studio door Friday morning, dreading the smirks from the staff after my performance last night. As soon as I entered the newsroom, people scattered. Only Gavin remained.

What the hell was this? "What's going on?" I asked. "Did I come down with leprosy or something?"

"They, uh, probably figured you wouldn't want be in the mood to talk after last night."

"Well, they're right. Anyway, I guess I've gotta talk to whatever guests you've lined up."

Suddenly he grew pale. "Yeah. Uh... your, uh, first guest is already in the studio." He pulled out his cell phone, looked at it, and said, "I gotta take this." He quickly turned and headed to his office.

Funny, I didn't hear his phone's ring tone. He obviously doesn't want to talk to me. Another coward. Whatever. I shrugged and headed to hair and makeup, then twenty minutes later I walked through the studio door.

"Well, look what the cat dragged in."

Oh, you gotta be kidding. I stopped dead in my tracks as Dexter was being miked up by a production assistant. "*You're* a guest this morning?"

"I'm always on after the first episode. Don't you watch your own show?"

"I wasn't on it last year." I slowly walked toward the set, not taking my eyes off him. "So, what exactly do you *always do* during these visits?"

"I recap last night's show, critique the contestants. Talk about who might be voted off."

Ouch. That stung.

I sat down next to him, grabbed my microphone and clipped it on the lapel of my royal blue blazer. "I'm sure you've got the appropriate text number on speed dial."

He smiled and said nothing.

The director's voice came over the loudspeaker. "Veronica, you ready?"

"Let's rock," I said, wanting to get this over as soon as possible.

The floor director adjusted his headset. "Tape is rolling. Stand by."

"So where do you want to start?" I asked.

"You're the one doing the interview. Start wherever you like."

I nodded. Fine.

"Ten out!" yelled the floor director, who then counted me down.

I sat up straight and looked into the camera. The red light came on. "And welcome back. Before we get to our guest Dexter Bishop this morning, I wanted to mention I'm very excited to be throwing out the first pitch at the Mets game tomorrow afternoon. So, the team's front office needs to have a jersey for me with a number *four* on it." I turned to Dexter as I saw the light on the two-shot camera come on and feigned a laugh. "So, I was *that bad* last night, huh?"

Dexter grew a worried look. "Miss Summer, I'm sorry if I offended you—"

I playfully waved my hand. "Pffft. C'mon, it's a game show! We're all there to have fun." I turned to my camera to talk to the audience. "Next week, ladies and gentlemen, in an effort to score higher than a four, my partner and I are going to do a mash up of the Bunny Hop and the Alley Cat. It'll be deja vu of every bad wedding you've ever attended!"

His face tightened a bit. "Perhaps I was a bit harsh with the score."

"Listen, I wanted to thank you for giving me such a lousy grade because I ended up in the final two... and that means more money for my charity every time people vote." I turned to the camera. "Hey, more money for the veterans!"

"You're certainly taking this well."

"No big deal, Dex. So, let's recap some of the stuff from last night. I mean, besides my stepping in a hole right out of the gate. And honestly, I deserved the four. I mean, I was moving around like a robot from a fifties sci-fi movie I was so stiff. Anyway, what's your take on some of the other contestants? I'm particularly inter-ested in our Olympic skater."

"Yes... her fall was rather... unfortunate."

"Not for her partner! I'll bet there are a bunch of guys out there who would love to learn *that* dance step!"

Dexter's eyes grew wide. He obviously had no idea how to deal with me, as he was expecting me to be pissed off and I was treating his show for what it was... a bullshit reality program.

For the next four minutes he went through the roster of dancers until I finally ended the interview.

"And... we're clear!" said the floor director.

Dexter exhaled as he unclipped his microphone. "May I speak

with you a moment?"

"Sure, what's up?"

"Away from the cameras and microphones. I don't want our conversation to become the flip side of that one you had with the Senator."

"Sure. Green room." I unclipped my mike and led him out of the studio, across the hall, and into the empty green room. "So, what's on your mind, *Dex*?"

"Are you deliberately trying to sabotage your tenure on my show?"

"Of course not. Whatever gave you that idea?"

"You're treating it as if you don't care and aren't taking it seriously."

"Why should anyone take it seriously? It's a reality program."

"And you're an employee of this network."

I shook my head. "I'm an employee of the *news* division. I have nothing to do with *entertainment*. If that's what you call it these days. Besides, since the show's rigged I know I can say just about anything and not get voted off."

He folded his arms. "That part is not necessarily written in stone."

"Bull. You need me. I checked the overnights and the ratings were through the roof, particularly in the last fifteen minutes, which is when I appeared. I'm your meal ticket this season. There's a new sheriff in town, Dexter Bishop. And you're lookin' at her. You wanted an *It Girl*, you got one."

He exhaled, looked to the side, and then back at me. "I think you'd understand things better if we could go somewhere private. Perhaps you would enjoy a full English since you're always head down."

Is he implying what I think he's implying? "Ex*cuse* me?"

"Maybe you'd fancy a couple of hot bangers."

Now I *know* what he's implying. "Oh, is that your solution for my attitude? You and me in a hotel room, giving me whatever the hell sexual connotations are meant by a *full English*? Is that your nickname for your Johnson?"

His face tightened. "What on earth are you talking about?"

"Look, you may be incredibly good looking with that perfect face and body and think you're God's gift to women, but not every woman's attitude problem, or in this case, *perceived* attitude problem can be solved with sex."

"Sex? Who said anything about sex?"

"You talked about banging me. And that my head is always down, so obviously you think it should be in your lap."

His face relaxed and he began to chuckle.

"What the hell's so funny?"

"Veronica, a *full English* is a breakfast with all the trimmings, including breakfast sausages, which is what we call *bangers*. And *head down* means you're working hard. You're at your desk with your head down, focused on your work."

Yikes.

My face flushed. "Oh," I said quietly, feeling exactly as I had when Bradley explained his "other date."

He flashed a sinister grin. "So, you think I have a perfect face and body?"

So much for my having the upper hand.

At this point I wished I had one of those cartoon holes like the Road Runner so I could escape. My face was probably approaching the color of my hair.

Dexter's smile grew. "How on earth did you interpret that as my invitation to shag?"

"To what?"

"Shag. Have sex."

"Shag is a fifties dance. To bang someone is to—"

"I get it, and perhaps I need to find you a primer on British slang. Look, I just thought it might be nice if we sat down to a hot breakfast and aired things out a bit. I think perhaps it would help if I explained what I do on the show and why I do it. How about tomorrow?"

I had no position to continue this argument, so the white flag went up. "Sure, Dexter."

"Fine. By the way, who the bloody hell is Johnson?"

***

Since we'd been saddled with a four from Dexter I asked Bradley if we could schedule a Friday practice session instead of taking the day off. (I also needed to know if he'd forgiven me, since I was so mad I forgot last night.) Anyway, he agreed to the session, as we might as well get the jump on the next dance in case I'm not voted off the show.

Besides, the next dance was the Lambada, a/k/a "the forbidden dance" which is so sexually charged I figured it might get Bradley thinking about me in a different way... just in time for the weekend. I was going to invite him over and cook dinner for him and get a "handle" on things. And hopefully make breakfast as well. Which would get me out of Dexter's "full English" with the world's best rain check excuse. "Sorry, I've already eaten. And I used Bradley's washboard abs as a plate."

Anyway, after two hours of rubbing against my sweaty bod Bradley seemed to be looking at me differently. The robotic glance from the previous night was gone, replaced by a smoldering lock on my eyes as we went through the steps. Surprisingly, I was better at this than the waltz. (I know what you're thinking. Don't say it. I'm not that kind of girl. I just desperately want to be that kind of girl right now.)

So without asking I assumed all had been either forgiven, forgotten or both, as Bradley was at this point thinking with the wrong head.

"I'm exhausted," I said, plopping down on our special out-of-camera-shot spot.

"Good work today," he said, sitting down next to me with his clipboard.

I quickly grabbed it from him. "Oh, my schedule's a little different next week. Let me write it down for you." I wrote, *Please let me cook you a great dinner tonight.*

He looked at the clipboard as I handed it back to him. "Sure. That will be fine," he said, shooting me a slight smile. "See you Monday."

***

An hour later after a shower, change of clothes and a quick cab ride, we were doing the lambada in my elevator as it headed much too slowly up to my floor. Fortunately I knew my ancient building did not have cameras in the elevators, so this would not end up on the Internet. Bradley had me pinned against one side of the car, dress slowly creeping up my thighs, and it was clear that dinner might be delayed slightly. I took one look at the little numbers on top of the elevator and saw that my floor was next. "Uh, we're here," I said.

He broke the embrace and straightened his shirt, then took my hand as I pushed down my dress. "Okay."

"Don't you wanna know what's for dinner?" I asked, as the bell rang, announcing our arrival at my floor.

"Right now I'm just interested in the appetizer."

The door opened and I quickly led him out of the elevator and down the hall to my apartment. I found the key in my purse, jammed it into the lock, opened the door and yanked him inside. I then took control, backing him against the door and shutting it in the process. I reached over his shoulder and threw the deadbolt while he bent down, wrapped his arms around my hips, and easily hoisted me into the air. I wrapped my legs around his waist and embraced my inner appetizer as he tried to devour me.

He finally came up for air. "Where's the bedroom?"

"Through the living room, down the hall, first door on the

right."

He started carrying me in that direction as I rested my head on his broad shoulder and breathed in his cologne. He headed down the hallway and turned into my bedroom, which was slightly illuminated by the setting sunlight filtering through the cracked blinds. He turned his back to the bed and sat down on the edge, leaving me straddled on his lap. He took my head in his hands, running his fingers through my hair and massaging my head as his mouth moved down to my neck.

That rain check for Dexter was looking good.

To say I was about to explode after months of being celibate Sister Veronica is putting it mildly.

Suddenly Bradley looked up at me as a single tear ran from one eye. *Oh my God, he's that sensitive about sex? I have hit bedroom powerball!* I smiled as I gently brushed away the tear. "Oooh, babe, don't cry. Let Veronica kiss it and make it better."

He started to blink very fast, then his hands quickly went to his face and he rubbed his eyes. He began sniffling as if catching a cold. "You have a cat."

Pandora must be right behind me. "Yeah. She usually sleeps with me but tonight that spot is taken." I patted the bed.

His eyes were quickly turning red but I ignored them and started to unbutton his shirt. "Oh, God."

"My, aren't we eager. But let me take you slowly. You'll enjoy it more."

"No, not that. The cat."

I looked around and didn't see her. "What about her?"

He put his finger under his nose. "I'm severely allergic. I gotta get home and get an allergy shot." He slid me off his lap onto the side of the bed and stood up. "Sorry, Veronica, I need my vaccine or I'll end up in the hospital."

He headed for the door and I followed. "So, let's go to your place. I can cook there—"

He turned and looked at me with a quickly reddening face.

His eyes already puffy. "It'll take all night for me to get back to normal. I'm really sorry but I gotta go."

Bradley hurried out the door.

Pandora started rubbing against my leg and let out a soft purr. "Great. You're the only action I'm getting tonight."

Full English and a couple of hot bangers, here I come.

As for Johnson, well... as Dexter would say, "Bloody hell."

***

Dexter was looking at his watch as I arrived ten minutes late to the restaurant on Saturday morning. Of course, I did it on purpose, just to get his knickers in a twist. (I also looked up some British slang last night since Bradley did the equivalent of hacking up a furball on our date.)

He stood up as I arrived at the table, a corner one next to the kitchen's swinging door. "Let me guess, you didn't have ten bucks to bribe the hostess for one near the window?"

"I like to eat in peace," he said, moving around the table and pulling out the chair for me.

"Thank you." Wow, talk about old school.

The restaurant was a throwback fifties joint, filled with loud conversation, the smell of bacon and the staff dressed like they were extras in *American Graffiti*. Old fashioned formica tables and wrought iron chairs added to the malt shop feel. "You become very adept at maintaining a low profile when you're internationally famous."

"I would think you'd love the attention."

He shook his head. "What's the old saying? People dream of being recognized and when it happens they go around the rest of their lives with sunglasses."

"Very true," I said, picking up the menu.

"Oh, you don't need that. Full English, remember? You're game, aren't you?"

I snapped the menu shut. "Of course. I'll try anything once."

"Good. This is one of the few places in New York that will serve one. I got them to put it on the menu when I moved here."

"Wow. You've got some clout."

The sound of glasses and dishes clanking filled the air as the kitchen door swung open and a middle-aged blonde waitress arrived at our table, hair put up with a pencil sticking through the bun. Her eyes were red and she was sniffling. Great, just what I need, to catch a cold.

"Take your order?" she asked, voice cracking a bit.

"Are you ill, my dear?" asked Dexter.

"Allergies," she said.

"Tell me about it," I said.

Dexter ordered two full English breakfasts and she headed for the kitchen. I folded my hands and rested them on the table. "So. Tell me about why you do what you do."

"You mean everything, or something specific?"

"Let's start with that *four* you gave me."

"Ah, so you *do* take the show seriously!"

I narrowed my eyes a bit. "Let's just say I don't like to lose."

"Very well. As you probably know, I'm the judge people love to hate."

I playfully slapped my face. "Who would have guessed!"

"Funny. So I use reverse psychology to manipulate the voting. Viewers naturally like to disagree with me, prove me wrong. So if I want someone to remain on the show, I give them a low score, and, as you would say, *rip them a new one* on national television. It never fails, Veronica. Trust me, that four I gave you was your ticket to staying on the show, and I don't even have to... enhance... the results."

"Seriously? So people are voting against whatever you say?"

He nodded. "It has worked numerous times."

"So what was my real score?"

"After your little opening pratfall, you did pretty well. I'd have given you a seven. Six at the lowest. But then you might have been voted off the show down the road. You needed the sympathy vote right out of the gate. And I need to piss off the viewers, give them a reason to tune back in and prove themselves superior."

Sonofabitch. It actually made sense. "So, let me get this straight. You're basically cultivating a reputation as a jerk and casting me as a victim?"

"I'm simply playing a part, Veronica."

"A part. Right."

"You'd understand that if you got to know me. And, let's be honest, news people are basically playing a part, aren't they?"

"Whoa, now, don't go comparing what you do on a reality show to journalism."

"Oh, come on. Journalism? I've seen those promos about the best news team is the one you can trust and you people don't even trust one another in your own newsroom. I dare say Gavin would sell out his own mother for ratings. And all those phony stories about sitting down and consoling victims of tragedy... it's really a bunch of vultures picking over the bones."

My blood pressure spiked. "*I* don't do those kinds of stories."

"I didn't imply that you did. But many of your cohorts specialize in adding drama to the news. What's that saying you have... if it bleeds it leads? And that old song about dirty laundry?"

"Don't lump me in with all that."

"Fine. Don't lump me in with all reality show stars."

"Fine."

Dexter looked toward the kitchen. "Wish our bloody food would get here."

Ten silent minutes, fifty looks at my watch and eighty sips of my coffee later it did. At least I'd have something to occupy my hands and keep my mouth full.

The full English actually looked good. Eggs, mushrooms, tomatoes, those double entendre sausages known as bangers, baked beans (obviously eaten for breakfast by Brits who work outdoors), fried bread and coffee. I tore into it the moment it arrived. Dexter looked up at me for a moment, then down to his own plate.

A few more quiet minutes later he spoke. "Your fry up good?"

"My what?"

"*Fry up*. Most everything on your plate is fried, so we call it a fry up."

"Actually, it's very tasty. I didn't think you people were known for your cooking."

"Perhaps you'd like some jam for your toast... might sweeten up your attitude a bit."

Dexter picked up the dish of blueberry jam and handed it across the table. On the way his hand brushed against my glass of tomato juice, knocking it over. It landed on a fork, which turned into a catapult, flipping up and stabbing his hand. He flinched and sent the jam in a perfect arc onto my white cotton dress. It was accompanied a nanosecond later by a flood of tomato juice.

I jumped up from my chair, my outfit now turned into a Jackson Pollock painting. "Look what you did!"

"Sorry, it was an accident." He looked at his hand, which now featured a drop of blood.

"Yeah, I'll bet." I grabbed my cloth napkin and tried to minimize the damage, but all the club soda in the world wasn't gonna fix this.

Dexter was biting his lip, obviously trying to keep from laughing.

"You think this is funny?"

"Well, the color scheme is appropriate for a Yank. Red, white and blue."

I noted he was wearing cream colored linen slacks. I sat down, pulling my chair forward so hard it slammed against the table and knocked over both his grape juice and coffee into his lap. He jumped up and started to say something but I cut him off. "Sorry. It was an accident."

Forty minutes later the waitress returned. "Anything else? More coffee?"

I had no desire to stay here any longer and have my profession run through the gutter while looking like Betsy Ross' nightmare. "I'm good."

"I'll take a coffee to go," said Dexter. "Light and sweet, like my companion."

"Sure," said the waitress, who wiped away a tear, then placed the check in front of Dexter.

"Don't wanna drink it here?" I asked.

"I have another appointment. At a dry cleaner."

"We could make it a double date."

Dexter pulled a leather billfold out of his inside jacket pocket, took out a hundred, and placed it on top of the check just as a manager arrived.

"Good morning. Just checking to make sure the food was okay?"

"The part we aren't wearing was excellent," I said. The manager laughed.

"Yes, quite," said Dexter. "Though you might give your poor waitress the day off. She seems to be suffering from allergies a great deal."

"She's a trooper," said the manager. "And it's not allergies, she's dealing with some upsetting financial news. Her ex cleaned out her bank account and stole her daughter's college tuition. If you feel she gave you good service, a nice tip would make her day."

"Done," said Dexter, patting the hundred. "Tell her to keep the change."

Just when I start to hate him again, he does something like that.

"That's very kind of you sir." He took a closer look at our clothes. "You know... I do have some wait staff uniforms in the back that you could borrow so you don't have to go out in public like that."

Dexter smiled and started to shake his head. "That would—"

"Be very nice of you," I said, shooting a big grin at Dexter. "C'mon, Dex, it'll be fun."

CHAPTER TWENTY-TWO

Yeah, it was fun all right. Until the paparazzi jumped out from behind a car and snapped a photo of us which ended up in the Sunday morning paper. Along with a story about why we were dressed that way.

On, you know, the front page.

YOU WANT FRIES WITH THAT?

By Jansen Reid

If you're a regular viewer of *Dance Off* you know the contestants are always dressed in outfits appropriate to the music, while the judges are decked out in formal attire.

That's why New Yorkers had their jaws drop yesterday when British judge Dexter Bishop and contestant/network info-babe Veronica Summer emerged from a restaurant dressed as a waiter and waitress.

Publicity stunt? Nope.

Are they a couple? Not according to another restaurant patron who dined at a nearby table. "They look as though they can't stand each other," said Billy Hember, who was within earshot of the two. "He spilled some food and juice on her, she got ticked off and rammed her chair against the table, spilling stuff on him. I thought it was going to escalate into a food fight. Their clothes were ruined so the managers gave them a couple of wait staff uniforms so they could get home without looking ridiculous."

Well, so much for that last part.

Bishop, widely considered one of the planet's most attractive men, was nattily attired in a form-fitting blue polyester shirt and black slacks, while Summer was rocking a matching blue jumper that made her look like a malt shop waitress from the doo-wop era.

A wave of snickers followed me as I headed into our usual Sunday brunch restaurant. I politely smiled as I saw Layla already at our table.

"Ah, finally," said Layla. "Can you take our order now?"

"Very funny," I said, as I sat down.

"Guess your poodle skirt is at the dry cleaners."

"Go ahead, get it all out of your system," I said.

"Coulda been worse. You could have been eating at Hooters."

"The outfit would have been less revealing than my blue spandex," I said.

"So how much of the story is true?" asked Layla, holding up the newspaper.

"Just about all of it. We can't stand each other—"

"I wouldn't say that," said Savannah, sneaking up behind me and patting me on the shoulder. She waited a beat and, as if on cue, a cute guy in his twenties magically appeared to pull out her chair.

She started to thank him but I beat her to it, turning on my attempt at the magnolia. "She always appreciates the *kahdness* of strangers."

She sat down and smiled at the guy, who backed up while staring at her. The back of his knees hit a chair and he went head over heels.

Savannah stood up. "Oh, my. Are y'all okay?"

"Sure," said the guy, brushing himself off as he got up, face red.

"Y'all be careful," she said, as she sat back down and shook her head. "I wish I didn't have that effect on men."

"Oh, give me a break," I said. "So what's this garbage about me and Dexter liking each other?"

"You may not like him, but he likes you."

"Really?" said Layla. "Do tell."

Savannah leaned forward a bit. "Well, last night he talked about her."

"Yeah," I said, "I'm sure he was filled with compliments after I covered him with food. And why the hell would he be talking about me when he's out on a date with you?"

"Really, I thought he was all puppy-dog eyed over you," said Layla. "That's not very nice that he takes you out and talks about another woman."

"Look," said Savannah, "it wasn't like that."

"What, he forgot your name and shouted *Veronica* during sex?" asked Layla.

Savannah rolled her eyes. "We do *talk* during dinner, you know. Do y'all think we just order room service and act like a bunch of rabbits? And, by the way, we simply enjoy spending time together. That doesn't necessarily imply we spend that time in the bedroom."

"So, you do it in the kitchen," I said, piling on.

"Can we just order?" she said.

"Not until you tell me what he said about me."

"And we are officially back in high school," said Layla.

"He said he admires you," said Savannah. "That you're so passionate about your career. He said he likes a woman who can obviously take care of herself."

"That's it?" asked Layla.

"Pretty much," said Savannah. "Except for..."

She left the words hanging in the air. "Except for... what?" I asked.

What she said next boggled my mind.

***

Gavin was wearing a huge smile when I arrived in the newsroom on Monday morning. Which, I figured, must mean he's either up to something or about to drop a bomb on me.

"You look awfully cheerful for a Monday," I said.

He held up a single sheet of paper in one hand while clutching an assignment sheet in the other. "I've got good news."

"Oh, shit. What now?"

"No, seriously Veronica, this is great. The Emmy nominations are out."

"And..."

"You were nominated!"

"For what, *Best Performance by an Anchor in Spandex?*"

He shook his head as he rolled his eyes. "Best Morning Anchor, of course. Scott was also nominated."

"Then please withdraw my name. I have no desire to compete against Scott."

"Sorry, too late. You shoulda told me that before I submitted our entries."

"You shouldn't have submitted both our names. You know we're close friends."

"You're allowed two entries. I have two anchors, so I entered both of you." He tossed the paper on a nearby desk, then handed me the assignment sheet. "Well, since that didn't cheer you up maybe your story this morning will."

***

I didn't recognize the address on the assignment sheet but it clicked when we pulled up in our news car.

It was the very same restaurant at which I'd debuted the Julia Child spring collection on Saturday.

The manager who had so thoughtfully provided our outfits

opened the door to greet me as I got out of the news car. "So glad to see you again, Miss Summer," he said, as he led me into the restaurant. "Sorry about what happened this weekend. I didn't think you'd end up on the front page."

"It goes with the territory," I said. "So, what's the deal? All I know is that some customer left a very large tip here that broke some kind of record."

"It's easier if I just let the waitress explain it to you."

I saw our photographer had already set up in the back of the restaurant as the umbrella light gave off a soft glow.

I also saw that the woman to be interviewed was the waitress who'd served us on Saturday. She smiled, stood up as I approached and extended her hand. "Miss Summer, I'm Elizabeth Franks. Nice to see you again."

"You too, and call me Veronica. So, you're the one who got the big tip?"

She nodded as we both sat down. "It changed my life. More like saved my life."

"Really," I said, as the photog handed me a microphone and I clipped it on my lapel.

"The whole thing is unbelievable. I was at the end of my rope, and then... it was like some guardian angel must have been looking out for me."

The photog focused on the waitress, then turned to me. "Anytime you're ready."

"Go ahead and roll," I said. He pushed a button and I heard the tape engage. I started as always, getting the spelling of her name correct and a little background information before proceeding with the questions. "So, when I was in here Saturday and you said you had allergies..."

"I'd been crying."

"Tell me why."

"Well, as you can imagine waitresses don't make a ton of money, but I get by okay. Anyway, my daughter is about to enter her senior year in college. Thankfully my ex husband and I had put money away for her education years ago, but on Friday I discovered he'd closed the bank account and taken off with all the money."

"How much?"

"A little over forty thousand. Just enough to pay for her last year. Anyway, Richie, our manager, started passing the hat among the regular customers, trying to raise money for me. I appreciated the gesture but I knew he'd never come close to getting that kind of cash. Until this morning."

"What happened?"

"I got a call from the university. It seems that some anonymous person paid her tuition, room and board, everything. Someone basically funded a full scholarship with the stipulation that my daughter receive it. And then when Richie opened the door to the restaurant, he found this." She pulled an envelope from a nearby table and held it up. "It had my name on it, and inside was a lot of money. Fourteen thousand dollars." She started to tear up, but this time they were tears of joy.

"Wow. Fourteen thousand? That's a pretty odd amount."

"I thought so too, until I found out there's a federal gift tax for anything over fourteen thousand. Whoever did this even knew the tax law. If they'd put one more dollar in the envelope the whole thing would be taxable. And that's why they set up the scholarship."

"That's incredible. Do you have any idea who your benefactor might be?"

"The University won't tell me. Apparently that was a stipulation." She shook her head as she wiped her eyes. "Our regular customers are pretty blue collar, they don't have that kind of money." Then she turned and looked directly into the camera. "I just wish I knew who it was so I could thank them."

"Elizabeth, I think you did just that."

And I had a pretty good idea about the identity of the guardian angel.

CHAPTER TWENTY-THREE

In the game of "tit for tat" between me and Dexter (I'll let you guess who has what) I thought he'd successfully ended the game with my little comment about his perfect face and body. I mean, you can't un-ring that bell.

And then Savannah came to the rescue.

The game is on again.

Monday is the recap/elimination half hour show, the moment of truth when one couple lives to dance again while the other is returned to the D-list. Or in my case, back to my coffin. Since the latter is definitely a possibility after our Saturday wearable food sampler, I wanted to play my card and assure myself of getting the last word.

But first there was an unanswered question that had been bugging me.

Was Dexter Bishop the "mystery tipper" who bailed out the waitress? He hadn't wanted any publicity on the swimming pool story... was he an old school philanthropist who did charitable works in private?

Inquiring minds wanna know.

But inquiring minds are confused. How could someone so totally obnoxious do something so nice? Was the part he played on television really the polar opposite of his real self?

And had I lost the ability to determine if a man was truly a nice guy?

Still, I was thinking the odds were good that he was the big tipper. I mean, my recollection of the clientele in that restaurant told me it was unlikely that it was anyone else, though it could be the owner of the place. But there weren't a lot of people in the category of those who can drop fifty-four thousand dollars as a tip for a twenty dollar breakfast.

Dexter was shuffling through some note cards as I approached him. He looked up and forced a smile. "Well, you certainly look... clean."

"Cute," I said. I gently took his forearm. "I need to ask you something personal." I nodded in the direction of his lapel microphone and he put his thumb over it.

"Certainly."

"Did you see my story about the waitress who served us on Saturday?"

He nodded. "Yes, as a matter of fact I did. Quite a nice happy ending, if I don't say so myself."

"Uh-*huh*. So let me ask you this... how many people who eat at that place have pockets deep enough to do that?"

I was hoping for some hint, some change in facial expression, but got nothing. He shrugged. "It's a busy place with good food. Any number of well-to-do people could have been the benefactor. Just because the food is inexpensive doesn't mean it doesn't have wealthy patrons. I eat there all the time."

Time for a reporter's trick. I leaned forward and dropped my voice. "I *know* it was you, Dexter. You left a clue in that envelope."

His eyes widened.

Gotcha.

His expression quickly went back to normal. "Why, Miss Summer, you are obviously mistaken."

"Uh-*huh*."

He took his thumb off the microphone.

"I'm not done," I said, as I put my finger over it. I looked around to make sure no one was in earshot. "It was nice to hear from Savannah you think I'm the most beautiful woman you've ever had on your show. And the smartest."

***

I was going to spend the rest of the evening basking in the after-glow of getting the upper hand.

But noooooo. Not thirty seconds had elapsed when the finger-nails ran across the blackboard.

"So, you're a prime time star now?"

The voice that had been my Kryptonite growing up brought my joy to a screeching halt. I turned to see the smiling face of my evil-bitch-from-hell sister Selina in the front row of the audience.

My eyes narrowed and jaw clenched as I practically spit my words at her in a guttural tone. "What are *you* doing here?"

"Hey, my sister's a network anchor and on the hottest nighttime show. I came to watch."

"Bull. You came because you wanted something."

I have avoided mentioning my sister to this point because I didn't want to subject you to her story but I guess now that she's shown up it's inevitable.

Selina is a year younger than me, and she's been nipping at my heels literally and figuratively since she was born. She has the same hair and eye color as I do, though she's a bit shorter and has more of a classic hourglass figure. Actually, you might say there's more sand in the top half, which she added to a few years ago with implants, making one wonder if said hourglass is in imminent danger of tipping over.

She morphed from annoying little sister to full blown nemesis when she arrived in high school. Not content to simply find her own boyfriends, she took great pleasure in stealing mine, which she did with great ease since I was the proverbial "nice girl" in

176

school. Selina, on the other hand, basically earned a letter from the football team in the form of kneepads as she was known as the "head cheerleader" even though she was a rookie on the pompom squad. You get the picture. And, of course, she had to attend the same college as I did, majoring in sex while continuing to target my dates. If there was a degree for being a party girl, she'd have a PhD.

We went our separate ways after college. She ended up with a most appropriate career in a perfectly named town; as a massage therapist in Babylon, New York. She's highly sought after for her rubdowns, though I'm sure her definition of "trigger point" is a little different from that of the average masseuse.

I had enjoyed three bliss filled years without even hearing from the little tramp. I wanted three more.

"I don't want anything," she said. "I came to support my sister."

"I don't suppose it has anything to do with the fact that I'm on a show with a bunch of great looking men."

"Sweetie, I've grown up. I'm not like that anymore."

"Uh-*huh*. So you're settled down with a husband and a bunch of kids?"

She shook her head and wrinkled her face, as I'd hit her with the one thing that made her cringe: the thought of being pregnant, changing a diaper and sleeping with the same guy more than once. "Hell, no. I haven't changed *that* much."

"So, who do we have here?" I heard Bradley's voice from behind me.

"This is my sister, Selina," I said, folding my arms as he arrived at my side.

"Well, I can certainly see good looks runs in the family," he said, his eyes running down her body and stopping about three quarters of the way up.

"Why thank you," she said, giving him the once-over, same as she did in high school, stopping halfway up. "So, you're my sister's partner."

He nodded. "Yep. She's doing really well. Do you live in Manhattan?"

"Long Island," she said, reaching into her purse and pulling out a business card. "I'm a massage therapist." She handed it to him. "I would imagine in your line of work those big muscles of yours get pretty tight and you need a way to relieve the tension."

"Yeah," said Bradley. "I usually get a massage about once every two weeks."

"Well, since you're helping my sister, I'd be happy to provide you with the first one free. My company has a franchise here in the city and I can use the facilities."

"Hey, free massage," said Bradley. "Can't turn that down."

"I promise not to rub you the wrong way," she said, running her tongue over her lips.

I threw my arms up. "Okay, that's it, time to go!" I said, grabbing Bradley's arm and heading toward the dressing room. I looked over my shoulder to shoot a glare at her just in time to see her mouth "call me" at Bradley, who was walking backwards, eyes locked on her.

"Good to meet you," he said, as I pulled him along. He turned and faced the direction in which I was headed. "She seems nice."

"Throw a bucket of water on her, and she'll melt."

***

After what seemed to be an endless recap of the previous week's dances, I was at the end of my rope. I couldn't believe I was so nervous about the outcome of the vote.

But I really couldn't believe I cared.

All of a sudden I wanted to stick around. And not necessarily because I wanted to avoid the vampire shift and spend more time with Bradley.

As previously mentioned, the *It Girl* doesn't like to lose.

I didn't expect to win the silver disco ball, but I didn't want to be the first person voted off. Unfortunately, it was out of my control as Bradley took my sweaty hand and led me out to the front of the stage during the last commercial break. We stopped about ten feet in front of the judges, standing alongside the ice skater and her partner.

Bradley leaned over and whispered in my ear. "Relax. There's no way they're voting you off, right?"

"I think," I said, as the commercial ended and we went live.

The theme music played as Dexter welcomed the audience back. "And now, the moment of truth. Which couple will be headed home? Brian and Janice, or Bradley and Veronica? It's time to tally the votes!"

A graphic filled the lower part of the monitor looking a great deal like the network's election system. Zeroes were next to our names, and then the numbers began to climb very fast.

Then they stopped and my heart sank.

A collective groan came from the audience as Dexter looked at me. "Oh, I'm sorry Bradley and Veronica, but it's time to say goodbye. The audience has spoken." He shot me a wicked grin. "Veronica, I trust you've had a good time."

I forced a smile through my disappointment. "Absolutely, Dexter. Everyone has been wonderful, and I couldn't ask for a better partner than Bradley. It's been a unique experience. And I'm very happy to have raised a few bucks for the veterans."

"Yes, very good. Glad you enjoyed it. So Brian and Janice, you two will—" Dexter stopped mid sentence and put his finger to his earpiece. "I'm sorry, my producer... hold on a moment... I'm being told that there's been a computer error. Oh, my! The vote totals were reversed! Bradley and Veronica, you're staying for another week! I do so apologize to both couples. And I'm sorry that we have to say goodbye to Brian and Janice. But we're out of time, so tune in tomorrow night for our next round!"

My heart leaped as I saw the ice-skater's face drop like a stone. I turned and gave Bradley a big hug as the credits rolled.

"And... we're clear!" said the floor director.

I broke the embrace with Bradley and turned to face Dexter. Just as he shot me a wink.

Sonofabitch.

There was no computer error.

He planned the whole thing just to torture me.

The man is sure one confusing guardian angel.

***

So here I was again having changed in a flash only to find out Dexter had bolted from the studio. I stormed out the back door of the studio, not wanting all the viewers who were camped out in front of the building to see me.

"So. You *do* care about winning."

I turned to find Dexter leaning up against the brick wall like Humphrey Bogart in an old movie, complete with steam rising up out of a manhole. All he needed was a cigarette, a fedora and a trench coat. I narrowed my eyes and marched toward him. "You sonofabitch!"

"Well, that certainly translates well in both countries. No need for a primer with that one."

I stopped a few inches from him. "How dare you do that... that..."

"What? How dare I do what?"

I slapped his chest with my palms, shoving him back a step. "Auuuugh! You're impossible!"

"Actually, I'm quite predictable. I simply needed to know if you actually cared about the contest. And I got my answer."

"You got nothing!"

"Oh, let's go down the checklist... after you were voted off I got the quivering lips, the misty eyes, the little wobble in your voice. If I'm not mistaken that's not the way you usually act when you anchor the morning show. You looked like someone had run over

180

your dog. The viewers were about to go through a box of tissues for poor little Veronica who had been wronged by that horrible Englishman. Made for quite a good bit of drama, yes?"

"You played with my emotions on national television!"

"Ah, so you *did* feel some emotion when you lost!"

"I didn't say that! Stop putting words in my mouth!"

"Don't like it when people play reporter's tricks on *you*, do you?"

Damn, he had me. I exhaled audibly, having run out of gas. "I wouldn't have to if people would be honest with me. If you'd simply told me that you were the mystery tipper in the restaurant—"

"What, you would have said that you cared about winning the contest?"

Damn, he had me again. That's *my* job, talking people into a corner. "Maybe... I don't know... we should call a truce."

"A truce? My dear, did you forget? We already tried that, and this is too much fun."

CHAPTER TWENTY-FOUR

The lambada went so well in episode two (gee, I wonder why) that we got good scores from the judges and escaped the dreaded elimination vote. After the two female judges gave us eights, Dexter gave us a six, eliciting groans from the audience but probably elevating my standing with the viewers should I end up in the bottom two again.

Which I was determined not to do.

Dexter Bishop was not going to beat me. Which meant one thing.

I was gonna have to win the damn contest.

But right now Dexter was not occupying my mind, Bradley was. And after a week doing the forbidden dance, I was hoping I was in his mind as well. Turns out I didn't have to wonder for long as he emerged from the dressing room. "Are you up for doing something?" he asked.

"Sure, I'm still wired. What have you got in mind?"

"Maybe something not involving a cat."

I hooked my arm around his elbow, resting my hand on his forearm. "So, where do you live?"

"Jersey shore, but the show provides us with a hotel room during the week so we don't have to commute. I'm over at the Briarwood."

"Nice place. I'm surprised Dexter doesn't stick you at the

YMCA."

We decided to walk, as it was only two blocks. But, just to keep the gossip columnists at bay we split up after signing autographs for the fans who were waiting in front of the studio, making sure our "see you tomorrow" goodbyes left no doubt that we were not an item. I went left, he went right. Of course no sooner had he taken off than I got surrounded by another horde of autograph seekers, so I was going to be a few minutes behind.

Ten minutes later I walked into the opulent hotel lobby. The Briarwood is classic old New York: gorgeous Italian marble floors, mahogany pillars and leather paneled walls. The bellhops are dressed in those old fashioned red uniforms with hats that in my opinion make them look like they're roadies for Devo, while the maids are actually famous for being hot and wearing French maid costumes. Supposedly the girls make six figures in tips. Then there's the famous bar that sits opposite the front desk, which used to be a meeting place for actors back in the fifties.

There was a definite spring in my step as I headed toward the elevators, Bradley's room number burned into my brain. Surely he was already tucked in, ready to go.

And then I heard his voice from the bar. "Hey, look who I ran into."

I turned to see him standing at the edge of the bar.

Next to my sister.

If I was a cartoon at that moment, steam would have been visible coming out of my ears. Selina was busy twirling a lock of her hair while sipping a glass of wine as I power-walked across the lobby. I glared at her as she swung around on her barstool to face me and flashed her phony smile. "Oh, hey sis."

"Selina was at the bar when I got here," said Bradley, not looking at me since he was too preoccupied staring at her legs, which were accessorized by what had to be five inch platforms and a tight, short leather skirt.

"Wow, *what* a coincidence," I said, trying to bore a hole through my sister with my glare.

"I heard this was a nice place for a drink," she said. "Then who should walk up but your dance partner!" She playfully ran one long red fingernail down his chest. "And he's such a gentleman! I can certainly see why you wanted him for the contest."

"Uh-huh," I said. Bradley's eyes had moved from her legs to her incredibly low cut top.

"Anyhoo," she said, looking at me as she hopped off the stool and finished her wine. "I don't want to be a third wheel as I'm sure you two need to go over your *dance routines*. I'm sure he can move those hips in any number of ways." She turned back to Bradley, then gave him a pat on the side of his leg. "See you tomorrow."

"Looking forward to it," he said, still obviously drooling over her.

She leaned forward and gave me an air kiss, which was prefer-able to the usual, considering where that mouth of hers has been. "Take good care of him, sis." She spun on her heels and turned her walk to the door into a production number, Bradley following it the entire way.

"So, you seeing my sister tomorrow?"

"Getting my free massage. You know, she's a really sweet girl." He drained the remainder of his drink, gently took my arm and led me to the elevator. "You don't usually find girls who are that pretty who are nice. I mean, she's drop dead gorgeous. Selina's got better legs than most of our dancers. And God, those great eyes."

I shook my head, rolled my eyes and stopped walking.

He stopped and turned to look at me. "What?"

"I just realized I'm pretty tired, Bradley. Between the dancing and the walk over here, I just hit the wall. I think I'm gonna call it a night."

His face twisted. "Really?"

No, I want you to be thinking of my sister while you're in bed with me. Maybe yell out her name at the appropriate moment. "Yeah."

His lower lip went out in a slight pout. "Well, okay. I guess it has been a long day for you. Rain check?"

"Yeah, sure. Rain check. See you tomorrow."

"Hey, great job tonight," he said. "You're turning into a really good dancer."

Yeah. And you're turning into a real disappointment.

And for some reason, on my walk home, I wondered what Dexter was doing.

***

"My sister is not going to out-sex me."

Layla furrowed her brow as she sipped her drink at the bar. "Is that actually a word?"

"I just made it up but I think it gets the point across. If she wants to play that game, then let's rock. I can dress just as cheap and talk like a porn star too."

She looked around at the Friday happy hour crowd, noticed a few people looking at us, then slid closer. "You do realize this is no longer about your wanting Bradley, which you clearly do not. This is about beating your sister."

"I still want Bradley."

She rolled her eyes. "Like I said earlier, we're back in high school. And I know you better than anyone. He's not right for you."

"Fine. I still want Bradley for purely physical reasons."

"And... C'mon, out with it..."

"Yes! I admit it! It would be nice to get the upper hand on Selina just once."

"Doesn't matter that he acted like a jerk last night."

"I've been out with much bigger jerks. And so have you."

"Point taken."

"Layla, I haven't had sex since Alexander. Can't I just act like a man for once?"

"You're acting more like your sister."

"Whatever."

"Whatever can get you into trouble." She reached across the

185

table and took my hands. "Veronica, this isn't like you."

"This is a unique situation. You know I hate to lose."

"Yeah, and that's part of your problem." She shook her head, obviously giving up on her attempt to talk me out of seducing Bradley. "So what's the plan? How are you going to keep your sister away?"

"I'm thinking I get him to order room service, we're having dinner, and then... I satisfy the sexual camel in me and get rid of my sister all in one shot."

"So you're thinking about spending the entire night in his room."

"Yep. So there's no way she can interrupt us."

"Better check under the bed first. Meanwhile, you know who you need to talk to."

***

As far as the art of seduction goes, no woman knows more on the subject than Savannah. It's almost like she's a Jedi Master, able to wave her hand and say, "These aren't the girls you're looking for. You want me." She can put any man into the equivalent of a hypnotic trance, so much so that he almost needs an antidote once she breaks up with him. (She always does.) One guy she dumped walked around in a daze for about a year. Savannah says that men often need the equivalent of romantic rehab after she dates them, as she so completely ties them in emotional Gordian knots that they are unable to function without her.

Think about it. She's probably the only woman on the planet besides me who can get a call from Dexter Bishop and let it go to voice mail. And then not call him back.

And since she goes out with some men simply for "exercise" and Bradley would possibly fit into that category, I figured she'd be able to advise me on keeping him interested in me and not my sister. I wasn't totally agreeing with Layla, as I thought Bradley was salvageable. I still like his personality and we get along well. Look, he's only twenty-eight and we all know men mature later than we do. He wasn't the first guy to become obsessed with Selina, but he's obviously turned on by her tactics.

Which I needed to adopt, and fast.

So I asked Savannah to be a "consultant" for lack of a better term. She invited me over to her apartment, the bedroom of which might be considered a lair if she were a sexual superhero, since I wanted to put my problem with Selina to bed, literally and figuratively, once and for all. Savannah had met her a few times, so she knows the type. I'd explained the situation with Bradley and she insisted it was easily fixable as she led me down the hallway to her boudoir.

Her bedroom was what you might expect from a Southern girl. A king size four-poster canopy bed, an antique armoire and matching dresser, a gorgeous ornate vanity, and a red leather chair with an ottoman in the corner.

"I've seen your bedroom before," I said, holding a glass of wine. "Why can't we just talk in the living room?"

She marched to one of her two large walk-in closets. "Because *this* isn't in the living room."

Savannah opened the double doors, revealing enough seduction "equipment" to open an adult superstore. Costumes that could only originate in the mind of a man filled one side of the closet, while the other had shelves stocked with various "toys" to accommodate any male sexual fantasy.

My jaw dropped as I took a quick inventory. "Whoa."

She smiled and playfully batted her eyes. "One never knows what will turn on one's date."

"I would think a woman who looks like you wouldn't need this stuff."

"Darlin', you have so much to learn about the male of the species. Rule number one of what every man wants: lady in public, whore in the bedroom. Throw in a fantasy and y'all can tuck his family jewels away in your purse."

I moved into the closet and started sliding the costumes along the rod. "French maid, dominatrix, Cinderella, Wonder Woman... you got a magic lariat?"

She picked one off the shelf and held it up.

"You've actually worn all this stuff?"

She nodded. "Look, I can satisfy the basic needs of any man, but why not take it to another level by fulfilling a fantasy?"

I turned to the other side of the closet, which featured a riding crop, various masks and a set of velvet handcuffs among other things. "I need all this to keep Bradley interested?"

"Look, y'all start with one fantasy, then if you decide to keep him around you can spice things up. You can mix and match things." She took one costume from the rack. "Cinderella with a riding crop has always been a big hit. Like I said, lady in public—"

"I get it, fantasy whore in bed. So where do I start?"

"What do you think would turn him on?"

"No idea."

"Well, what do you think he finds attractive about your sister?"

"You mean other than the fact that's she spends more time on her back than the Jets quarterback?"

"No, what attracts him physically."

"He did mention she had better legs than most of the professional dancers."

She nodded, reached out and grabbed the dominatrix outfit, complete with thigh-high black vinyl boots. "I've got just the thing to show off yours. How about this?"

"I dunno. He's a dancer and used to leading... not sure he'd want to be led."

"Can you do a fake French accent?"

"*Oui, madame,*" I said, which didn't sound bad.

"French maid it is." She grabbed the costume and handed it to me. "Try it on."

I swapped out my outfits and moved in front of the mirror

on the back of the door. I had to admit it did show off my assets very well.

"He won't be able to resist you," she said. "So when you go to his hotel room, have this on under a raincoat, then do the big reveal. Trust me, you'll be in control the rest of the night."

"And my sister will be gone?"

"She'll move on to someone else, but remember, there will always be party girls. It's like playing a game of whack-a-mole: get rid of one and another will pop up."

"As long as she pops up back in Babylon, I'm good."

CHAPTER TWENTY-FIVE

Well, Operation Margaux the French maid (yes, I gave my alter ego a name) was on hold since there was a much more important event that I absolutely could not postpone.

Dinner and dancing with Dexter Bishop.

No, hell hasn't frozen over. It's prom night.

Remember those two kids in the pool? Well, tonight we're supposedly making them the most envied kids in high school.

I had mixed emotions about the whole thing. On the one hand I'll be doing something very nice for a very special young man. On the other hand, I've gotta spend several hours with Dexter, and even though I'm starting to see him in a different light we're still playing this game of one-upsmanship. But the former outweighs the latter by a good deal.

Dexter already sent over a detailed itinerary of the evening, in a parchment envelope sealed with wax. Like I said, he's old school.

-Limo picks me up at six, then picks up the kids. (Which means I'll be alone in the limo with him for awhile.)

-Dinner at one of the city's most exclusive restaurants at seven.

-9pm, arrive at prom.

-Midnight, leave prom for afterparty at one of the other student's homes. (Visions of scenes from the movie *Risky Business* dance through my head, followed by a headline in the tabloids linking me to a teenage prostitution ring.)

-1:30am, leave afterparty, "breakfast" at an exclusive restaurant that Dexter has bribed to stay open just for us.

-2:30am, drop off kids, head home. (Which means I'll be alone in the limo with him for awhile.)

So I spent the last hour getting gussied up. I found an appropriate "prom dress" for the event; not too sexy, but nothing that screams "teenager" either. It's a knee-length turquoise off-the-shoulder number that reveals no cleavage. After all, I figured I'd be meeting the kid's parents and didn't want to look like a party girl. As opposed to Margaux, who will rival her evil nemesis, Selina.

The doorman buzzed me, telling me the limo had arrived, so I made my way downstairs. I found Dexter in a tuxedo chatting with the doorman as I stepped off the elevator. He turned and smiled at me as I headed in his direction.

"You look lovely," he said.

"Thank you. So do you."

He stuck out his elbow as the doorman held it open. "Shall we?"

I curled my hand around it. We walked into the street and found a chauffeur in uniform standing next to a rather unusual looking limo. He held the door open for me, revealing some sort of silver metal contraption attached to the floor. "Watch your step, Miss."

"What is this thing?" I asked.

"I had a limo modified to accommodate a wheelchair," said Dexter.

Damn, that was thoughtful. "That's, uh, very nice of you," I said, as I stepped over the device into the limo.

"Just a small alteration," he said, as he climbed into the limo and sat opposite me. The chauffeur closed the door and headed for the driver's seat. Dexter pointed to a fully stocked bar. "Care for a cocktail?"

On the one hand I didn't want to meet parents with liquor on my breath. On the other hand, I sorta needed it and I had a supply of breath mints. "Sure."

"Champagne?"

"Bring it on."

Dexter pulled a bottle of champagne from a silver bucket, poured two glasses and handed one to me. "Cheers." He held out his glass.

"To doing good deeds," I said, as I clinked his glass. I sipped the champagne, which was terrific. Not dry, not sweet. "Excellent choice."

"Thank you."

I leaned back and stretched out my legs. "So where do the kids live?"

"About thirty minutes away in New Jersey. They actually attend the same school, so they're in the same neighborhood." He paused a moment, then pointed at a television monitor. "Care to watch the telly?"

"Why would I want to watch television?"

"I assumed you wouldn't be interested engaging in conversation with me."

What the hell, cut the guy some slack. "Hey, you're doing a great thing tonight. I think I can put aside our differences for one evening. Maybe actually honor our truce."

He smiled and exhaled audibly. "I'm glad to hear that. I wouldn't want any perceived animosity to ruin the evening for our dates."

I finished the glass of champagne, which had a quick effect on me due to my empty stomach.

Dexter noticed. "Would you like another?"

"I'd better wait till dinner."

***

Dinner was amazing, and probably cost Dexter a thousand bucks. Heather, his date, had tears in her eyes when she saw the limo had been specially equipped for her. Her mom actually cried when she saw what Dexter had done for her daughter.

Jim's parents were equally impressed that a network anchor was escorting their son.

It was the first ride for both kids in a limo. Had this happened before I got the network gig, it would have been mine as well.

We arrived at the prom to a standing ovation and were escorted to a table in the center of the gymnasium, which had been turned into a colorful dance hall complete with red streamers and a disco ball. Thankfully there was a decent band instead of what I had feared: a disc jockey playing nothing but rap music. (That's actually an oxymoron.)

Dexter had an easier time dancing with Heather than I did with Jim. He danced around her wheelchair while she expertly popped wheelies and rolled under his arm as he "twirled" her. Jim was propped up on his braces, so he couldn't use his hands. I kept my arms around his waist and we basically swayed back and forth to the music.

Of course like most teenagers they didn't want to spend the entire night with adults, so Dexter and I ended up dancing with a bunch of teachers who were there as chaperones. And for some odd reason, there were an awful lot of female chaperones. But after two hours of drinking punch I was in serious need of some alcohol. Luckily the teachers had kept Dexter's dance card full so I hadn't had to spend much time talking with him.

Jim and Heather were elected king and queen of the prom and managed to share a dance in the center of the floor, capping off their magical evening. He used the handles on her wheelchair to keep himself upright. There wasn't a dry eye in the house.

And then, a curve ball.

The class president stepped to the microphone as the band finished the song. "May I have your attention please." Everyone stopped dancing and quieted down. "While we've already elected our king and queen, we wanted to extend a very special thank you to two incredible people who made this evening unforgettable. So please give a round of applause to tonight's *honorary* king and queen, Mister Dexter Bishop and Miss Veronica Summer."

My jaw dropped as I looked across the room at Dexter, who was genuinely as surprised as I was. We moved toward the center of the floor as the class president hopped off the stage to meet us. Jim and Heather came forward with crowns; Jim put mine on my head while Dexter kneeled down so Heather could crown him. The crowd applauded again and I thought we were done.

Damn, those curve balls.

"So," said the class president, "what would you like for your first dance as honorary king and queen?"

"Oh, no, that's not necessary," I said.

"You two have to dance," said Heather.

"Really," said Jim.

"We've never danced together," I said.

Dexter ignored me and turned to the band. "Quickstep. Can you fellows play something fast?"

The bandleader nodded as everyone backed up to give us room. My eyes grew wide as Dexter took my hands. "What are we supposed to do?"

"You and Bradley did very well on the quickstep," he said. "And I was a dance instructor. I taught him the routine you've been doing."

"Okay."

"Just let me lead."

"Don't get used to it."

The music started and suddenly Dexter was pulling me around the floor, using the same steps I'd been taught. The muscle memory took over, and I was surprisingly in tune with him, more so than Bradley. Dexter was looking at me, but in a way he'd never done before, locked on my eyes... I don't know, I couldn't put my finger on it. "Stop looking at me like that," I said, low enough so no one else could hear.

"Like what?"

"Like you're doing."

"Do you want me to look at your feet? One is supposed to look at the partner's eyes."

"You're staring."

"I am not."

A photographer came out of the crowd, moved closer to us and started shooting pictures. I forced a smile and turned to the camera.

Dexter's hand gave me a gentle tug, making me snap my head back toward him. "What?"

"Focus on your partner. Not the camera."

Again with the look.

The song finally ended, we stepped apart and clapped along with the crowd.

***

I'd put off a trip to the ladies room as long as possible since I had no desire to share a mirror with a bunch of teenage girls. Fortunately there were none as I entered to freshen up. The quickstep had made me glow a little.

A thirtysomething pert blonde teacher was touching up her lipstick. "Hi, Miss Summer."

"Veronica, please."

"Veronica, I'm Cassie Davies. I teach creative writing. I admire your work, you can really turn a phrase."

"Thank you, I often wonder if viewers notice that stuff," I said, as I put my purse on the counter and pulled out a compact.

"So, I gotta ask. Are you and Dexter dating?"

I stopped and turned to face her. "Oh, no. I'm just a contestant on his show."

"Oh. You guys make such a nice couple. I just figured—"

"Well, thank you, but we don't really have much in common."

"Well, you're both very nice people to do this tonight, so that's something you have in common."

"Really, it was nothing."

"It wasn't nothing to those two kids."

"No, I suppose not."

"Anyway, if I had a shot at Dexter Bishop, I wouldn't give a damn if we had anything at all in common."

"Yeah, you would."

She laughed. "Maybe after awhile. But *awhile* would be a lot of fun, know what I mean?" She turned back to the mirror. "I really thought I had a celebrity scoop. Honestly, the way he looks at you I figured you two were an item."

"What way?"

She pulled out her cell phone, touched a few buttons and handed it to me. The screen was filled with a photo of the two of us during our dance together. Dexter had that look I'd seen earlier, but somehow, seen from a different point of view…

"If I didn't know better I'd say that was the look of love," she said.

***

My feet were barking as I took off my shoes in the limo and stretched out my legs. We'd dropped off the kids and were headed home. I took a quick look at my watch, which read a quarter to three, and laughed.

"What's so funny," asked Dexter.

"I was just thinking… I'd have gotten up forty-five minutes ago if I was back on my regular shift."

"Well, lucky for you that you're a good dancer."

"You mean lucky for me the show's fixed."

"Honestly, Veronica, I haven't had to tamper with the show at all. You've done remarkably well."

"Oh, *remarkably*? Does that mean you're surprised?"

"Young lady, you seem to surprise me on a regular basis."

Bang!

The loud noise from the front of the car made both of us jump. I turned around and saw smoke coming out from under the hood as our driver pulled over onto the shoulder.

"That didn't sound good," I said.

Dexter shook his head, said, "No, and it doesn't look good either," then got out of the car. I watched as he met the driver at the front of the limo. They opened the hood and thick black smoke billowed out. They waved away the smoke, studied the engine, and then the driver pulled out his cell phone as Dexter headed back.

"So, you a mechanic too?" I asked as he got in.

"I worked on my own car when I was younger."

"So what is it?"

"Some sort of problem with the engine, so we're not going anywhere in this vehicle."

"So we're stuck here?"

"For the time being. Unless you fancy walking back to Manhattan."

"Wonderful."

The driver tapped on the window and Dexter lowered it. "They'll have another car here in thirty minutes, Mister Bishop."

"Thank you, Henry. That's not bad considering the time of day." The driver walked back to the front and got in the driver's seat while Dexter rolled up the window.

I realized I needed a little help to get through the next hour until I got home and eyed the bar. "You got anymore of that champagne?"

"Excellent idea," he said, as he reached for the bar and pulled out a bottle. "I've had my fill of punch for the evening."

"No kidding." Though we'd had "breakfast" I was still hungry from all the dancing. "You got anything to eat?"

"Macadamia nuts or chocolates?"

"Yes."

"Which?"

"I said yes. That means both."

He handed me a jar of nuts and an expensive looking box of chocolates. I tore into them as he attended to the champagne. He popped the cork, poured two glasses and handed one to me. "I must say, it was an enjoyable evening."

"Yeah, I think we made a big deposit into the karma bank. But you did a lot more than I did."

Dexter shrugged. "I didn't do anything different than you."

"Oh, come on. You had the limo outfitted for the wheelchair, sprung for a really great dinner. All that wasn't cheap."

He started to laugh.

"What?"

"Veronica, you're new to the seven-figure salary club, but I assure you, there are only so many lobsters you can eat. I couldn't possibly spend all my money in a dozen lifetimes, so I might as well do some good with it."

"Does that mean you wanna come clean on the big tip at the restaurant?"

"Are we off the record?"

I made the zipper motion across my lips, turned the imaginary key and threw it away. "I'm a vault."

"Well, there's a Bible verse my mum used to read me, about charity. The left hand is not supposed to know what the right hand is doing, that charitable acts should be done in secret."

"That's very noble, but you didn't answer the question."

"I believe I just did." He smiled and sipped his champagne. I did the same.

Five minutes later I needed another glass.

Fifteen minutes and two more glasses later I was seriously buzzed, but really loosened up. The usual tension I felt around Dexter had melted away. "So, I gotta ask. What's your problem with Bradley?"

"I don't have a problem with him."

I wagged my index finger at him. "Ah, but you do. You always stick him with a contestant who can't win. I checked. And you were going to do it again this time. You also said the partner you originally paired me with was a better person."

"Fine. Bradley has been... at times... difficult."

"Difficult how?"

"I don't appreciate the way he treats the contestants. And he has a bad attitude about the show. He should be grateful he's part of a network hit and not having to do cattle calls on Broadway."

"So why don't you fire him and get someone else?"

"Because he's immensely popular with the viewers. Which is the same reason Gavin doesn't sack you."

My face tightened. "Ewwww. Why would I want to sleep with a creep like Gavin?"

"Getting sacked means getting fired."

"Oh." Then it occurred to me what he had said and I flashed a huge smile. "So, if I'm reading your analogy correctly, Bradley is to you as I am to Gavin. We're both very popular with the viewers, but both very difficult to deal with."

"You seem to wear your snarky attitude as a badge of honor."

"Damn straight. So, Dex," I said, stretching out the length of the bench seat as I talked through a mouthful of nuts. "Moving on from Bradley, what are your intentions with Savannah?"

He furrowed his brow. "How do you mean?"

"Well, are you serious about her?"

"A gentleman never kisses and tells."

"C'mon, Dex, just one little detail."

"We enjoy spending time together."

"Dammit, you two really got your story straight." I shook my head and rolled my eyes. "That's not gonna make the tabloids. C'mon, I saw the way you looked at her when you first met. Practically tripped over your tongue." I stuck my leg across the compartment and gave his a gentle push. "C'mon, I'm getting drunk and I probably won't remember anything you tell me anyway."

He shook his head.

"Fine. You wanna tell me why you talk about me when you're out with her?"

I spotted a slight flush in his face. "We talk about the people who are important to us. I simply asked about your relationship."

"Uh-*huh*. So, she didn't mind you calling me the most beautiful woman you've ever had on the show."

He shook his head. "I was merely complimenting her friend."

"Were you being honest?"

Now I got a better flush.

"Ah-ha!"

"Ah-ha, what?"

"You *do* think I'm attractive!"

"I would venture to guess that most of the men in New York and the rest of the country agree, so my opinion is not at all unique."

"But coming from you, that means something. You're Dexter Bishop, voted the best looking man on the planet. You're rich, famous. A guy who can have any woman he wants."

"Contrary to popular belief, Veronica, that last part isn't true."

***

Around four in the morning our replacement limo pulled up in front of my apartment building. I had left *buzzed* in the rear view mirror and was about to pass *sloshed* on the autobahn on the way to *hammered*. Thankfully I didn't see any paparazzi around as the world did not need to see a morning anchor who is supposed to have *gravitas* falling down drunk after a high school prom of all things.

The chauffeur opened the door for me and I got out, only to find Dexter already on the sidewalk extending his hand. "What are you doing?" I asked.

"I'm being a gentleman and escorting you to the door."

I waved my hand. "I'm fine." I started to walk and was seriously unsteady on my heels.

"I think you could use a hand."

"I can make it." I narrowed my eyes and focused on the quickly blurring front door. Then I started to sway and fall. I felt a strong arm catch me, then in an instant found myself lifted off the ground. Dexter was carrying me toward my building. "Hey, put me down!"

"Must you always be so difficult? You can't even walk, Veronica."

"I can walk." My head started to spin so I leaned it against his chest and wrapped my arms around his neck, holding on for dear life. "Whoa. Well, maybe not."

"Finally, the poster child for stubbornness stops fighting me."

He carried me into the building and across the lobby to the elevators. I expected him to put me down, but instead he managed to hit the up button with his shoe. "Hey, where do you think you're going?"

"Your flat."

My head snapped up. "I am not! You've seen me in that blue spandex!"

"Veronica, a flat is an apartment."

"Oh. I thought you were commenting about my boobs." The elevator door opened and he carried me inside. "You can just drop me here."

"You want to spend the night riding up and down on the lift?"

"Excuse me? You're not sleeping here!"

"A lift is our name for an elevator. Must you think everything I say has sexual connotations? Now what floor do you live on?"

"Sorry. Seven." I reached out and pushed the button. The door closed, we headed up and my head began to spin again. I tightened my grip around his neck. "Whoa."

"Are you alright?"

I leaned my head back against him. "I just need to go to bed and sleep it off. Damn champagne."

"Revenge of the grape," he said, as the elevator door opened. I directed Dexter to my apartment and he carried me there. Again, he didn't put me down.

"You're not coming in."

"You think you can make it all the way to your bedroom without passing out?"

"Of course."

"Fine."

Dexter put me down. "Good night," I said, just before the world spun for the final time and went black.

CHAPTER TWENTY-SIX

As far as waking up after you've passed out goes, I'll take lobster bisque in my hair any day compared to the massive hangover that greeted me at the crack of noon. My bedroom came into focus as I rubbed my eyes and grabbed my head, which felt like it weighed twenty pounds. I slowly swung my legs over the side of the bed, got up, and staggered to the bathroom, steadying myself against the wall on the way. Priority one was mouthwash. I took a slug straight from the bottle in an effort to get rid of my horrible breath which, as Savannah would say, would knock the proverbial buzzard off a shit wagon. After spitting out the stuff I leaned on the counter, looked in the mirror, and was greeted by light socket hair and makeup that looked like it was applied in the dark.

Then I noticed something. I stepped back and saw I was still in my dress from the previous night. Must have been too tired to take it off.

Come to think of it, how did I get in my bed?

I replayed the fuzzy memories from the previous night. I remembered Dexter carrying me into the building and to the door of my apartment. After that, I remember thinking I was going to pass out. So I must have passed out in the hallway.

Did Dexter put me to bed? And if so—

A knock at the door interrupted my train of thought. I walked to the door, deciding that if it wasn't someone really close to me I was not going to open it looking like this.

I relaxed when I saw Layla through the peephole and let her in.

Her jaw dropped. "Good God, did you just get home?"

"No, I just got up. C'mon in before anyone sees me."

"What time did you get back?"

"Around four. Our engine blew on the Jersey Turnpike and we had to wait for another car. So we raided the liquor cabinet in the limo."

"You look like you raided a liquor *store*."

"I feel like it. What brings you by?"

"We were going for a drive down the shore, remember? Hit that old fashioned malt shop with those cheeseburgers you love, do some shopping."

"Oh, dammit, I'm sorry. I totally forgot. Give me a few minutes to hop in the shower and then we can go."

"If you're not up to it—"

"No, the fresh air will do me good."

"So, you were too hammered to take off your dress?"

"I'm, uh, pretty sure I passed out and was carried in here."

"By who? Your doorman?"

"No. Dexter."

"Really." Her eyes widened as she grabbed a chair in the kitchen, smiled, propped her elbows on the counter and rested her head in her palms. "Do tell."

"Well, as far as I can remember, we pulled up to my building, I almost fell, he caught me, carried me inside because I was too drunk to walk, then dropped me at the door. After that I don't remember a thing because I'm pretty sure I passed out."

"You think Dexter put you to bed?"

"It's the only logical explanation."

"If that's true, he could have taken off your dress to check under the hood."

Yeah. But he didn't.

Dammit, conflicted again.

***

"How's your ankle?"

Hal the newsstand guy looked at my feet as he handed me the Sunday paper. "Huh?" I asked, half asleep.

He pointed at the front page. "I read that you twisted it."

I handed him a ten, then turned the paper around right side up.

There it was, a grainy screen grab from the security camera in our lobby. Dexter Bishop carrying me like a bride. "Oh, shit."

"Big Brother's always watchin' these days, Freckles."

I opened the paper to page two and the headline threw a bucket of cold water in my face, making me wide awake.

CHIVALROUS BRIT SAVES DAMSEL IN DISTRESS

If you thought Dance Off judge Dexter Bishop and network info-babe Veronica Summer were an item after looking at the above photo, taken at four in the morning, you'd be wrong.

Turns out the sarcastic-but-dashing star from across the pond was simply being a gentleman.

How the two ended up like this in the middle of the night is a long story, but one worth telling. Turns out Bishop and Summer were escorts for two physically challenged teenagers to their high school prom in New Jersey. Their limo broke down on the Jersey Turnpike on the way back to Manhattan, which explains their very late arrival back home.

As for the photo that looks like the final one in a wedding album, Bishop cleared it up.

"Miss Summer was exhausted after dancing the entire night and turned her ankle when she exited the limo. She was unable to walk on it, so I gave her a lift up to her flat." (That's British for "apartment.")

And if you think that sounds like a bogus story to cover up any romantic sparks between the two, you'd be wrong. Security cam video shows that Bishop left the building a few minutes later.

As for their good deeds that had been kept quiet, well, the secret's out. Students and teachers from the high school flooded social media with photos and glowing comments.

"It was the best night of my life," said Heather Starling, Bishop's "date" who is paralyzed from the waist down. "Mister Bishop picked me up in a limo specially equipped for wheelchairs. He took us out to a really expensive dinner and was such a gentleman all evening, dancing with me and anyone who asked. I'll never forget it."

Miss Summer's companion, Jim Larsen, echoed the sentiments. "She's as beautiful inside as she is outside. I was the envy of every guy at the prom. I wish I was ten years older."

Bishop and Summer were named honorary king and queen of the prom, which explains the many photos of them dancing together. However, we're disappointed that the two are not dating, as they would possibly be the snarkiest couple on the planet.

The opposite page was filled with photos from the prom.

Hal's voice broke my concentration with a sing-song grade school rhyme. "Veronica and Dexter, sittin' in a tree. K-i-s-s-i-n-g."

I glared at him and he stopped.

"So, how's that well-turned ankle of yours?" he asked.

"Uh, oh, it's fine. I put some ice on it. Nothing major."

"Good. You don't need to be on the disabled list for that show." He reached out and tapped the photo which showed Dexter and me dancing. "So, you two aren't... together?"

I shook my head. "Nope. Just work for the same network."

"Huh. Sure looks like you oughta be."

***

Savannah, who had spent Saturday with Dexter, quickly cleared up the mystery at brunch as to how I'd made it into bed fully clothed. My theory was correct. I'd passed out in the hall and he had put me to bed. "I told you he was nice," she said. "Any other guy would have ripped off your dress and done God knows what to you."

"I suppose I owe him one. Right after I get our overnight security guard fired. Can't believe he sold those tapes."

"Oh, come on, all those photos were innocent," said Layla. "And now the world knows what *we* do."

"What's that?" I asked.

"That once you peel away the snarky, sarcastic bitch suit you wear on the morning show you're really a softie."

"Shit, there goes my reputation."

"He said you two had a nice evening, by the way," said Savannah.

"Don't you get tired of him talking about me all the time?" I asked.

She shrugged. "As I said before, we do discuss things during dinner."

"You two still getting along?" asked Layla.

She nodded. "We really enjoy spending time together."

Boy, they've got that line down pat. "I'm happy for you," I said. "I hate to admit it, but I think you're dating a nice guy."

And that maybe, just maybe, I missed something special.

No, wait. He's Savannah's guy, and I'm happy for her.

Yeah, let's go with that.

CHAPTER TWENTY-SEVEN

Friday was a big day. I actually had to get to the studio at seven to go live at seven-thirty, but I didn't mind since the guest was the woman who would be President, Senator Sydney Dixon. Gavin didn't want to pre-tape something this important and be stuck holding it till Monday. Not a big deal since I'm going to be flying the friendly skies of Air Force One. Though she still hadn't formally announced her candidacy.

I was already on set when the Senator strolled into the studio during the commercial. I stood up to greet her, got *the look*, and shook her hand. "Senator, nice to see you again."

"You too, Veronica. How's that ankle?"

"Oh, you saw that story, huh?"

"*Everybody* saw that. My immediate reaction was, hey she's a smart girl using the old 'fake sprained ankle to get the guy to carry me' trick."

"Well, the story was actually true."

"Hey, no one would blame you for going after a guy like Dexter Bishop."

"You *like* him?"

"I'm married, I'm not dead. Anyway, you two look good together."

Good God, I'm even getting it from the next President of the

United States. What did everyone see that I didn't?

"Ten out!" yelled the floor director.

I sat up straight in my chair as Senator Dixon did the same. Adrenaline shot through my veins like it always did during a big story, except this one had personal implications.

The floor director counted me down and the red light atop the camera came on. "And welcome back. Joining us this morning is Senator Sydney Dixon, just back from that wild session in Washington. Senator, thanks for coming by."

"My pleasure, Veronica."

"So, let's get right to it. Is the proposed Senate budget dead, or do you think there's hope of some bi-partisan support?"

"Well, Veronica, I'm sorry to say you can stick a fork in the bill, because it's done. We're not getting any help from across the aisle, so we're going back and re-drafting a new proposal which will hopefully be more appealing to our friends in the other party."

"So does that mean—"

"However, I do want to share some other news this morning."

"You're moving forward on the farm bill?"

"No, I'm moving forward on the campaign. Today I am officially announcing my candidacy for President of the United States."

***

I was walking on air as I escorted the Senator to the door. "I absolutely cannot believe you announced this on our show."

"Like I said, we redheads have to stick together."

"I can't thank you enough for thinking of me."

"Sure thing. Well, I'm off to make the rounds with your competition."

"As long as you stopped by here first, fine with me."

She turned to face me as she reached the door and handed me a plain white business card with nothing but a phone number on it. "Listen Veronica, that's my private number. Anytime you need something from me, don't hesitate to call."

"Thank you, that's very kind."

"Hey, Big Red's gonna take care of you."

***

As if this day hadn't been great enough, tonight was the night I was going to exorcize the demon known as Selina and make that girl's head spin like Linda Blair in *The Exorcist*. Yes, Margaux the French maid had an appointment at seven with Bradley, bringing new meaning to the term "room service." I had my hair up, which would come down later. A big pair of glasses, which would be removed later. And my costume under a raincoat, which would come off later. I wasn't sure what I was supposed to do with the feather duster Savannah had given me, so I left it home. Layla kept reminding me that I really didn't need Bradley, but I explained to her that there was a difference between *want* and *need*. And right now I needed to want what my sister wanted because she needed whatever guy I wanted but didn't necessarily need. Got it?

Bradley had already given me a room key in case I arrived first, but I was determined to make him wait. Savannah said a little bit of torture would help turn the tables in my favor. I got off the elevator on the top floor of the old hotel and followed the sign that directed me to room 2314. I passed a pair of french doors with the sign "Presidential Suite" and found Bradley's room right next door. No one else was in the hallway so I removed the raincoat, took a deep breath, knocked and said, "Housekeeping" in a bad French accent.

Bradley opened the door. "I didn't need anything..." His eyes widened as he saw my outfit.

"Monsieur, would you care for turn down service?"

"I'm not turning down any service from you."

Damn, Savannah was right. I'll just tuck your Johnson away in my pocket for the rest of the evening.

"Oui," I said, as I moved into the room and he closed the door. I noticed a room service tray filled with food next to a table near the window.

"Good God, Veronica, I didn't expect this."

"Who ees thees Veronica? I am Margaux." I folded my arms. "Are you seeing another woman behind my back?"

He smiled, ready to play along. "No, of course not. This is all for you. Would you care for some champagne?"

Bradley looked like his clothes had been covered with itching powder as he sped through dinner, obviously impatient to get to the main course, Margaux. I continued to torture him during the meal, running my foot up his leg and making a big production number of eating chocolate covered strawberries and then seductively licking my fingers. I'd gone easy on the champagne, not wanting a replay of last week.

"Let me freshen up," I said, getting up and heading toward the bathroom.

"Not going anywhere," he said. His look told me I'd left Selina in the dust.

I grabbed my purse, entered the bathroom and closed the door. I was about to touch up my makeup when I heard voices from the next room coming through the heating vent. It was obvious the two people were having a wild tryst.

But what I heard made me stop. The woman's voice sounded so damn familiar.

I needed to get my ear closer to the vent so I hopped up on the vanity stool.

And what came through next nearly made me fall off.

"Big Red's gonna take care of you."

Ho-lee shit! My eyes widened as I realized Senator Sydney Dixon was in the Presidential suite.

The man's voice was muffled, as he was probably farther away from the vent. But I could tell it belonged to someone much older.

Someone who wasn't her husband?

Could it be? Could the slam dunk candidate and the next President be so stupid as to have an affair? And who the hell ever heard of a female politician cheating?

Nah, obviously she and her husband were just enjoying a weekend getaway in the Big Apple and he had a deep voice. But the next words that came through the vent shot that theory to hell.

"Of course we can keep doing this. I'm not gonna let my husband give up his teaching job. A candidate can't ask for a better job for a spouse."

Damn.

"Hey, Margaux, you okay in there?"

Bradley's voice brought me back to reality. But what I'd heard was more important. This could be the story of the century.

I needed visual confirmation.

I knew I had to somehow get in that room.

I'm wearing the same uniform as the maids in the hotel... even if the hemline is a foot higher...

Time for more reporter's tricks. I pulled out my cell, looked up the number to the hotel, and dialed it.

"Good evening, hotel—"

"Oh, sorry, I was trying to dial room service."

"One moment, I'll connect you."

It only took a few moments to connect. *"Room service, may I help you?"*

I lowered my voice, trying my best to sound as husky as Senator Dixon. "Good evening, we're in the Presidential Suite. Could you please send up a bottle of champagne right away? Like in five minutes?"

"Certainly, madame. It is on its way."

"Hey, Margaux! You're date's gettin' cold out here!"

Now I had to stall Bradley for a few minutes. Incredibly, getting even with Selina had to go on the back burner. I grabbed some money from my purse, left the bathroom and found him already undressed, and in the antique oak bed. He patted the side. "Need a little of that room service over here. I wanna be... tucked in."

I forced myself not to roll my eyes at that one. "In a minute," I said, grabbing the ice bucket. "I need some ice."

His face tightened. "Ice?"

"Yeah. Be right back." I headed for the door.

"You can't go out looking like that."

Well, actually that's part of the plan, but... "Oh, right." I grabbed my raincoat and put it back on, then headed out into the hallway just as I heard the elevator ding.

A young room service waiter, probably around twenty with short dark hair, was carrying an ice bucket with a bottle of champagne in it, headed toward the suite.

I put up my hand. "Excuse me..."

"Can I help you?"

"Yes, and you can help yourself." I pulled a hundred dollar bill out of my pocket. "How 'bout you let me deliver that champagne."

"You serious?"

I reached out and shoved the bill in his shirt pocket. "Deal?"

He held out the bucket. "Knock yourself out."

I took off my raincoat and handed it to him. "Hold this."

His dark eyes widened as he saw my outfit. "Uh, we don't allow *working girls* in this hotel."

"Do I look like a hooker?" He raised one eyebrow and smiled. "Don't answer that. But I'm not."

"Stripper?"

"No!" *But thank you for thinking I have the body for it.*

"So, is this some sort of elaborate practical joke?"

"Something like that." It was clear the kid still didn't believe me. "Look, if I were a prostitute or a stripper I wouldn't be giving *you* money. It generally works the other way around."

"Yeah, you've got a point. Sorry." He studied my face for a moment, then his eyes got that look of recognition. "Hey, aren't you Veronica—"

I put one finger on his lips. "Look, I'm undercover on a story." I pulled out another hundred and stuffed it in his shirt pocket. "You never saw me here."

"Damn, I need to switch my major to journalism. But yeah, you were never here."

"Wait at the end of the hall. It'll just take a few minutes."

"Oh, hold on." He pulled a slip of paper from his pocket. "They have to sign for this. Give them the top copy."

"Sure."

He took my raincoat. I set my cell phone to record video, then slid it into my pocket, the lens peeking out. I took the bucket and the room service ticket, headed for the door to the suite, then politely knocked. "Room service," I said, in my bad accent.

"Just a minute," said the male voice. I heard footsteps moving toward the door, the deadbolt being turned.

Then the door opened and what I saw knocked the air from my lungs. It was all I could do to keep my jaw from dropping.

The man wasn't the Senator's husband. But he was someone every American would recognize.

He was our network's main anchor, Bill Recker.

CHAPTER TWENTY-EIGHT

My heart slammed against my chest. *Oh my God, he's going to recognize me!*

"Well, come in, young lady," he said. For once the my-eyes-are-up-here thing was working to my advantage, as his were laser locked on my boobs. "Syd, did you order champagne?"

"No," came the answer from the Senator.

"Compliments of zee house," I said, as I walked to the table and set the bucket on it.

"How nice. I didn't know maids delivered room service," he said, tightening the sash on his hotel robe. I noticed the bed sheets were already rumpled and there was a pair of fur-lined handcuffs and an actual whip on the nightstand.

"Monsieur, we are, how you say, shorthanded," I said, careful not to make eye contact even though mine were distorted by huge glasses. My hands were shaking so I put them behind my back. I took a quick look to the right and saw the Senator, also in a robe, seated at the desk, talking on the phone. She was only a few feet away and thankfully not paying attention to me.

"Well, I must say, the housekeeping department is certainly looking good."

It should be noted that Bill Recker has a reputation as a major hound. He's married, but right up there with Roper the Groper, though the silver-haired smooth talker has movie star looks and can charm the skirt off any woman.

"Thank you, monsieur."

Recker grabbed the bottle from the bucket, poured two glasses, and handed one to the Senator. I backed up a step hoping my cell phone was getting a decent two-shot. She smiled, took the champagne, reached out, grabbed his crotch through the robe and gave it a squeeze.

Whoa!

Meanwhile, I couldn't depend on just the video, because everyone knows those things can be doctored. I pulled out the room service check, which was printed with her name on it, and handed it to Recker. "Please sign."

"Oh, certainly," he said. He took a pen and signed the ticket.

But I was not going to give him the top copy. That was mine. His name on her room service check. His fingerprints on it as well.

Talk about a paper trail.

I turned to leave when his words stopped me.

"Wait just a minute, young lady," he said.

Uh-oh. Busted. Beads of sweat began to blossom on my forehead.

I turned as he grabbed his wallet from the desk, opened it, pulled out a twenty and handed it to me.

"Merci," I said, taking the money. I headed for the door. "Have a pleasant evening."

"Oh, we will," said Recker. "Please thank the manager for the champagne."

Hmmmm... I was dressed like a hooker and taking money from married men. Do the math.

I pulled off the top copy of the ticket, careful to handle it by the edges and shoved it in a pocket as I left the room. The room service waiter was leaning against the wall. "That was fast," he said.

"I told you, five minutes."

"Yeah, I guess a real hooker would have taken longer."

"Funny." I finally exhaled as my heart downshifted, then handed him the bottom copy of the check. I took my raincoat back and put it on. "Listen, you guys have security cameras in this place, right?"

He nodded. "Yeah, but just in the lobby. It's an old hotel. We're not exactly high tech."

"You think the person manning the security office would enjoy a big tip?"

He smiled. "He's a student like me. I know he would."

"Lead on, my young friend."

Ironically, I now needed a security guy to leak some video. Funny how that works, huh?

***

An hour later I had broadcasting gold in my purse: a time stamped security cam copy of both Bill Recker and the Senator entering the hotel a few minutes apart; a room service slip with her name, his signature and fingerprints on it (in a Ziploc bag); and a great piece of video from my cell phone of the next President of the United States grabbing a network anchor by his Johnson.

But wait, there's more! (That's my game show host tease.)

The kid manning the security cameras went back a week and found the same thing on the previous Friday. And the Friday before that. And the one before that. So this was a regular deal with the two.

I clutched my purse close to my body with one hand as I rode home in a cab.

But broadcasting gold or not, there were a whole bunch of problems with breaking this story. And as the cab pulled up to my building and I got out, it hit me that I might be making more trouble for myself.

-First, breaking a story about a Presidential candidate being unfaithful would be huge, but how would my network feel about fingering its main anchor as the man in her life? Would they consider making the relationship public to get rid of an overpaid anchor with slipping ratings?

-If the network did let me use the story, Recker would no doubt be fired. Not only for the morals clause violation but the bias factor. He'd have no credibility covering the campaign of a woman with whom he'd had an affair. Therefore...

-If Recker was fired, would I get *The Chair* now? Would the network pull me off mornings with the ratings off the charts? The current substitute anchor, Jeff Garlen, would be heavily campaigning for the job.

-And what about *Dance Off*? Would they use my commitment to prime time as an excuse to *not* give me *The Chair* if Recker was immediately fired?

-Finally, what would happen if Gavin simply killed the story and dumped me permanently in the doghouse for even suggesting we run it?

-Worst case scenario: Bill gets fired, they give the job to someone else, I bank fifteen million over three years and then find a nice reporting job with normal hours.

It was like the math formula from hell. If A then B which equals C. Way too much to think about as I got out of the cab and headed into my building. I was going to need serious help sorting it out. The good thing was that no other reporter had any clue about the story, and the two people involved had no idea I was the person in their hotel room. So I had time. But I also knew that every politician considers himself bulletproof; sooner or later they all screw up. The exclusive had an expiration date, but I had no idea what it was. And it was too risky to just sit on the story. I'd kick myself forever if someone else broke it.

Right then, though, I was still wired. When a reporter finds a huge story, the adrenaline kicks in at a level that's hard to believe, a rush that courses through your veins and gives you an incredible natural high. It takes a while to come down from the excitement. So I was headed for a little help in the form of a big bottle of wine I had in the fridge as I entered my apartment.

I tossed my keys on the kitchen table and took off my coat.

Then I went cold as I realized I was dressed as a French maid.

Bradley!

Oh.

My.

God.

I totally forgot about him! He was still back at the hotel probably wondering if I got kidnapped when I went out for ice!

I whipped out my cell, which I had put on vibrate during my clandestine spy mission, and saw he had called four times. I quickly dialed his number. He picked up on the first ring. "Veronica, my God, are you okay?"

"I'm fine, Bradley. God, I am so, so sorry."

"I've been worried sick about you. I've been looking all over the hotel for you. What the hell happened?"

"I know this will sound hard to believe, but I stumbled onto a huge story and I lost track of time."

Long silence. "You found a story." The emotion was gone from his voice. "In the hotel."

"It's the truth."

"Uh-huh."

Oh, shit. "I'll be back in ten minutes—"

"Don't bother." The line went dead.

***

After a miserable Saturday spent divided between trying to figure out what to do with the story and how to possibly do damage control with Bradley, I needed my friends more than ever. But since I couldn't possibly discuss things in public and risk the chance of someone overhearing, I'd ordered in and invited Layla and Savannah over to my apartment for Sunday brunch.

Along with the one friend in the news business who could look at the situation objectively.

Scott.

And after telling them everything and showing them the videos (the one with the Senator grabbing Bill Recker actually made Scott blush) I was poised to take notes with a legal pad as we all sat on my sectional sofa around the round glass coffee table in the living room. I had drawn a line down the center of the pad, making two columns. Pro and Con. "Okay," I said, clicking my pen. "Layla?"

"Sell the video to a supermarket tabloid for a million bucks?"

"C'mon, be serious," I said.

"Actually not a bad idea," said Savannah. "Gets you off the hook for breaking it."

"Okay," said Layla. "I don't think you should tell your own network about it. From what you and Scott told me about Gavin, he'd probably sit on the tape, have a talk with Recker, put him on notice, and bank on Senator Dixon being President so you'll be in the inner circle at the White House. I'm sure Gavin's future is somehow tied to yours."

"Trust me," said Scott, "he's dying to get that evening producer job. The guy campaigns more than the President."

"Okay, good points," I said. "Savannah?"

"Well, if this were a male politician I would say it wasn't a big deal anymore, since the country's gotten used to that and they even re-elect men who have had affairs. But a woman... that really changes things. There might be a backlash against you... you'd be the girl who kept the first woman President out of the White House."

"I hadn't even thought of that," I said.

"You can't be the one to break the story," she said. "And if we're using my argument about the voters not caring, are we being sexist by telling the world she's cheating? Maybe the story needs to die."

"Those are valid arguments," I said, seeing the biggest scoop of the decade slowly slipping away. Why couldn't the woman cheat with an anchor from another network, dammit? "Okay. Scott?"

"Well, let me ask you a question," he said. "If you were any other reporter, if your future at the network wasn't at risk and there would be no repercussions against you, what would you do?"

"I'd break the story. I wouldn't even hesitate. But I'm not someone else."

"I know that, but take yourself out of the equation and put on your journalism hat. Take yourself back to Mister Hastings' class. What do you do?"

"I break the story."

"You wouldn't let it die?"

I shook my head. "No way. The public needs to know that the Senator isn't what she appears to be, even if half of them don't care about affairs anymore. It's not about killing her campaign, but getting the truth out. If they still want to elect her after that, at least I've done the right thing."

"Okay, so that's settled. The story needs to get out. But, as your friends have pointed out, you can't be the one to break it. I agree. That would be career suicide, even though you'd be doing the right thing. Trust me on this one, I know these people at the network. And Savannah's right about women being pissed at you. You might find yourself a pariah and out of the business."

That last part hit me like a shot to the soul. "Which leaves me back where we started."

Scott shook his head. "No, it leaves you with one option, and only one option. You have to give the story to another reporter."

I bit my lower lip and felt my eyes well up. This was the kind of story reporters dream of, and I was going to give it away? No!!!

This cannot be happening. "I... uh..."

"And you can't give it to another network and help the competition," said Scott. "It has to be someone in print, and a paper without a relationship with a broadcasting company."

"But it's video," I said. "It has to be a TV person."

"No, he's right!" said Layla. "The story about Dexter carrying you home broke in a newspaper and it came from a piece of video. The paper uploaded the clips on the website. Veronica, it works!"

"Okay, so who do I give it to?"

Suddenly Savannah sat up straight. "Guys, you're all missing the obvious! You don't give it to a print journalist."

"Well," said Scott, "we can't give it to a television reporter. And it's useless on radio."

"You don't have to give it to another reporter. You give it to the *other political party* and let them leak it. And I know just the person who'll kill to get it."

CHAPTER TWENTY-NINE

With Savannah off on a political mission I was free to take care of problem number two: patching things up with Bradley. He still wouldn't take my calls yesterday and wasn't at the hotel when I dropped by so I decided to hit the practice studio before it officially opened to the contestants. I knew he always got there an hour before I did to warm up and do Pilates, and the cameras wouldn't be rolling at that time because the crew didn't report in till later. Though I wasn't serious about the guy what I did was unforgivable, even if my original motivation was to simply top my sister.

So it didn't surprise me that I was greeted by an icy glare and a sarcastic comment when I arrived.

"Why don't you go out for some ice before we get started. Might find a big story."

I moved toward him quickly. "Bradley, please let me explain—"

He put up his hand. "Nothing to explain. I spent two hundred bucks on room service lobsters and champagne, you got me all worked up with your French maid routine and then you took off. I thought something bad had happened to you. You didn't even answer your damn phone."

"It was set on vibrate."

"How convenient."

"Bradley, I really did find a story. I'm not making this up."

"So what's this big story you found that was so important you forgot about me?"

Oh, shit. "I, uh, can't tell you."

"Again, how convenient."

I shook my head as I realized I was fighting a losing battle. "Well, I guess there's nothing I can say since you're obviously in no mood to accept an apology."

That seemed to strike a nerve. He quickly moved toward me, eyes filled with rage. It actually scared me so I backed up. He kept coming and I eventually backed into the wall. He closed in on me, grabbed my arms and started yelling. "So you just thought you could march in here with that bullshit excuse and all would be forgiven? Did you really believe I'm that stupid?" His face was inches away.

"Bradley, calm down—"

"Well, excuse the hell out of me for being pissed off!" His grip tightened on my arms.

Now I was really scared. "You're hurting me!"

He didn't let go.

"Get your bloody hands off her!"

We both turned our heads as Dexter barged into the room carrying a stack of newspapers. Bradley gave me a shove against the wall in the process of letting go. "This has nothing to do with you, Dexter," he said.

Dexter moved closer, placing his body between me and Bradley. He dropped the papers and folded his arms. I wrapped mine around my waist, as I was shaking.

One paper landed with its front page facing up, and the headline made my adrenaline spike even higher.

DANCE OFF PATERNITY SUIT SCANDAL!

"Get out," said Dexter. "You've embarrassed the show."

Bradley took a look at the newspaper. "What? That? C'mon,

Dexter, I would think that kind of publicity would be a ratings bonanza."

"*Dance Off* is a family show, and there's no place for that kind of behavior."

Something from Journalism 101 told me the headline had something to do with Bradley. "Guys, what are you talking about?"

Dexter bent down, grabbed the top newspaper and handed it to me, keeping his eyes on Bradley. "Read it."

I flipped the front page and saw a shot of Bradley and me on the dance floor. "I'm not pregnant!"

"It's not about you," said Dexter. "Read it out loud."

"Okay," I said, the paper shaking as I started to read. "The horizontal mambo is not one of the featured routines on *Dance Off*, but professional partner Bradley Hart may find he can't tap dance his way out of a paternity suit. Filed Friday in Manhattan, the lawsuit contends Hart is the father of an unborn child. The plaintiff, Selina Summer—" I dropped the paper and whipped my head up at Bradley. "You knocked up *my sister*?"

"Veronica, you can't file a paternity suit until a child is born—"

"*That's* your explanation? When the hell did you sleep with Selina?"

"I didn't exactly sleep with her the first time. The, uh, massage therapy got a little out of hand."

Curses, she beat me again!

Meanwhile, I came *this close* to sleeping with someone who'd been with Selina... and needing a bucket of penicillin.

"Clean out your locker and get out," said Dexter. "You're sacked."

"I'm what?" asked Bradley.

"It means you're fired. Out. Now."

Bradley moved closer. "You're actually serious? You're going to fire me in the middle of the season? This thing will blow over in a few days."

Dexter glared at him, said nothing and pointed toward the locker room.

"Fine," said Bradley. "I'm sure you weren't going to let me cash a bonus anyway."

"Excuse me?" said Dexter.

"Oh, don't give me that. You've been sticking me with loser partners since the show started. Then just when I think you've done me a favor with someone who can actually dance, it turns out I get stuck with a lying cock-teasing bitch."

Before I had a chance to say something, Dexter's hand balled into a fist and he swung, catching Bradley square on the jaw. Bradley fell back and landed on his ass. He grabbed his jaw, looked at his hand, saw blood, got up and charged at Dexter, ramming his shoulders into Dexter's stomach. I backed out of the way in the nick of time as they both slammed into the floor-to-ceiling mirror, shattering it and scattering shards of glass everywhere. They got up and started trading punches.

For the first time in my life I was paralyzed by what was happening in front of me. Finally I yelled. "Stop it!"

And, like typical men, they didn't hear me.

The barroom brawl went on for another minute, with both men landing punches to the face. Finally Dexter connected big time, nailing Bradley square in the nose. He went down in a heap and didn't get up.

Both men were bloodied and out of breath.

"Now get out," said Dexter, doubled over, breathing hard, resting his hands on his knees.

Bradley said nothing, managed to get up and staggered into the dressing room.

Dexter turned to look at me, blood dripping down his forehead, lower lip twice its normal size. "Are you all right?"

"*Me*? We need to get you to the emergency room."

He shook his head. "I'm fine."

"Fine, my ass. You're going."

"Stop trying to lead."

"This time you're the one being stubborn." I moved forward

and took his arm. "C'mon, I'll take you."

"No. Nothing's broken and the last thing I need right now is more bad publicity for the show. I just need to clean up and go home before the crew gets here."

Bradley was already gone when I returned to the locker room with a bag of ice from the break room. Ironic, huh? I ended up going out for ice anyway. Dexter was sitting on the long wooden bench in front of the row of red lockers, bare-chested, having thrown his bloody shirt in the trash. Some bruises were already visible on his chest, he was surely going to get a black eye, and the lower lip had swollen even more.

"Put this on your lip," I said, handing him the ice bag.

"Thank you," he said softly.

I grabbed a washcloth, ran some cold water on it and sat next to him, then gently began to dab the blood from his face and scalp. "You look awful."

"You should see the other guy," he said. "It doesn't hurt as much when you win."

"Yeah, right. What the hell were you thinking?"

"What do you mean?"

"I mean, you fired him and all, why did you have to start an actual fistfight?"

"Veronica, where I was raised a gentleman doesn't insult a lady like that."

"I kinda had it coming." He furrowed his brow. "Long story that I don't wish to repeat."

"Regardless, what he called you was inexcusable."

I continued to wash away the blood, which kept coming. "What, you were defending my honor like some medieval knight?"

"I'm sure Manhattan has laws against jousting."

"Well, anyway, I'm glad you came in when you did. I was afraid he was going to hurt me."

Dexter nodded toward one of my arms. "It appears that he did."

I looked and saw a dark welt forming where he had grabbed me. In all the commotion I hadn't noticed it. And I had a matching welt on my other arm as well. "Wow." I went back to washing his face, then grabbed a first aid kid and put a few band-aids on the cuts as the blood flow finally stopped. "I think you're as cleaned up as you're gonna be. But you need stitches."

"Thank you. Would you be so kind as to go down to wardrobe and get one of my shirts?"

"Sure, Dexter. But you'll need an hour with the makeup artist before you can go on TV tonight."

"We're pre-empted tonight. Remember? Your President is speaking. I'm going home."

"Well, you've still gotta get out of the building. And people are going to notice your face."

Fortunately there's that daily soap opera produced in our building, so after picking up a shirt for Dexter I stopped by that studio and borrowed a fake beard from their makeup artist, telling her I needed it for a practical joke. Then I swung by my desk and grabbed a Mets baseball cap.

Dexter was lying stretched out on the bench when I returned, obviously not feeling well. He raised his head a bit as I sat next to him.

"Okay, got you a clean shirt and a disguise to get you home."

He smiled as he saw the fake beard. "You really think this will work?"

"Hey, all we've got to do is get you in a cab and into your building. I already ordered a taxi to do a pickup at the back door."

"You're very resourceful. I can see why you're such a successful presenter."

"A what?"

"Oh, that's what we call news anchors in the UK."

He put on the shirt and disguise, stood up, staggered a bit and steadied himself against the wall. I moved toward him and wrapped my arm around his waist. "Lean on me."

"I'm fine."

"Bullshit, you're about to fall over. I'm not some ninety pound waif, you can lean on me."

He exhaled, apparently realizing that arguing with me was a losing proposition. He put one arm around my shoulders and leaned on me as we headed for the back door. A few minutes later a cab rolled up. Dexter was unrecognizable with the hat, glasses and beard.

"Thank you, Veronica," he said, grimacing in obvious pain as he reached for the door to the cab.

"Don't talk, your voice is very recognizable."

"Good point."

I told the cabbie the address and paid him in advance with cash. Dexter smiled at me as I shut the door.

And as the cab pulled away, I knew damn well that wasn't enough.

***

Savannah was speechless at lunch for the first time since I'd known her. Between the main event featuring Dexter and Bradley and the undercard featuring my dance partner knocking up my sister, she sat there transfixed as I recapped the morning's events.

Finally I finished and the sphinx spoke. "Wow. How romantic."

"*Romantic?* The guy I almost slept with nailed my sister and you call that *romantic?*"

She shook her head. "Not that part, silly. The fact that a man defended your reputation. That's some serious old fashioned chivalry y'all saw today."

"Well, fiddle-dee-dee, there's no romance involved and we're not going to the cotillion. Dexter obviously is very protective of women, that's all."

"Sure. Y'all can spin it anyway you like."

"Hey, you're the one dating him. You get the romance, not me."

229

"You know, for such a smart girl you're sometimes clueless. Anyway, I already have news on that little video project I'm working on."

I looked around to make sure no one was within earshot. "Do tell."

"I'm using an intermediary to make the deal, but it will probably happen within a day or two. The buyer wants to check the tape and make sure it hasn't been doctored. For that kind of money, they want to be sure."

I lowered my voice to a whisper. "Money? You're selling it? I can't have any paper trail that gets me money for this."

"Of course not. The deal is that the buyer will make a sizable anonymous donation to a certain charity you feel strongly about."

I relaxed. "Wow, that's a great idea. You come up with that?"

"Of course. I also came up with the price tag. The other part of the deal is that it will be released on Saturday night, so all the Sunday morning political shows will have it. It gives your network twenty-four hours to deal with it before you have to go on the air."

"Damn, Savannah, you're brilliant. I hadn't even thought of that."

"I didn't want you to be the person reporting the breaking news on the person you're going to replace."

"Sounds like everything is in motion. Meanwhile, you might want to check in on your boyfriend this afternoon. I'm sure he could use a little TLC. I thought we could go by the deli and get him some goodies."

"Great idea, but you're the one he saved. You should be the one to drop by."

CHAPTER THIRTY

So after a stop at a seriously decadent deli, dropping a hundred bucks on all sorts of exotic treats, and trying unsuccessfully to talk Savannah into being the delivery girl, I was headed up to Dexter's apartment. He sounded surprised on the intercom when the doorman announced my arrival but said to send me right up. I still felt like I was cheating on Savannah, but she was the one who told me to do this and I had no intention of stealing a man from a good friend. Not that I was interested in Dexter anyway.

Yeah, let's go with that.

Anyway she was right that it should be me. Dexter saved the lying cock-teasing bitch, not Savannah.

This was one of those penthouse apartments where the elevator opened right into the living room, so he was standing there waiting to greet me when the door opened. The swelling on his lip had gone down some, his right eye was definitely on its way to a shiner. A butterfly bandage highlighted his forehead near the hairline and I could see a few surgical stitches peeking out. "You look... a little better," I said, as I stepped off the elevator.

"I don't feel any better. I have a massive headache."

"Oh, I'm sorry if I disturbed you. Were you asleep?"

"No, my head hurts too much for that."

A quick look around surprised me. While the apartment had

a spectacular view of lower Manhattan, it was sparsely furnished, with a simple beige couch and loveseat, coffee table, and a large flat screen atop an antique credenza. The dining room held a simple maple table for four. The walls were bare, as if he'd recently moved in. Homey it wasn't. The place was sorely in need of a woman's touch. Or at least a decorator.

"You just move in?" I asked.

"Been here three years," he said. "Why?"

"Just curious." I pointed to the bandage. "I told you that you needed the emergency room."

"I had a concierge doctor come by. Just five stitches."

"Ouch. Well, you can afford a plastic surgeon when it heals up."

He waved his hand. "No big deal."

"You're going to keep a scar on that famous face?"

"What's the old saying? Chicks dig scars. Besides, my hair pretty much covers it up."

I held up a big brown shopping bag. "Anyway, I brought you some stuff to hopefully make you feel better."

"Is there a gallon of bourbon in there?"

"Funny. You haven't eaten dinner, have you?"

"No, I was going to send out. Don't feel well enough to cook."

I furrowed my brow. "You know how to cook?"

"No, little elves come by every evening and whip up a seven course meal. Of course I know how to cook. I wasn't always rich, and I enjoy fooling around in the kitchen. Eating out every day would get old in a short time."

I pointed toward his dining room table. "Well, take a seat and I'll get you all fixed up."

"Veronica, this is very nice but you didn't have to go through all this trouble."

"Hey, you were my white knight this morning, so shut up, sit down, and let me thank you."

"Still trying to lead, eh?"

I narrowed my eyes at shot him a glare.

"Very well. I'm in no mood to argue with a Jedi Master in confrontation."

"Ooooh, I like that."

Dexter sat down at the table while I brought the bag into the massive kitchen and began to unpack it. While the rest of the place was barely furnished, the kitchen was just the opposite, the counter cluttered with all sorts of cooking utensils and appliances. He obviously wasn't kidding that he liked to cook. The appliances were all top of the line, while a rack of copper pots hung over the black granite island in the center. I found the dinnerware and utensils, fixed the main course, carried it into the dining room and slid it in front of him.

His eyes widened a bit. "This looks and smells wonderful. What is it?"

"Chicken soup from the best deli in town. Hunks of chicken, bits of pasta, homemade broth, carrots, celery, lots of spices."

"I thought chicken soup was for colds."

"What the hell, it makes you feel good."

He dipped his spoon into the soup and took a sip. "Oh, this is lovely. Excellent choice. Won't you have some?"

"No, I brought it for you. There's enough for four bowls so you can have some for tomorrow."

"Veronica, you're not going to stand there and watch me eat."

"Well, if you twist my arm. I love the stuff." I headed to the kitchen, fixed a bowl for myself and returned, taking a seat next to him. "So, heard from Bradley's attorney yet?"

"No. Why would I?"

"I figured he'd sue you for wrongful termination or something. And then maybe assault since you threw the first punch."

"He violated the morals clause in his contract. As for our fisti-cuffs, those bruises on your arms would be my defense, so snap a photo when you get home just in case. But trust me, he doesn't want it out in public that he was getting physical with a woman."

"Good point. I hadn't thought of it that way." I sipped some of the soup, watching Dexter as he seemed unsteady. "So, now that I'm without a partner am I supposed to do some interpretive dance like a beauty pageant contestant?"

"You're not without a partner. I've already arranged for a replacement. He'll be practicing with you tomorrow."

"Aw, darn it. I was already working out a ballet routine to *Wipeout*."

He laughed a bit. "I couldn't very well have our *It Girl* lose the contest because some bloke left your sister up the spout."

"Whaaaat?"

"Pregnant."

"Oh. I'm not sure I wanna know where *that* term came from. Anyway, thank you for getting me a new partner. I'd kind of resigned myself to being out of the running with Bradley gone and starting from scratch with someone else."

"You'll be fine. Have you spoken to your sibling?"

"We don't really get along, Dexter. Never have. She's been a thorn in my side since I was a kid."

"That's unfortunate."

"It's okay. I have great friends."

We continued to enjoy the soup. Dexter finished his and wanted a second bowl. After that I served dessert, a decadent slice of raspberry cheesecake. He took a bite and smiled as he savored it. "Oh, this is wonderful. Aren't you going to have some?"

"I only brought the one slice. Didn't know I was staying for dinner."

"Well, get another fork and we'll share." He slid the plate toward me a bit.

I patted my belly. "Hey, if I'm still on the show I need to fit in those costumes."

"Nonsense. You don't have an ounce of fat anywhere. Go and fetch a fork."

I couldn't help but smile at the compliment, as I headed back to the kitchen. We split the remaining cheesecake and he leaned back in his chair.

"Feeling better?" I asked.

"Yes, much. I was feeling so badly I just realized I forgot to eat lunch."

"Might be part of the reason for your headache. By the way, if you get hungry later there's a whole bunch of goodies in the bag. Chocolates, cookies, dipped strawberries, a few specialty items you might not get across the pond."

"Thank you, Veronica, you've been very kind."

I leaned back as well. I couldn't believe that I was actually enjoying his company. "You know, I can't believe I'm saying this considering how we started, but Savannah is a lucky girl."

"You're lucky to have her as a friend. She may be the most unselfish person I've ever met."

"You're right on that."

We traded hilarious stories about television. Then he wanted to know more about my initial interest in journalism while I was curious about his life before television. For the first time "the game" we were playing had faded to the background. He sat at one end of the couch while I'd gotten comfortable at the other, shoes off and legs tucked under me as I leaned my head on a pillow. I saw his eyes getting a little droopy. "Looks like you need a nap."

He covered a yawn. "Yes, perhaps. The doctor did give me some medication for the pain."

"Well, I'll get going." I looked at my watch, and my eyes bugged out. I had been there four hours. "Listen, if you need any help with anything, or feel sick, I'm just a few blocks away."

"I'll be fine. Thank you again." We both got up and he escorted me to the door. "It was very nice spending time with you, Veronica."

"Yeah, it was. So, should I show up at the regular time tomorrow? Will Bradley's replacement be there?"

He nodded. "Oh yes."

"You gonna tell me anything about him?"

"Just get ready to work."

***

I arrived early at the studio the next day, wanting to get a head start with my new partner. I figured starting with a clean slate would leave me behind the pack, so any extra practice would help.

But he hadn't arrived yet, so I stretched out on the floor and unfolded one of the city's daily tabloids.

There I was again on the left side of page three, being carried into the building by Dexter. The right side featured a shot of me dancing with Bradley.

BRIT SAVES DAMSEL ONCE AGAIN

Last time he saved her from a sprained ankle. This time Dexter Bishop made sure Veronica Summer wouldn't be stepping out alone when *Dance Off* continues this week.

Her partner Bradley Hart found himself high stepping to the unemployment office yesterday after the revelation that he was the defendant in a paternity suit and his confirmation that he'd had a sexual relationship with the plaintiff. His actions apparently violated a morals clause, and, had he remained on the show, would have been a huge distraction. Even worse was the fact that the woman filing the suit was Ms. Summer's sister, Selina Summer. Talk about sibling rivalry.

"*Dance Off* is a family show," said Executive Producer and judge Dexter Bishop. "I have no tolerance for such behavior, and I know the viewers would not have looked kindly on us had we kept him on the program."

The firing temporarily left celebrity partner Veronica Summer alone at the ball. But Bishop apparently has a deep bench, and said a replacement had already been found.

Meanwhile, Hart was seen carrying two large suitcases and

checking into a midtown hotel. His wife has apparently thrown him out of their New Jersey home.

My eyes widened as my jaw dropped. "His *wife*?" I said aloud, just as Dexter entered the studio. I looked up at him. "Bradley's *married*?"

"You didn't know?"

"No, he conveniently left out that little detail. He told me you provided him a hotel room during the week so he wouldn't have to commute from Jersey."

Dexter shook his head. "Not true. I would assume his use of hotel rooms would have been for after-hours activities with your sister."

"That sorry sack of shit."

"I don't quite get the metaphor, but it sounds appropriate."

I rolled my eyes as I tossed the paper aside. Not only had I come *this close* to picking up whatever Selina was carrying around as a walking petri dish, but I came *even closer* to being the *other woman* and breaking up a marriage. Beating my sister would have been a career killer. Along with leaving me feeling guilty for, you know, forever.

Thank goodness Senator Dixon was having an affair and interrupted me. Ironic, huh?

Anyway, back to the present. Dexter's swollen lip had amazingly returned to normal, his hair had been combed to hide the bandage, and he apparently was wearing enough makeup to cover up his black eye. "Well, you're looking much better."

"Thank you. I feel much better, but I'm still a little light headed. The soup and goodies you brought certainly helped."

"Glad to hear it." I got up and moved toward him. "So, what time's my new partner getting here?"

"He's already arrived."

"Good, can't wait to meet him."

"You already have."

I nodded, realizing he was pairing me with one of the dancers who'd already been eliminated in the previous rounds. "So, is it Kyle?"

"No, Veronica. I'm you're new partner."

Jaw drop number two.

"I... uh... don't understand. How can you be my partner when you're a judge?"

"I've delegated my judging duties to someone else."

"You can do that?"

He raised one eyebrow and smiled. "I'm the Executive Producer, remember? I can do anything. Look, I was a dance instructor and I felt a certain chemistry with you at that high school dance. Viewers have been clamoring to see me dance for years, wanting to see if my criticism of other dancers is backed up by talent. I saw it as the perfect opportunity. Sort of a *put up or shut up* thing. Like I did to you when I got you on the show."

"You already knew this when I came by last night?"

He smiled. "Yes. Actually it was not my idea, but I must admit it was brilliant."

"So whose idea was it?" He started to answer but I put up my hand. "Wait. Let me guess." I narrowed my eyes. "Gavin?"

"No. Savannah."

***

The question had been driving me crazy all day, especially since Savannah had been tied up in meetings and hadn't been able to answer her phone. So I simply texted her to meet us for dinner at the Italian place. As always, Layla and I had already arrived and had gotten a head start with the wine when we saw her approach our table.

"Sorry ahm late, meeting ran a bit long." She turned to me and smiled. "The deal is done."

I put my burning question aside for the moment. "So,

238

everything's a go for this weekend?"

"It will be dropped on the Sunday morning producers late Saturday night. Newspapers will get it in time for their Sunday editions which, as you know, are the most read of the week. And an anonymous donation in the amount of one million dollars for the Wounded Warrior Foundation is in the mail."

"A million bucks? Damn!" I said.

"My little French maid outfit paid a nice benefit, huh?"

"They actually mailed a check that large?" asked Layla.

Savannah shook her head. "Figure of speech. They sent a courier this afternoon to their headquarters in Florida. The cashier's check is untraceable from a bank in the Cayman Islands."

Layla rolled her eyes. "One of our national political parties stashes money offshore? What a bunch of patriots."

Savannah smiled and shrugged, then turned to me. "So, how'd your day go with your new partner?"

"Funny you should ask," I said.

"Oh yeah," said Layla. "Did you get somebody good?"

"Oh, I got somebody good all right," I said, looking at Savannah. "So, this was your idea?"

She smiled as Layla furrowed her brow. "Well, who the hell is it?"

"Dexter Bishop," I said.

"Huh?"

"Yeah, and it was apparently Savannah's idea that he should find a new judge and be my partner for the rest of the season."

"Wow," said Layla. "You lucky bastard."

"Yeah, wow," I said, still staring at Savannah. "So, let me get this straight. You're dating a guy who is supposedly the most desirable bachelor on the planet and for some bizarre reason you keep throwing him in my direction. Mind explaining that one?"

"While you're at it, mind explaining why you didn't throw him in *my* direction since Veronica doesn't like him?" asked Layla. "What am I, chopped liver?"

Savannah got that kid-caught-in-the-cookie-jar look and

shrugged. "I guess it's time you both knew."

"This oughta be good," I said.

"Well," said Savannah, "when I told you we enjoy spending time together, I was being literal."

"I'm still confused," said Layla.

"That's *all* we do," said Savannah. "Spend time. We're not in love or anything. We've become platonic friends."

"Now we're getting into the realm of science fiction," said Layla. "You mean to tell me that after the two of you drooled over each other when you met, and, given your history of going through men like Kleenex, that you two go to dinner, then go home and play Monopoly?"

"Actually, he likes chess," said Savannah. "He's quite good at it."

"Come on," I said. "Do you expect us to believe that you two never—"

She shook her head. "Look, on our first date we went back to my place and were playin' tonsil hockey and we both realized there was no chemistry. I know this sounds hard to believe considering how attractive he is, and his initial attraction to me, but it's the truth. He's just a nice guy who could have taken advantage of me and didn't. He's become a friend. I guess I've realized some attractive men are good for things other than sex. I'm growing up."

Layla pointed out the window. "Oooh, look, a bunch of pigs just flew by. Veronica, call your weather department and see what time hell froze over."

"Hush," said Savannah, playfully slapping her shoulder.

"That still doesn't explain why you're sending him in my direction," I said.

"Because," said Savannah, "and don't you *dare* tell him I told you this... he's crazy about you."

CHAPTER THIRTY-ONE

I have one of those talking smart phones. You know, the ones that let you ask a simple question and give you a polite, politically correct answer from a somewhat sexy sounding female android.

I think cell phone companies could make a fortune if they offered different "attitudes" for the voice, from sultry to sarcastic with everything in between. (They could pay off the national debt with the money men would spend on this.) Personally, I wish mine had a "New York" setting instead of the default one which bores the hell out of me. For instance, when I asked it how the New York Giants did after slaughtering the Packers, it responded in that robotic voice, "The Giants soundly defeated the Packers today, thirty-four to nothing." With a New York setting, it might, in a wicked nasal accent, say, "Fuhgeddaboudit! The Giants kicked the living shit out of the Packers, toity-foah to nuthin, an' sent dem cheeseheads back ta freeze their asses off in Wisconsin!"

So if I asked the Big Apple version of my phone, "What the hell do I do about Dexter Bishop?" it would reply, "What's your praaaab-lem? Wake up an' smell the cawfee! He's a catch! Are ya friggin' blind?"

No, I'm not. And sadly, there's no magic 8-ball to tell me what to do about this situation. Sure, I've got Savannah and Layla trying to help me sort it out, but it's still very confusing considering the recent revelation about his feelings for me. Besides, with all the other stuff going on in my life right now, the last thing I need is someone with a high school crush, especially someone who's going to be spending a lot of time up close and personal with me. I mean, I've got the French maid tape about to leak, which may or may not further my career. The local tabloids are having a field day with that paternity suit, as my sister has turned into a media magnet reaching DEFCON 2 on the Kardashian scale, with DEFCON 1 meaning she's cut a deal with Playboy. Rumor has it she's going to use her new fame to launch a line of lingerie called "Summerwear" which means my last name will be embroidered on thongs across the country. And I need to extend my stay off the vampire shift by kicking ass on *Dance Off.*

So, the answer to the question of "What do I do about Dexter Bishop?" is... wait for it... I don't know. While it is nice having the upper hand in that I know he has a "thing" for me, I'm not going to use Savannah's tactics because I'm not really interested. Definitely not. I mean, he's turned out to be a nice guy and all that, and he's smart, and he didn't take advantage of me that night I was hammered, and he defended my honor like some medieval knight, and he rescues broke waitresses, and he goes out of his way to do something special for kids who can't walk, and the locker room image of his chiseled chest is burned into my brain, and he looks right into my soul with those incredible eyes of his... but we're simply not compatible.

Yeah, let's go with that.

He was already warming up in the practice studio when I arrived. This was to be our first full dance practice, since he was light headed yesterday and we really didn't get anything done together. He simply put me through some steps, much as Bradley had done when we first started.

"How you feeling today?" I asked.

"I'm almost full strength. But it's a good thing we're pre-empted this week."

"We still going with the cha-cha?"

He shook his head. "I've changed my mind. I want something that's going to knock their socks off for our first time together, and the cha-cha isn't that hard. We're doing the mambo."

"But not the Bradley version, right?" I shot him a grin.

"Funny. No, this one will remain vertical." He reached for the stereo on the shelf and turned it on. The room filled with upbeat Latin music as he extended his hands. I moved toward him and took them. "The mambo is about the hips."

"Yours or mine?"

"Both. It is a very fast but sensual dance, and must convey the passion felt between the couple." Dexter pulled me a little closer and placed his hands gently on my waist. "Sway your hips in a circle."

I moved my body back and forth.

"No, no. Just your hips. Try to keep your upper body from moving." His grip on my waist got firm.

I did my best to keep my upper body in one place while moving my hips. "This reminds me of the hula hoop."

"Not quite, but you're on the right track." He looked down and slid his hands down my sides onto my hips. I felt a slight rush of electricity as he pushed my hips side to side. "More of an exaggerated motion."

He was close now, near enough for me to take in a breath of his musky cologne. He nodded in approval. "Now you're getting it."

"What about *your* hips?"

"Same thing." He moved closed and our bodies lightly touched as he began to sway his hips. His hands slid back to my waist. "Hands on my shoulders," he said.

"This part of the dance?"

"Just an exercise to get your muscle memory going."

Problem was, what we were doing had my muscle memory thinking back to my old boyfriend.

Three hours later, I was wiped out. I'd been lifted, twirled, flipped, dipped, you name it. If Dexter Bishop had wanted to take an inventory of my entire body with his hands, he'd done it. But for all the close contact, he never did anything that was unprofessional. You'd never know the guy had a crush on me. I may as well have been a seventy year old librarian. I had waited the entire session for one suggestive comment, one pass, one double entendre. Nothing.

He remained a perfect gentleman. As if he knew I wasn't interested and shouldn't take a shot.

I gotta admit, I felt a little, well... disappointed. I mean, I had some really snappy comebacks ready to launch. So I could stand there and let him *know* I had the upper hand. And then... nothing. Well, I did get that soulful look, which he apparently can't turn off. He had dipped me to end the dance and held me there, supporting my back as I bent backwards, for what seemed like an eternity, locking eyes with me. For a brief instant, and I do mean brief, I felt... I don't know, something I've never felt before.

Like I was welcoming him into my soul.

Chalk it up to being in close quarters with a very attractive man. I mean he's nice and—

Damn, I need to change the subject. Ya think?

Anyway, here's the other thing. I felt more comfortable dancing with him after one day than I did in all the weeks I spent with Bradley. That thing he said about two people becoming one on the dance floor... I felt it for the first time.

"You did well today," he said.

"You're a great teacher."

"Helps to have a talented student. So, miss Bradley?"

My face tightened. "Are you serious?"

"I meant his dancing. As a partner. How do we compare?"

"Well, you're very different. Bradley was more mechanical, with more repetition. With you... I don't know... you're fluid. It's like

what you talked about on day one... two dancers becoming one.
I never felt that with him."

"But you feel it now?"

"I *understand* it now."

Go ahead, say it.

Liar.

***

Savannah had told me the video would be sent out at midnight
on Saturday night. Every network executive and producer would
get a copy, as would every newspaper, magazine, major website,
political blogger, etc.

So at one minute before the witching hour, I pulled out my
cell and put it in the middle of my coffee table.

"T-minus one minute and counting," said Layla.

Savannah was on her cell with the person responsible for
sending out the tape. She nodded, smiled, and hung up on her
call. "It's on its way to everyone as we speak."

"Well, this is it," I said, raising my wine glass. "I hope we're
doing the right thing."

"To doing the right thing," said Savannah, as we all clicked
our glasses.

Layla patted my hand. "Don't worry, you are. Regardless of how
it turns out." She nodded toward my phone. "So how long before
you hear from someone at the network?"

I took a sip of sweet red, savoring the taste. "Within the hour,
I think. Gotta figure it'll take awhile for the old boys club at the
network to look at it. I'd love to be a fly on the wall 'cause they'll
look like they had a prostate exam with an eggbeater. Then there
will be some all night meetings with the heads of news and entertainment to figure out how to deal with the Senator and how to
spin the Bill Recker situation."

"Really? I figured they'd call everyone in the morning." asked

245

Layla.

"Hell, no. They'll have a gag order out within the hour. Because print people and the competition will start calling every employee at my network for a quote."

"Why is entertainment involved?" asked Savannah. "Wouldn't it just be a news division problem?"

I shook my head. "News is a cash cow. Cheap to produce, and brings in money to spend on entertainment. Same deal with The Morning Show."

"I sure hope this works out for you," said Layla.

"Speaking of things working out," said Savannah, "how are things going with Dexter?"

I knew where she wanted to go with this line of questioning, so I changed the topic. "He's an amazing dancer and a great teacher."

"I didn't mean on the dance floor."

"Well, that's all we're doing."

"Uh-huh."

"What, *uh-huh*?"

Layla jumped in. "Can we go over that checklist of the perfect man we had years ago?"

"What for?"

"I'm your best friend. Humor me." She looked up at the ceiling, as if searching for inspiration. "Ah, yes. Let me see. He had to be a gentleman, right?"

"Yeah. Still does."

"And Dexter is a gentleman. You've said so yourself. And he had to be kind, right?"

"Yes."

"Let's see. Now Savannah, would you say what he did for that girl in the wheelchair was a kind act?"

Savannah nodded. "I'd say it was incredibly kind."

"Guys—"

Layla put up her hand. "Let me finish. And he had to be old fashioned, the kind of guy who would protect you if necessary.

And since he ended up with stitches defending your honor, I'd say Dexter qualifies."

"You done?" I asked.

"Just about. If I remember correctly he had to be smart, driven, have a great career, and finally, be good looking. And he had to be head over heels for you."

I finally had enough. "Stop using logic on me!"

"Well, y'all are too stubborn to use it on yourself," said Savannah.

Layla reached out, took my hands and looked into my eyes. "You're fighting it, Veronica. Let yourself go. Put away the journalism credibility outfit and let the wave take you where it wants. Stop thinking with your head and follow your heart. Give the guy a chance."

"I'm not fighting anything."

"Yes you are," said Savannah. "Everyone can see it but you."

"You're a reporter," said Layla. "You know the truth when you see it, right?"

"Yeah."

"Then look in the mirror."

***

At three minutes to one, my cell rang.

It was Gavin.

"Hello?"

"Veronica, it's Gavin. Sorry to call you in the middle of the night and I hope I didn't wake you."

"Nah, I'm hanging out with my friends. What's up?"

"Listen, a major story has broken about Senator Dixon. She's apparently having an affair."

"Holy shit! Are you kidding me?"

"Nope, we've got video. It got dropped on us an hour ago and I understand every news organization in the country has it. Our tech guy already confirmed the video is legit. And you're not gonna believe who she's having an affair with."

"Someone else in Congress?"

"Nope. None other than our own Bill Recker."

"Damn, Gavin, that's unbelievable!

"You're telling me."

"Have you talked with Bill?"

"Not yet. His voice mail message says his mailbox is full. What a friggin' nightmare. And I thought the Katrina Favor situation was the worst I'd ever have to deal with."

"Jeez, Gavin, I'd hate to be in your shoes." At this point I smiled and flipped the bird at my phone. "So what is the network gonna do with him?"

"I don't know. I'm about to go into a conference call with the west coast people. We'll probably be up all night figuring out how to deal with this. Meanwhile, if anyone contacts you for a reaction—"

"Say nothing, got it. I have no idea what they're talking about and should refer them to the network's PR department."

"Which is conveniently closed on the weekend. We'll talk more tomorrow, Veronica. Right now we gotta decide how we'll handle this on the Sunday morning show."

"Okay, Gavin, thanks for the heads up." I hung up and smiled at my friends. "Okay, the shit has hit the fan. Now I have to hope none of it gets on me."

CHAPTER THIRTY-TWO

Were it not eight in the morning, this would call for popcorn, chips, guacamole and a barbecue.

Alas, I needed one of the basic food groups for breakfast, so I would have to settle for a mimosa while watching the Sunday morning shows.

I'd set the DVR to tape every network, but we were going to start with mine.

Layla and Savannah had spent the night, an old fashioned slumber party. Scott had dropped by an hour ago with bagels, croissants, fruit, and all sorts of delicassies to make this the ultimate Sunday brunch. Those in the news business love to cheer on a good fall from grace, especially when it involves a previously squeaky clean politician. When there's a burning at the stake, we bring the marshmallows.

We'd already had plenty of stuff to read, as papers were strewn across the floor of my living room. Every newspaper's front page was plastered with a screen grab of Margaux's surveillance tape featuring Senator Dixon grabbing Bill Recker in the crotch. Best headline: "Home Recker", which was accompanied by a cartoon of our anchor reading from the set with the Senator under the desk wearing a Cheshire cat grin and a bib, smiling. Though "Recking Ball" wasn't bad either, with our anchor doing a Miley

Cyrus impression.

I hadn't had much sleep. Can you blame me? This was an anxiety filled Christmas morning, since I didn't know if I'd find the ultimate gift under the tree or a stocking full of coal.

We all took our places in front of the television armed with drinks and sustenance. I practically inhaled a croissant topped with raspberry preserves, my stress already burning through calories at an alarming rate. The moment I finished that pastry I reached for a bagel.

"You trying to make the weight?" cracked Scott.

"Just nervous," I said, as guilt forced me to grab a bowl of fruit instead. I saw the network animation for the Sunday morning show fly across the screen, so I fired the remote at the TV and turned up the sound. "Here we go."

The animation dissolved into the serious face of Jack Krenshaw, the elder white-haired statesman of the network who'd spent forty years covering Washington and had moderated the Sunday morning show for two decades. "Good morning, Americans. If you've already picked up your Sunday paper from the driveway you know the top story today is a bombshell which not only has rocked the political landscape but also this network. The video you're about to see is not suitable for children and you might find it offensive."

"Still the best tease in television news," said Scott. He was right. Nothing makes viewers stop dead in their tracks than the notion that disturbing video is coming up.

The anchor voiced-over the video as it rolled. "Late last night this videotape was released showing Presidential candidate Senator Sydney Dixon in what appears to be a hotel bedroom with this network's main evening anchor, Bill Recker." The video rolled, looking impressive on my giant flat screen television.

"For a French maid, you're not a bad photographer," said Layla.

The anchor continued. "Our technology experts confirm that the tape is legit and has not been tampered with. So far, we've had no comment from Senator Dixon or her campaign, though we understand there might be a statement later in the day or tomorrow morning. As for Mister Recker, we're joined now by the President of our news division, William Fincastle. Sir, thanks for joining us this morning."

"I would say it was my pleasure, Jack, but this has been a very upsetting night for all of us at the network. To say I'm shocked by the behavior of one of our oldest and most trusted employees is putting it mildly."

"I understand you've talked with Bill Recker."

Fincastle nodded. "Yes. He was very apologetic and may or may not make a statement of his own at a later time. He admitted to the affair with the Senator, which has apparently been going on for a long time. He and I both agreed that his intimate involvement with a Presidential candidate has severely tarnished his credibility. That said, he tendered his resignation early this morning."

"Did you ask for it?"

"I didn't have to."

"Yeah, right," said Scott. "Fincastle would have waterboarded him to get him to quit."

"How do you feel about all this?" asked the anchor.

"Look, we can't expect the viewers to trust an anchor who can't be trusted by his own wife."

"Ouch," said Savannah. "That one left a mark."

"C'mon," I said. "Ask Fincastle who gets *The Chair*."

"So," said the host, "where does this leave the network as far as a main anchor is concerned?"

I leaned forward. "Here it comes."

"It's too soon to make a permanent decision," said Fincastle, "as we have to weigh our options. We of course were planning to have Bill Recker anchor our evening news for a few more years until his retirement. For the time being we'll go with substitutes, as we have a deep bench at the network. Unless, Jack, you want to move to New York."

The host smiled and shook his head. "Happy right here in DC, but thank you for the offer."

The rest of the show was a political feeding frenzy, as the sharks in Washington smelled blood in the water. While media people enjoy the fall from grace, politicians will provide the shove off the cliff. The other party slammed Senator Dixon for being a hypocrite while speculation was already running rampant from her own party as to who might be the candidate in the next election since she was now "unelectable."

After our show ended we watched the others. Of course the competing networks piled on big time, one even coming up with a montage of clips showing Recker's now obvious bias toward the Senator.

By the time we were done one anchorman's career and reputation had sunk like a stone while a slam dunk Presidential campaign had hit an iceberg and was taking on water. With my future possibly stuck in steerage.

"So, what happens now?" asked Layla as I turned off the TV.

"They put Jeff Garlen in as anchor for right now," said Scott. "Knowing him, he was down at the network this morning starting his campaign. Luckily we're not in ratings so they don't have to make an immediate decision. Besides, Veronica still has a month left on *Dance Off*."

Savannah turned to me. "How do you think it went?"

"Well, I thought they'd simply fire Bill Recker, but the outcome is the same. The fact that Fincastle was non-committal about his replacement was good. I think." I turned to Scott. "You think I should call Gavin today?"

He shook his head. "Play it cool for now. Garlen is going to be hounding management all day. You should be the one to act professional."

So I was supposed to do the right thing again.

That wouldn't necessarily get me the dream job. Because acting professional with people who weren't might not be the right way to go.

I didn't have to play it cool very long. Gavin called late Sunday afternoon.

"How's your day going?" I asked.

"Finally going home to get some sleep. I was here all night. Listen, I need you to come in at six-thirty tomorrow morning. We need you to be live."

"Something special?"

"I can't talk about it."

What the hell was this? Were they going to announce me as Recker's replacement? Were they going to have me announce someone else as Recker's replacement?

"How about a hint?" I asked.

"Sorry," said Gavin. "See you tomorrow." He ended the call.

Oh, shit, another sleepless night.

I tried to act casual as I entered the newsroom Monday morning but my heart was a triphammer. Gavin was talking with Scott, who spotted me and shot me a worried look that told me something wasn't going well. Gavin smiled as he noticed me. "Come with me to the green room," he said.

"What's in the green room?"

"You'll see in a minute."

He led me across the hall to the lavish waiting room. When he opened the door and I saw who was inside, my jaw dropped.

Senator Sydney Dixon.

And her husband.

"I'll leave you to chat for a minute," said Gavin, "then get over to makeup."

"Sure," I said, as he left and closed the door.

"Hi Veronica," said the Senator, with very little life in her voice. Her face was drawn, eyes bloodshot. Her husband sat next to her, holding her hand while looking like someone who was in mourning. "This is my husband, Francis."

I nodded and said nothing to him, as, "Nice to meet you" would have made no sense. "I must say, I'm surprised to find you here," I said.

"I needed to come clean," she said. "And you're the most unbiased journalist I know."

"So you wanna do a Bill and Hillary thing on the couch, like 60 Minutes?"

She nodded. He looked at the floor.

"Fine," I said. "Just know I'm not throwing softballs this morning."

"Wouldn't expect you to," she said. But her eyes begged me to do the opposite.

While you don't kick someone when they're down, that rule doesn't apply to journalism. Besides, she made her own bed. Literally.

***

After getting made up I pulled Scott into his office and shut the door. "I can't believe she picked our show for this," he said.

"When did you find out?"

"About two minutes before you walked in. Gavin obviously knew about it yesterday."

"Why didn't the network promote the hell out of it?"

"He said he didn't want the competition to know they were in town and be waiting outside the door with a limo for them to make the morning show rounds. And the Senator insisted it be kept quiet because she only wants to do this once. Let's face it, the other networks are going to hammer her anyway."

"Good point. How do you think I should handle this?"

"Well, it's not like you're breaking the story, so women aren't going to blame you for taking her down. I'd be tough but fair. But don't hold anything back."

"Wasn't planning to."

"You do realize this is probably the most important interview you'll ever do. So do it like you're the next main anchor. *Gravitas.*"

***

Senator Dixon was doing her best to put on a brave face as she sat next to her husband on the couch opposite me. Scott had opened the show with the announcement that they were the guests, then he tossed it to me.

"Thank you, Scott. Senator Sydney Dixon and her husband Francis join us this morning. Thank you both for coming by."

"Thank you for giving us the opportunity," she said. Her husband said nothing.

"Let's get right to it. How long has this affair with Bill Recker been going on?"

She bit her lower lip. "About three years."

"Francis, did you have any idea this was happening?"

He shook his head. "No," he said softly.

"Have you two been having marital problems?"

"I didn't think so," said Francis, his eyes filled with hurt. "But obviously she had a different point of view."

"Senator?"

"I love Francis a great deal," she said. "I'm away from home a lot and... well, I made an error in judgment."

I wanted to roll my eyes at this standard *mea culpa* from a cheating politician, but resisted. "Senator, with all due respect, an error in judgment is painting the kitchen the wrong color. You cheated on your husband. That's not an error in judgment. It's breaking a sacred vow, and judging by the look on your husband's face, something that has hurt him a great deal."

Her eyes widened and began to grow misty, as she obviously expected me to buy the "error in judgment" thing. "I don't know what else to say," she said. "It was a terrible thing to do. You don't have to tell me that I've hurt my husband, I already know that."

"And considering you had an affair with a very influential member of the media, I have to ask... what was the motive? You've already been accused of doing this to curry favorable coverage during the campaign."

"It was... uh... just two people who made a huge mistake. It had nothing to do with bias. There was no motive to get favorable coverage from him during the campaign."

"Francis, are you two planning to stay together?"

He nodded. "We'll get through this." But his eyes told me he was lying and probably had agreed to stay with her through the campaign, if she still had one.

"Do you still love her?"

Short pause. "Of course."

"What about the campaign, Senator?" I asked. "Are you still running for President?"

"The campaign is suspended for the time being," she said. "We plan to take time to fix our marriage and then we'll see what happens."

"If you do still run, do you think the American people will trust you?"

"Americans believe in second chances," she said. "History has proven that with politics."

"But we've never before had a female politician who's been unfaithful. Do you think there will be a double standard?"

She paused a moment, looked down, then back up at me. "I can't answer that."

"One more question. You seemed to have the world by the tail and were a slam dunk to be the next President of the United States. Women all over the country were excited about the prospect of the first female President. And you seemed to have the perfect family. I hate to be blunt, but this is the question everyone wants answered. How could you jeopardize all of that by doing something so incredibly stupid?"

CHAPTER THIRTY-THREE

VERONICA SUMMER: CROSSING THE LINE OR SIMPLY ASKING THE OBVIOUS?

By Jen Harlen

When The Morning Show host Veronica Summer asked unfaithful wife Sydney Dixon what is now known as "the question" many of us were taken aback as much as the Senator, whose face jerked like she'd been hit with a blow dart.

But was Ms. Summer simply asking the question we all were thinking?

"How could you jeopardize all of that by doing something so incredibly stupid?"

The general protocol among journalists when asking a pointed question is to preface it with, "With all due respect." (Which we all know actually means, "You're full of it, but I'm trying to be classy and not say it.") In this case, Ms. Summer threw high heat at the politician, instead of the usual softballs lobbed by many so-called journalists.

The response was almost as surprising as the question. The Senator, obviously shocked at the blunt nature of the question, said nothing for a full five seconds until her husband finally ended the pregnant pause by saying, "We all make mistakes." (The guy gets newly minted Tammy Wynette "Stand By Your Woman" award.)

The reaction to the interview brought a lot of strong opinions. Some politicians in the Senator's party seemed to think Ms. Summer crossed the line, while viewers overwhelmingly supported her style of holding nothing back.

"I don't tell my anchors or reporters what questions to ask or how to ask them," said The Morning Show's Executive Producer Gavin Karlson. "Every politician should know Veronica Summer is a tough journalist, and if they're looking for softballs they need to join a beer league. I think she asked what we all were thinking. And for those who think we give politicians questions in advance, I think the Senator's reaction told you we don't do that at this network."

Sources say the Senator stormed off the set and out the back door after the live interview. We're told she selected The Morning Show figuring she'd get a fair shake instead of other network offerings which have traditionally supported the other party.

Ms. Summer was not available for comment, but her co-anchor Scott Winter chimed in. "Any politician who thinks they're going to get special treatment from Veronica should think twice. She's always been a tough reporter but a fair one. And what she asked was a tough but fair question."

So, had I passed the *gravitas* test? Time will tell. Scott spent the rest of the morning using his private bathroom snooping device and found out the network is planning to give the current sub a month to see how the ratings play out. Interesting timing, since that's the same amount of time I have left on *Dance Off*.

Which means the decision may be out of my hands, and in those of the viewers.

But he did say the network's *old boys club* was impressed with my interview.

Meanwhile, back to my dancing shoes.

***

After three days of rehearsal with Dexter, I felt like a professional tonight as I prepared for the competition. Not a professional like my sister, but a professional dancer.

I couldn't believe how he'd taken my dancing to the next level. Working with him was so easy, so natural, with a fluidity that usually only comes with someone you've known a long time. He seemed to know my moves perfectly, and how to guide me through them flawlessly.

Still, he hadn't said anything that would even hint he was interested in me.

Though I'd gotten *the look* every day when he dipped me at the end of the routine.

During our last rehearsal this afternoon he'd held me longer than normal, maybe five seconds. I found myself not saying anything, just staring into his spectacular eyes. Then he broke the trance, blushed, shook his head as if to clear it, and said, "Uh... excellent rehearsal, Veronica."

Had he asked me out, I doubt if I could have remembered a snappy comeback.

Layla's wave was lapping the shore, and I felt myself being pulled in.

I couldn't get the look out of my head as I took one final glance in the dressing room mirror. The emerald green sequined halter dress was flashy and showed a good deal of leg when I twirled, but nothing approaching skimpy. I looked at the clock, saw that we just had a few minutes left and headed for the green room, where I found Dexter waiting with another couple.

He smiled as I entered. "You look stunning," he said.

"So do you," I said, admiring his outfit. An open collared pale green shirt and dark slacks.

A production assistant entered and called out the other couple, leaving us alone in the room. We were to be last in the competition.

"You should know," he said, "that viewers are licking their chops waiting to get even with me for all the snarky comments over the years. So if we're eliminated, it's nothing you've done. It's not you, it's me."

"We're *not* going to be eliminated," I said. "They like me more than they dislike you." I shot him a wicked smile.

"You certainly have a unique way of looking at things. Though I would surmise you're probably right."

"We're also the best dancers."

"Excellent point."

We turned our attention to the monitor as the other couple started their routine. They were good, but not great, and I knew we could beat them. Hell, our rehearsals had been better than all the couples I'd seen. It was just a matter of not screwing up.

For whatever reason, I knew that was impossible.

If I simply let myself go.

***

The first three minutes of the dance went flawlessly. I never looked at my feet once, didn't have a single misstep, and glided around the floor as Dexter guided my moves. We were incredibly fluid. I'd even managed a sultry expression, which he said was essential to conveying the meaning of the dance. Even the viewers who hated Dexter would have to admit we'd blown away the competition.

With thirty seconds to go we were a slam dunk to not only avoid elimination, but to get the highest score of the night.

It went off without a hitch.

He dipped me, held me there.

The music stopped.

Again with *the look*.

Suddenly, something happened to me that had never happened

261

before.

Everything disappeared. The studio, the crowd, the judges... the rest of the world did not exist.

My God, those eyes...

I felt my head raise up, our eyes still locked, my lips parting slightly to meet his—

"Earth to Veronica and Dexter!"

The judge's words snapped us out of the trance. The rest of the world flooded back as we whipped our heads toward the judges, who were all smiling. The crowd was delirious, on its feet. Dexter raised me up to a standing position and we headed toward the judges.

I couldn't be sure, but I'm guessing my face matched my hair.

***

This time I beat Dexter to the alley at the back door. I leaned against the brick, much as he had done, my heart skipping a beat each time the door opened, then downshifting when I saw it was someone else.

I had to know. And I had to know *right now*. Suddenly I was a reporter on a major story, needing the one piece of information that served as confirmation. And I was ready to let the story take me wherever it wanted to go.

Finally, he stepped out into the night, dressed in his usual suit and tie.

"Mind telling me what just happened out there?" I asked.

He turned his head and offered a soft, shy smile as he walked in my direction. "I could ask you the same thing."

"I asked you first."

He moved forward until he was standing before me. I moved slightly closer, dipping my head and looking up at him through my eyelashes, giving him my bad little girl look. "Don't you ever let a woman take the lead?"

"On the dance floor, no."

"How about off the dance floor?"

He shrugged. "Depends on the woman."

"Oh, really? And what sort of woman would be the type that would be allowed to lead?"

"Hmmm. Well, she would have to have a combination of qualities. Obviously she'd have to be very confident, because she would need the resolve to take the lead. It would be nice if she were independent, and smart. Able to take care of herself but not minding if a man offered to play a traditional role. She would have a career, one that she was passionate about. Generally women who are passionate about their work are the same about love. And she would have a life force that is off the charts, with a fire in her eyes that could never be put out."

"I see. You didn't mention anything about the woman's appearance. About what your *type* might be."

"There's the problem. You see, Veronica, some women are so incredibly beautiful that I find myself unable to think straight."

"You seemed to think straight around Savannah, and she blows me away in the looks department. I'm not even in her league."

"Ah, Veronica, but the overall beauty is more than just physical. It's the total package, with all the qualities I just outlined. And in that case, it is actually preferable if the woman would take the lead."

So if this was going to happen, it had to be my decision.

I had to know.

I moved closer, ran my hands under his jacket and up his chest. I heard him inhale quickly. "So, you're telling me certain women can render you powerless? As if they're made of some sort of sexual Kryptonite?"

"That's... uh... quite a good analogy."

I snaked my arms around his neck and locked my fingers. "And turn the great Dexter Bishop into a shy high school boy afraid to make the first move?"

He gulped. "There you go again. Trying to lead."

"Damn straight." I grabbed his necktie with one hand, gently pulled him toward me, leaned up and kissed him, long and hard, not caring if the paparazzi or anyone saw us, because just as it had been on the dance floor, the world around us disappeared.

I broke the embrace and looked around. Dead silence. No one was watching.

I turned back to Dexter and got *the look* again.

"So," I said. "Let's mambo. My place... or mine?"

***

I woke up from what seemed to have been the best sleep of my life. The sun was already sending fingers of light into my bedroom while the clock told me it was almost nine. No big deal, I had the day off.

I rolled over and saw the other side of the bed was empty.

Oh, you've gotta be kidding.

Typical man.

They're all the same. Well, nice while it lasted.

I shook my head, got up, grabbed my robe, wrapped it around me and headed for the kitchen.

The smell of frying bacon greeted me as I opened the bedroom door.

I quickly moved down the hall and saw Dexter, clad in only boxer shorts, busy cooking in my kitchen.

He looked up and smiled. "Good morning. I didn't want to wake you. You looked so peaceful."

"You're here."

He shrugged. "Where else would I be?"

"And you're cooking breakfast."

"Well, I was starving. I've had to get a little creative since your cupboard was a bit bare, but I think this will suffice."

I moved toward the cooking island and saw he had several pots and pans going. "What are you making?"

"Crepes. Bacon. A few other goodies." He noticed a little flour on his chest and brushed it off. "Oh, I couldn't find an apron."

Yeah, like I wanna cover him up. "I have one, but I'm not giving it to you."

He actually blushed a bit. "Leading again, I see."

"You seemed to like it last night."

He offered a soft smile as the buzzer on the oven went off. He turned, opened it, pulled out a cookie sheet, and set it on the counter.

My eyes went wide. "You made biscuits? From scratch?"

"They're not very difficult. I would have made croissants but you were out of butter."

"So, is there anything you can't do?"

"As I said last evening, I am rather powerless around a certain woman."

I smiled, quickly moved forward and wrapped my arms around him, laying my head on his chest. He put one arm around my shoulders. "So, were you ever gonna make the first move?"

"Probably not. Fear of rejection, which I was reasonably sure of in your case."

I leaned back and looked up at him. "*You're* afraid of rejection? You can have any woman on the planet."

"Veronica, underneath it all I'm like any other man. And I didn't want *any* woman on the planet. I wanted a *specific* woman."

"Me?"

He nodded.

"After the way I treated you? I was a total bitch."

"You thought the real me was the persona I portray on television. I would surmise you finally realized I'm nothing of the sort."

"Yeah. I surmised. Took me awhile, but I got there. With a lotta help from my friends. I'm a little stubborn, in case you hadn't noticed."

"I hadn't. Perhaps I should call your network to break into programming with a news bulletin to that effect. We interrupt our regularly scheduled program to tell you Veronica Summer is an immovable object."

"Smart ass."

"Alas, you're also an irresistible force. I realized the tough, take-no-prisoners journalist is the persona you portray, not the real Veronica. You simply couldn't turn it off after hours."

"You're right about that. Still, I'm curious. Why me?"

"You still don't get it, do you?"

"Get what?"

"Why you're so special."

"No, I honestly don't. Enlighten me."

"Because I felt *it*."

"*It*?"

"You're not only the *It Girl* for the show, but you have the intangible my heart craves."

"And that intangible would be...?"

"Don't know. But you're the only woman I've ever met who has it. Perhaps it's the fire in your eyes, your life force, your incredible mind, your bold personality, your independence, your cute little freckles. A combination of everything. One cannot define attraction. One cannot define *it*. And you're my *It Girl*."

"For what it's worth, I felt *it* last night too."

"Still feel *it* this morning? Or was I simply a bit of exercise?"

"You don't get off that easy, Mister. *It* is still there."

He smiled as he turned off the burners on the cooktop. "So, hungry?"

"Are you kidding? I had the *full English* last night."

CHAPTER THIRTY-FOUR

An hour later I was trying my best not to look like I was walking on air when Hal's voice cut through the sounds of the city.

"So, why didn't you just kiss him?"

The newsstand guy smiled at me as he handed me the morning papers. "I wasn't planning to."

"Pfffft. Yeah, right. I suppose it was all part of the routine."

"It was."

"Right. And denial is a river in Egypt. Veronica, I've been married too long to miss something that obvious. You've got it bad for that guy, and the whole world knows it. I got a high-def TV, you know. I can see your eyes. And you got the look."

"What look?"

"The woman-in-love look."

I actually wanted to tell the world about the new relationship, to shout it from the rooftops, but it wasn't the time. And I had a ways to go before saying the 'L' word anyway. Plus, I knew Dexter valued his privacy as much as I did. "Believe what you want, Hal."

"Sure, kiddo. Just make sure I get a wedding invitation." He glanced at the small portable television he always had playing in the newsstand. "Hey, isn't that your old partner?"

He pointed at the screen which was filled with Bradley's face.

My pulse spiked when I saw the graphic below.

***

I was out of breath as I jammed the key in my door and shoved it open.

Dexter was gone.

I saw a note on the kitchen table and quickly ran to it.

Veronica,
Had to put out a fire at the network. Will call later.
-Dex

Just as I finished reading my cell rang. I saw it was Layla. "Hey."

"You got your TV on?"

"No, why?"

"Put it on."

"Which channel?"

"All of them."

I ran to the living room, grabbed the remote and fired it at the television. The screen cleared and filled with Dexter's face. "How long has this been on?"

"Just started."

"Call you later." I hung up and turned up the sound.

Dexter was beginning a news conference from the lobby of his production office. And, from the looks of things the sharks were in the water.

"Thank you for coming," he said. "I'll make a short statement, and then take questions. This morning, a former employee of our production accused *Dance Off* of not being on the level, saying that the outcome of the show was pre-determined. As the Executive Producer of the show I stand before you today to categorically deny those accusations. They are simply the ramblings of a disgruntled former employee who was recently let go due to a violation of our morals clause. While the outcome of *Dance Off* has always been up to the judges and the viewers, their opinions are subjective. You may not always agree with the choice of the winning couple, or with those voted off each week, but the competition has always been on the up and up. I'll now take your questions."

The horde of reporters fired questions at the same time. One cut through the chatter. "Bradley says the voting process is rigged, that the viewers' votes mean nothing. How do you respond?"

"As has been the case from the beginning of the program, the viewers' votes have counted as a percentage of the final tally. Anyone who has watched the show will notice that when we flash the numbers on the bottom of the screen, there is a notation clearly stating that the viewers' votes do not comprise one hundred percent of the vote. The judges' votes are factored in as well."

"Why not let the viewers' votes count for one hundred percent?"

"Well, a few years ago there was a similar talent show with a contestant who was just dreadful. An internet campaign was mounted to gather votes on his behalf; an electronic flash mob if you will, designed to make a mockery of the competition by keeping the worst contestants on the show. Our system prevents that from happening. Having the judges' input factored in with the viewers' votes is a fail-safe method. Should we ever see an obvious anomaly in the viewers votes, the judges would have the right to overrule."

"And you were one of the judges until a week ago."

"Yes."

"Was there ever an occasion where you had to employ that fail-safe method?"

"Thankfully, no. But my input, as well as that of the other judges, was always factored in. In many cases a contestant may have been the top choice of the viewers but not the judges, or vice versa. You add everything up and get the results. It's the same as many beauty pageants that incorporate votes from viewers. It's just part of our interactive society."

"Bradley claims he got this information from Veronica Summer, who was told she didn't have to worry about being voted off the first week."

Oh, shit.

Dexter nodded.

Ho-lee shit.

I broke out in a cold sweat. Had I sabotaged something wonderful?

"That is true," said Dexter. "But let me explain. You don't want a contestant walking on eggshells, or in this case, dancing on them, worrying about being voted off. I surmised that she would be more relaxed if she believed she could not be voted off, and it worked. However, had she been dreadful, she would have been shown the door."

"Bradley says you always put him with a contestant who had no chance of winning."

"Well, up until this week he'd been dancing with Miss Summer, and I'm sure you'll agree she has an excellent chance of winning."

"Speaking of Miss Summer, did you think she was going to kiss you last night?"

He shook his head and smiled. "Of course not. It was part of the routine. The mambo is a sensual dance so we thought we'd have a little fun and tease the viewers. And we did end up with the highest score of the evening."

"So you two aren't dating?"

He shook his head. "She's merely my dance partner. Nothing more."

Ouch.

The news conference ended and I turned off the television.

A single tear rolled down my cheek.

I was the source of the problem.

More important, was I *merely his dance partner* now?

***

My heart hadn't stopped pounding. I flew out of the cab and ran into the production building. "He's expecting me," I said to the receptionist, who waved me on but didn't smile.

Uh-oh.

Everyone's blaming me for this.

I'll be lucky if he even speaks to me.

The elevator seemed to be taking forever to get to the penthouse floor. "C'mon, c'mon, c'mon!" I paced around the car until it came to a stop and the door finally opened, revealing Dexter on the phone behind his desk.

He didn't look pleased. He looked up at me and didn't smile.

"Yes, it will blow over," he said, to whoever he was talking with on the phone. "Yes, Sir. I think the viewers see this for what it is, a former employee being angry. Yes, thank you. Chat soon."

He hung up and exhaled deeply, then looked at me.

I moved quickly toward him. "Dexter, I am so, so sorry. When I told Bradley all that stuff I was mad at you—"

He put up his hand. "I understand."

I bit my lower lip and started to cry. "I can't believe he did this and put you in this position. I know you probably hate me."

He reached out, took my shoulders and pulled me close. I wrapped my arms around him and my emotions exploded as I buried my head in his chest. He started to gently stroke my hair and kissed the side of my head. "It's not that bad, Veronica."

I leaned back and looked up at him. "Not that bad? This is a huge scandal!"

He wiped away my tears with his thumb and offered a soft smile. "It's just an entertainment show. It's not like we're doing brain surgery here. Trust me, this will blow over."

"I can't believe you're not furious with me."

"Why on earth would I be furious with you?"

"Duh, because I'm the cause of this problem. I put you in a horrible position."

"And I just got through explaining it all to the media. It's done.

Everyone will see through Bradley's motivation."

"What about the part where I found out I couldn't get voted off the show?"

"That was absolutely true in your case. You needed confidence in your dancing, and you would do better if you honestly believed you wouldn't get voted off. It's been done before with other contestants. Trust me, if you'd been dreadful you would have been gone. Even the network wouldn't keep you on if you were obviously the worst dancer, because that *would* have made the show appear to be fixed. They asked me to do everything I could to keep you on, as they've done with other contestants, so we simply got you in a confident mood. And I also think you wanted to succeed to get back at me."

"But when I let you know that I might reveal the show was fixed, you looked scared."

"Even the accusation from a respected journalist would have been devastating. Do we give more help to contestants we know are popular with viewers? Absolutely. And we pair them with the best dancers. If that means the show is fixed, then I'm guilty as charged."

"No, I'm the guilty one."

"Please stop beating yourself up, Veronica. Everything's fine."

"You're honestly not mad at me?"

"Veronica, I finally got the woman I've been enchanted with to notice me. Why on earth would I be upset over something so trivial?"

"It's not trivial."

"In the grand scheme of things, it is. We all make mistakes, we all do things we regret. None of that changes the qualities I admire in you."

"So I'm not *merely your dance partner* like you told reporters?"

"After the wonderful night we just spent? You shouldn't have to ask that question. You need to learn to separate my television persona from the real me. Look, I knew you didn't want our relationship to go public. It's just a bit of misdirection. I certainly hope I didn't hurt your feelings." His eyes looked right into my soul and gave it a hug. My eyes welled up again and I started to cry. "Oh dear, apparently I have hurt your feelings. Veronica, please don't be upset with me."

"I'm not upset," I said, hugging him tighter. "Typical man. You don't understand tears of joy."

CHAPTER THIRTY FIVE

ONE MONTH LATER

We all have days that can significantly change our lives. From big forks in the road to the smallest decisions, at some point we can all look back and replay the times when our lives took a turn for the better or worse.

This was one of those days.

It was the last episode of *Dance Off*, and I was one of the two finalists. But whether I go home with a garish trophy or not won't affect my career.

It was also the day when the network would make a decision about who gets *The Chair*. The current sub has had a month, and the ratings are really no different than Bill Recker's, which weren't great to start with. So I think I've got a pretty good shot. Of course, neither Gavin nor any of the higher-ups has told me this will be a red letter day. I'm simply going on Scott's bathroom surveillance. So tonight I might be the happiest dancer ever on *Dance Off*.

Or the most depressed.

Of course, if it's the latter, I have a very special man who I know will be able to cheer me up. And if it's the former, I have a very special man who will hit the jackpot in the bedroom when we get home.

Yes, the last month has been the proverbial whirlwind romance. I simply cannot believe how much we have in common and how compatible we are. Once I took off my journalism hat and let Layla's wave take me I finally realized what everyone else did. We really enjoy teaching each other fun stuff about our respective cultures. Amazingly we've been able to keep the relationship quiet and out of the tabloids, though once *Dance Off* is over we won't be able to use that as our excuse for being together.

But pretty soon I won't care if the whole world knows.

While neither of us has said the "L" word, we know it's inevitable. I already feel it, and I think he does as well. I, of course, have been stubborn (so what else is new?), having never been the one to say it first. Seriously, is there anything worse than saying "I love you" and having the other person not say it back? Talk about high risk. He's still the shy high school boy when we're alone, having that fear of rejection demon lurking in the back of his head. Some babe must have done a real number on his head when he was younger. Can you believe the most desirable man on earth is afraid of losing *me*? I sure can't. I'm nothing special, but he seems to think I am.

Not that I'm complaining.

I'd just gotten off the set when Gavin walked through the studio. "Veronica, can I see you for a minute?"

This was it.

"Sure," I said, trying my best not to let him know my heart rate was off the charts. I followed him to his office. He opened the door, gestured toward the chair in front of his desk. I took a seat as he closed the door and sat down behind his desk. I grabbed the arms of the chair and began to squeeze the life out of them.

"Okay," he said, folding his hands on his desk. "I wanted you to hear this from me before the gossip train gets rolling."

Here it comes.

"I'm not going to be producing The Morning Show any longer."

"Oh." This is *not* the news I want right now. Personally, I couldn't care less if Gavin is leaving to become a toll collector on the Jersey Turnpike. "Well, it's been nice working with you. Where are you going?"

"I'm not going anywhere. The network has reassigned me." He flashed a big smile. "I've been named as the new producer of the evening newscast."

"Wow. Well, congratulations, I know you'll do a fine job." C'mon, tell me, yes or no! "So, who will I be working with?"

"You'll be working with me." His smile got bigger as I realized what he was saying.

"Are you kidding me?"

"Veronica, it's my pleasure today to offer you the lead anchor position on the evening news. You're going to be the face of the network."

***

I blew through the door of the practice studio, knowing Dexter would be there early before the cameras were turned on. He was working on some dance moves. He saw me and smiled as I ran toward him, jumped into his arms and wrapped my legs around his waist.

"Well, if you miss me this much after just a few hours I should go away for a weekend."

"I got it!"

"Got what?"

"Duh! The job! The main anchor job with the network! No more mornings, no more crazy hours!" I hugged him as tight as possible, then gave him a big kiss. "You just kissed the most powerful woman in television news."

"I think you had that title before."

"Smart ass."

"That's wonderful news, Veronica, I know this means a lot to you and I'm thrilled for you. Congratulations. We'll have to celebrate after the show tonight."

I wanted to take him right then and there. "Damn, I wanna celebrate right now!"

"The floor is a bit hard."

"Yeah, and we have to rehearse, I know. But get ready for the best night of your life, Mister."

***

I was bouncing up and down on the balls of my feet in the green room as we watched our competition. I had to admit, they were fabulous, and their mash-up routine of music and different styles of dance was spectacular. Dexter had put together clips of songs that would show off our strong points, and the rehearsals had gone flawlessly. But it would be hard to beat what I was watching.

What the hell, nothing could ruin this night.

A production assistant stuck his head in the door. "Five minutes."

"Thank you."

The guy stood there in the doorway. "We're sure gonna miss you around here, Mister Bishop."

"I'll miss being here," he said. The production guy nodded and left.

What the hell was this? "What was he talking about?" I asked.

"This is my last show."

"Yeah, of the season."

"No, in the American version. You knew that."

"No, I didn't. And I'm not sure I understand why this is your last show if you're the star of the highest rated show on the network."

"Veronica, everyone knows I've been on loan from British television."

"Well, *I* didn't know that." Suddenly I was getting concerned. "Wait a minute. If you're on loan... does that mean... you're going back to London?"

He nodded. "Veronica, I'm so sorry, but I hadn't any idea you didn't know."

"I never watched your show or even knew who you were before this. How would I know? When are you going back?"

"In a few weeks."

"And you didn't think to discuss this with me?"

"Honestly, things were going so well I've been avoiding the subject... and I assumed you were doing the same. I knew we'd have to deal with it eventually, but I didn't want to put a damper on things until absolutely necessary."

My mouth hung open. I couldn't believe it. "So, you're going back there to host the British version of *Dance Off?*"

"Yes."

"Dexter, can't you just quit?"

"I'm under contract, Veronica."

"Yeah, but you've got millions."

"Those people gave me my big break. And if I should leave, the show will collapse. There are almost eighty employees of the show who are depending on me. I know a girl with a heart as big as yours wouldn't want me to leave all those chaps out of work."

Dammit, I hate when other people hit me with stuff that makes sense. "The needs of the many outweigh the needs of the few," I muttered. "Or the one."

"I'm not sure Mister Spock's logic applies here."

"You know Star Trek?"

"It's the famous line from Wrath of Khan. Though in your case, I must meet your needs as well. They are not outweighed, they are equal. The needs of the one will be taken care of."

"So... did you have any sort of plan regarding our relationship?"

"It involves private jets on weekends and long distance video chats during the week. While the show is in production for four months. After that, I can live here for eight."

"Four months? And what happens if you fly over here and the network has me somewhere else?" I felt myself begin to tremble.

He took my shoulders and pulled me close.

"Veronica, we'll work this out. True love always finds a way."

A tap on the door broke our embrace. The production assistant stuck his head in. "You're up."

Dancing was the last thing I felt like doing.

***

The mash-up Dexter had put together was nothing short of brilliant. We were to start slow, pick things up, slow down, speed up, then end with something soft. And as luck would have it, every damn song seemed to have been written for me; about lost loves, taking chances, soul mates. If I wasn't so upset I would have gotten a cavity. The first song was Donna Summer's "On the Radio" which starts slow and then morphs into a quick disco tune while talking about relationships. Then a bunch of short clips showcasing the mambo, jitterbug, and meringue. After that another song that started slow and picked up, Madonna's "Like a Prayer," the lyrics of which always made me emotional. The final tune was Bette Midler's "The Rose" which took care of the people afraid to take chances on love. As an added touch we were to end up at a specific spot on the stage, with Dexter on one knee so he could pick up a single rose that had been placed there and hand it to me as the song ended with its slow piano instrumental.

As before, the rest of the world disappeared as the music started. I heard the music, the muscle memory kicked in flawlessly.

But my mind was a mass of conflicting emotion as we moved around the floor. Donna Summer's words tore at my heart.

The man who I was pretty sure was Mister Right would be gone for four months. A long flight away on weekends that we might be able to get together. Accent on the *might*, depending on the whims of the network. We'd be stealing moments together.

And I knew from the experiences of many friends that long distance relationships rarely worked.

279

If love was going to find a way and the needs of the one were equal to the needs of the many, I needed more Star Trek in the form of a transporter. Beam me over to London, Scotty.

Lovers were not supposed to be separated by thousands of miles.

And the ultimate dream job wasn't supposed to pop up at the most inopportune time.

Dexter's eyes were locked on mine as he led me around the dance floor while Madonna's words of love and spirituality tugged at my soul.

His soulful look told me he was racked with guilt, thinking he'd committed some unforgivable sin by not discussing the future, blaming himself for my not knowing.

Right now I wanted the damn show to be over so we could go home and sort this out.

And I wanted it to be over because I was seriously about to lose it on national television.

The music segued into The Rose. The end was in sight. Thirty seconds to go.

We floated across the stage, locked in each other's arms, eyes connecting with souls. I could feel mine welling up and bit my lower lip, trying desperately not to cry. The lyrics to the song pushed me over the edge, and trumped my efforts to stop the flood of emotion.

Dexter took a quick look at the rose on the stage. We hit our mark as the song wound down, he kneeled at the perfect time, grabbed the flower, looked up and handed it to me as the song ended.

And a single tear rolled down my cheek.

The audience applauded as Dexter got up, gave me a hug, then led me over to the judges.

"Wow!" said one of the judges. "Veronica, you really got into it at the end."

"I'm sorry," I said, wiping away the tear. "That song reminds me of someone."

"A lost love?" asked the judge.

"No such thing," I said. "Someone very special to me says true love always finds a way."

***

What should have been the happiest night of my life complete with hours of incredible sex had turned into a gut wrenching no-win situation. Dexter ended up holding me the entire night, and all I could think of was that he wouldn't be there to do that simple act every night.

I needed to sort this out, and I needed to do it immediately.

I couldn't do it myself.

I needed help, as I was an emotional wreck incapable of making rational decisions.

I convened an emergency conclave with Layla and Savannah in my apartment. If anyone could figure out a solution to this puzzle, they could.

Still, I'd gone over dozens of scenarios, and all were stopped cold by this simple fact. We'd be three thousand, four hundred and sixty five miles apart. Over seven hours by plane. (I looked it up, which made it worse.) Take fourteen hours out of a weekend, add a good dose of jet lag, and you don't have a weekend. I even had this crazy idea that we could meet halfway in Iceland, but let's be serious.

Layla reached over and took my hand. "In all the years I've known you, I don't think I've ever seen you so emotional."

"I think this is the first time in my life I have absolutely no clue about what to do," I said, wiping my eyes.

Savannah pulled a tissue out of a box and handed it to me. "Sweetie, we're gonna figure this out."

"How? It's impossible. It's like the universe said, 'You can have a perfect man or a perfect job, you can't have both.' My whole life I've had this goal of getting *The Chair*, and then I get it and...

281

dammit, I want it all!"

"What does Dexter want you to do?" asked Layla.

"He says he'll do whatever it takes to make me happy and will support my decision, but he absolutely cannot abandon his commitment, and I agree with him on that. Too many people depend on him."

"That's awfully noble of you," said Savannah.

"Yeah, but it doesn't make me feel any better."

Layla put her arm around me. "Are you absolutely sure he's Mister Right?"

"About ninety-five percent," I said. "Let's be honest, we haven't been dating that long."

"I hate to say this," said Layla. "But you could just quit and move to London."

"I thought of that and Dexter won't let me do it. He says I'd be bitter giving up a career I love. And dammit, I know he's right. I'd end up resenting him. So I'm gonna be stuck three thousand miles away and instead of getting off work and spending the evening with a great guy I won't even be able to call him up because he'll already be asleep! If I didn't get my dream job and if he didn't have a commitment—"

"And if a bullfrog had wings he wouldn't kick himself in the ass every time he jumped," said Savannah.

Layla and I looked at each other and shook our heads. "I'm not even gonna try to figure that one out," she said.

"I guess I'm doomed to a long distance relationship. At least it's better than in the old days. I can see him on Skype."

Suddenly Savannah sat bolt upright. Her eyes widened.

"What?" asked Layla. "You remember another Southernism about flying bullfrogs?"

"No," she said. "Something Veronica just said."

"What did I just say?"

"It doesn't matter." Her face beamed. "You *can* have it all, Veronica. Because I have the solution. And I can give it to you in two words. However, you will have to make one huge sacrifice."

CHAPTER THIRTY-SIX

"Good morning, everyone, I'm Scott Winter in New York."

"And I'm Veronica Summer in London. Top of the morning from across the pond."

Hosting a national morning show in New York is an absolute bitch when you have to get up at two in the morning.

Doing it from London when you're on the air at the crack of noon, no problem.

After giving Gavin an ultimatum that the network would lose me unless they allowed me to co-host the morning show from London, they did the math. The Morning Show is a cash cow, and they didn't have another snarky anchor on staff to take my place. Evening newscasts were no longer appointment television, and ratings on all networks have been dropping like a rock since the Internet became popular. So any ratings spike I would have gotten at night wouldn't have made up for the drop on The Morning Show.

And of course I owe it all to Savannah's two words that will be forever burned into my brain.

"Time zones."

My mention of Skype had given her the idea. If I could talk to Dexter across the Atlantic, I could talk to a national audience as well. And at an hour that would let me sleep until a normal time.

It was so damn simple, but leave it to someone like Savannah to figure it out.

True love found a way with a little help from satellite technology.

So I anchor out of the London bureau. The network loves it since it gives the show an international flavor, and more of an opportunity to cover the Royal Family, which fascinates American women. Morning shows are predominantly watched by women anyway, so that worked out perfectly. I have a cushy nine-to-five job and am home in time to have dinner with my sweetie. Some nights he's off to work on *Dance Off*, but other nights I don't share him with anyone.

Sure, I gave up *The Chair*, but when you think about it, I swapped a piece of furniture for Dexter Bishop. That's a pretty damn good trade it you ask me. A sacrifice? Hardly. In the grand scheme of things, it's just television, not brain surgery. I was really liking this "ride the wave" thing. I've become an emotional surfer girl.

Oh, almost forgot. The dream of Air Force One and rubbing elbows with the first woman President went down the tubes anyway, as it turned out Senator Sydney Dixon had a thing for male anchors around the country. She resigned from Congress in a tearful speech, admitting she suffered from a mental condition and had been diagnosed as a "sex addict." (The politically correct euphemism for "party girl.")

As for my friends, I do miss having them close by on a daily basis, but we worked a deal with a private jet company to bring them here or take us there anytime we want.

And I love it here. The people are so friggin' polite... excuse me, I meant to say they're *lovely*. That's the popular word over here. Good things are lovely. Nice people are lovely. Great things are "brilliant." (So Savannah's idea was brilliant, regardless of the country of origin.) Anyway, sometimes I have to remind myself to turn off my Noo Yawk attitude when I leave the studio.

As for the living arrangements, Dexter has a gorgeous penthouse and I've got a swanky apartment. Excuse me, a *flat*. I know that sounds old fashioned, but I've never believed people should live together until they're married. They can have sex until they drop, but they need separate mailing addresses. Besides, we've only really been dating a few months and by now you should know I'm a practical girl who doesn't rush into things.

But don't worry, everything's going along just fine. I know he's *the one*.

I said the "L" word first, in case you're wondering.

***

It was deja vu all over again as I slipped into my outfit from the *Dance Off* finals. We'd lost, by the way. Well, kinda sorta. The viewers had apparently been so touched by my tear that we narrowly won the voting, but Dexter and I agreed the other couple was much better. So did the judges. He asked me if I had a problem with giving them the trophy, and I told him they deserved it. It was the right thing to do.

So in the end, having a show that was "fixed" was a good thing.

Anyway, to kick off the new British season of the show, Dexter and I are reprising our routine. The Brits never got to see him dance, and there was a massive demand, so I agreed to go steppin' out one more time.

But in this case there was no competition to worry about, no emotional tsunami in my head. This was going to be pure fun, and also a nice way to introduce myself to the UK on television. The tabloids have gone wild with our romance, as it's common knowledge I moved here to be with Dexter.

"No stress this time," he said, as he led me to the studio.

"No kidding."

"Nervous?"

"Absolutely not."

The crowd went wild (for him, not me) as we stepped into the spotlight after being introduced. We took our places in the middle of the floor, the music started, and off we went.

This time it was pure joy, two dancers becoming one as Dexter had said during that first day of orientation. I did my sultry thing the whole time, thoroughly enjoying the routine, this time not wanting it to end. Savoring every moment.

Alas, the music segued into the final song. I looked over at the stage where we were to end up. It was missing.

"They forgot the rose," I said.

Dexter looked to the spot, then turned back to me. "Unfortunate."

It was. That was the very cool ending to a great routine.

Whatever, the audience was loving it anyway.

The song came down to its final notes, Dexter swept past me and landed on one knee. Since I wouldn't be receiving a rose I figured I'd better turn to the audience and smile when the song ended.

So I did.

The crowd applauded, then started chanting. "Yes! Yes! Yes!"

I mouthed a "thank you" figuring this was another British tradition I didn't understand. Most people simply applaud. Why the hell they were yelling "yes" was beyond me.

"Veronica?" said Dexter.

"What?" I was busy smiling and waving to the crowd.

The applause died down and they started to laugh for some reason.

"Veronica?"

"So why are they laugh... ing." My words trailed off as I turned and saw Dexter, still on one knee.

Holding up an engagement ring. Nothing gaudy, despite his wealth. It was silver and very ornate, obviously an antique, probably checking in at one carat.

In this case, size didn't matter.

My jaw dropped and the crowd went dead silent.

Dexter looked into my heart. "Veronica Summer, will you do me the great honor of being my wife?"

The six month engagement was filled with excitement and something fun every day. Between the British tabloids going wild over Great Britain's most eligible bachelor being taken off the market and my own network promoting the hell out of our wedding, our nuptials had taken center stage on two continents.

Of course when I finally marched down the aisle, it was a private ceremony in an old stone church with one stationery camera hidden behind a plant, the video from which would be shared by everyone. I didn't want a media circus. The only guests were family and friends. We'd chartered a jet to fly in people from New York; I even brought Hal the newsstand guy and his wife. Of course, I knew damn well he'd say, "I told you so," when I first saw him, and he didn't disappoint. His gift was a hoot: a digital subscription to all the New York tabloids.

Dexter had kept the honeymoon a secret, and it was a great one. A two week trip around the UK countryside, staying in a different castle every night. He said he wanted to treat me like a fairytale princess, and I certainly felt like one. When we returned home I discovered he'd purchased an abandoned castle in the country and had the interior remodeled to modern standards while keeping the charm and history intact. There's nothing quite like cooking dinner in a stainless steel convection oven while looking out a window across the moat. We even got into a little routine if he had to leave for the studio after dinner. I'd climb one of the turrets, hold a long scarf and wave goodbye with it, and he'd say, "Alas, fair damsel, I shall return!"

Layla and Savannah fly over once a month, and we do the same to New York. But I'm quickly becoming a British lass, picking up all the lovely expressions and adapting quite well to the brilliant local customs.

In fact, I've gotten in the habit of starting each day with a full English.

After that, I get out of bed and make some eggs.

BONUS MATERIAL

Wing Girl

CHAPTER ONE

"Dating you would be like dating Mike Wallace," said the dark haired hunk who could easily be considered for a certain magazine's Most Beautiful People issue.

Before you get the wrong idea about that comment, let me say that I do not in any way, shape, or form physically resemble the legendary reporter. I'm actually a slender redhead with emerald green eyes, classic high cheekbones with a constellation of freckles, little dimples when I smile, and a whiskey voice that sounds like it lives in a smoky bar and channels Demi Moore. Tonight it's all packaged in a brown paper wrapper consisting of a bulky sweater and pants, while my hair is up (as it always is) in a tight bun and my eyes peer through Coke-bottle glasses. Gotta maintain the journalistic credibility. If you wanna be taken seriously as a woman in my business, you can't play the glamour card.

But as for the Mike Wallace comment, I am the city's most recognizable and feared investigative reporter who channels the *60 Minutes* icon every chance I get.

So I sorta get what the guy's saying, but then again I don't. Does he mean that he admires my work as much as that of the broadcasting legend? Or that when he kisses me he'll be thinking of an eighty year old guy who's dead?

So I said, "I'm not sure how to take that."

He leaned forward and I felt his knee gently brush mine, sending a subtle jolt of electricity through my body. "Oh, it's a compliment," he said with a smile. "I mean, everyone knows you're the best reporter in town."

I tried to hold back a smile but couldn't as I looked at this Greek god with the chiseled jawline sitting before me in a dark gray windowpane suit. The rest of the bar faded to grayscale as he provided the only color in the room. His deep blue eyes became beacons as I caught a faint whiff of Fendi cologne. A subliminal daydream whipped through my mind and I saw myself being carried to the bedroom by those broad shoulders, my legs wrapped around his slim hips.

However, given enough ointment, there's always a fly.

"But..." he said.

Oh shit, here it comes.

Again.

"I just know if I asked you out you'd probably run a background check on me and unearth any skeletons I have in my closet. And I would never be able to lie to you. I mean, no one lies to Belinda Carson and gets away with it."

Investigative reporter red flag alert. "Does that mean you lie to all the women you date?"

"I didn't say that—"

I leaned forward, eyes narrowed. "But you *have* lied to women before or you wouldn't have brought it up."

"Why do you think that?"

"Your previous statement implies that you have been less than truthful with previous girlfriends. What aren't you telling me?"

He looked to one side, flashed a crooked smile. "Geez, lady, turn it off."

"Turn off what?"

"The investigative reporter thing. What's next, hot lights and thumb screws?" He downed the rest of his drink and stood up. "Look, I don't think this is gonna work. It was nice meeting you,

Belinda." He shook his head and smiled. "Wait till I tell the guys at the office I got interrogated by the Brass Cupcake."

Yeah, that's my nickname in the Big Apple, courtesy of those clever headline writers at *The Post*. Great for journalism, a killer when trying to meet men.

The colors returned to normal in the trendy watering hole. Half the crowd leaned against the brass rail running the length of the dark oak bar, while the Tiffany lamps above the small round tables provided subdued light to the other half. My best friend Ariel Baymont slid her tall, willowy frame into the next chair and quickly noticed the previously occupied seat at our table was now empty. "What happened to the total package who was here five minutes ago?"

I exhaled, shook my head and looked down into my nearly empty glass.

"You did it again, didn't you?"

"Yeah," I muttered, then slugged down the remainder of my rum concoction.

"Trying to drown your sorrows?"

"I would, but the little bastards have learned how to swim."

She wrapped her arm around my shoulders and I leaned my head on hers. "Aw, sweetie, we're going to have to work on your bedside manner."

"You're assuming a man has been remotely close to my bed."

She pulled back and gave me a soulful look with her ice blue eyes. "Well, all is not lost. We'll try again this weekend. Anyway, the cute guy who was hitting on me earlier wants to *go someplace where we can talk.*"

"So you're taking him home."

She shrugged, then started to twirl her honey-blonde hair with one finger. "We can talk there as well as anyplace."

I raised one eyebrow. "Talk. Right."

"You know, I can see why you're such a good reporter. You really are a human lie detector."

"Yeah, I might as well change my name to Polly Graph."

"Cute. Anyway, we still on for Saturday night?"

"Thanks to my aforementioned bedside manner, my dance card is clear."

She leaned over and kissed me on the side of the head. "Great. I'll see you then. Hang in there, Wing Girl."

***

Before we go any farther, I should explain the "Wing Girl" concept and how it applies to me, since that is my current after-hours nickname.

As most women know, a good looking guy will often cruise the bars with a "wing man" at his side, the theory being that men in pairs can separate women in mismatched pairs (one attractive, one not), using a divide and conquer tactic designed to liberate the good-looking woman from the skank. This presumes that the hot girl will not take off and leave her unattractive friend to fend for herself. The wing man swoops in like a dog after a pork chop and takes one for the team, chatting up the skank while his friend moves in on aforementioned hottie, who no longer feels obligated to keep her homely friend company and is thereby freed to engage in extracurricular activities.

It's a little different for those without a Y chromosome, and totally opposite in my case. Here's the deal. When it comes to attracting the opposite sex, I am to my friends what a puppy is to a single guy.

Ariel and my circle of friends have dubbed me "Wing Girl" because I end up taking one for the team every time. However, the strategy my friends use is backwards. Since I am a very recogniz-able member of the media, it's a case of moths, meet flame. I'm not sure if it's the fame thing or the challenge of possibly nailing the Brass Cupcake, but it works, drawing in attractive men who I naturally turn off, leaving my friends with very delectable leftovers. My friends always end up with positive results while I finish the evening without so much as a request for a phone number. My Wing Girl moniker started out as a term of endearment, something fun, but lately it's beginning to wear thin.

I don't mean to repel men like a Star Trek force field. Really, I don't. But as I approach the big three-oh, I'm beginning to wonder if I'll ever be able to drop my "prosecutor from hell" persona when I'm off the clock. And I really want to. Before that other clock, the biological one that's ticking louder every day, strikes twelve.

Because, and don't ever tell my boss this, beneath the brass lies a real cupcake looking for her perfect icing.

***

"Cupcake, you really nailed the Senator last night."

My boss, the grizzled Harry Coyne, whose face is so wrinkled it would tie up a dry cleaner for a day, smiled as I took a seat at the conference room table for the morning meeting, his daily sit-down with the dozen reporters on the dayside staff.

"Thanks," I said.

Now, before we get the PC police involved in this, let me explain a little about newsroom language. We usually call each other by last names or, in my case, nicknames. And you might think that a man calling a woman "Cupcake" in the office would violate a litany of sexual harassment laws and cause thousands of dollars of "emotional stress" to the recipient of said nickname. But since I'm cool with it and the rest of the staff knows it, it's not a big deal.

Of course, the first time Harry called me Cupcake the Human Resources troll happened to be within earshot and her harassment sniffing dogs confirmed that this improper term of endearment was, in fact, being used by men in the newsroom. I explained to her that it originated in *The Post*, we all thought it was funny (as well as dead-on appropriate), I actually liked the nickname, and considered it a compliment. The troll, a two hundred pound fire-plug, actually typed up a release form which I had to sign saying I approved of the term and would not sue the station nor hold anyone accountable should I suddenly decide to become offended. That night after the troll went home, one of our photographers went down to her office with a chisel and added the prefix "In" to the "Human Resources" nameplate outside her door. Now she had the nickname "Inhuman Resources" which spread through the station like wildfire and stuck like superglue.

Back to the original comment, in which Harry highlighted the fact that I nailed the Senator. While this might have meant something sexual had I been a Washington, DC intern in a blue dress, the term "nailed" in the news business meant that I exposed some serious shit about a politician, in this case, a New York State Senator.

And you have to understand where Harry's coming from. He broke into the business in the dinosaur age, when smoke-filled newsrooms were populated by nothing but men and the only women in the building were secretaries. When the women's move-ment was making inroads into the biz, the men lived by the mantra "keep the broads out of broadcasting" as they fought an unsuc-cessful battle. Harry is still old-school on the subject of equality in the television news industry, thinking most women are simply eye candy, but he loves me because he says I'm "one of the guys."

You beginning to see my problem?

Harry just turned sixty, and doesn't look a day over seventy-five. The shock of white hair and the closely cropped matching beard doesn't help. His gray eyes are framed by a flock of crows feet. He's short and stocky, maybe five-six, with a bay window from too many trips to the tavern across the street for a cold one after the newscast. The trademark red suspenders harken back to a bygone era. He paced around the glassed-in conference room channeling DeNiro with that baseball bat in *The Untouchables*, whacking a ruler into his hand as he recapped the previous newscast. "Yessir, damn fine reporting." Tap, tap, tap. He stopped behind the reporter who would be this morning's victim, fortyish general assignment reporter Bob Evanson, then rested the ruler on the man's shoulder like he was knighting the guy. "She woulda done a better job on *your* piece last night."

Evanson looked over his shoulder as fear crept into his dark eyes. (Evanson, it should be noted, is a product of Catholic school and therefore has a genetic fear of rulers.) "All the facts checked out, Harry. What was wrong with it?" he asked, voice cracking.

"Oh, nothing was *wrong* with it," said Harry, continuing his parade around the room. "You didn't go for the kill shot. You had the guy and you let him off with a slap on the wrist. Softball questions." Tap, tap, tap. "Just lob the damn things over the plate like it's a beer league."

"I thought my questions were valid."

"Yeah, they were valid, but soft. The Cupcake woulda nailed his ass to the wall and lit up a cigarette afterwards on the set." (Interesting visual that would no doubt land me on the front page of *The Post*.) He stopped, then turned to face the reporter. "You know the difference between you and her, Bob?" He pointed the ruler at Bob, then me.

Evanson rolled his eyes and exhaled audibly. "No, Harry. What?"

"You're too nice. You never go for the jugular. What makes her a great reporter is that she's a bulldog with absolutely no social skills."

My head jerked back like I was hit with a blow dart.

"Ouch," said feature reporter Stan Harvey, who was sitting next to me. "That one left a mark."

Harry glanced at me with his best attempt at an apologetic look. "No offense, Cupcake."

"None taken," I said, lying through my slightly quivering lips.

And for the first time in my eight years in the business, I almost showed emotion.

Almost.

But I felt it.